FAMILY VALUE

FAMILY VALUE

(392 CHESTNUT STREET)

D-L NELSON

FIVE STAR
A part of Gale, Cengage Learning

GALE
CENGAGE Learning

Detroit • New York • San Francisco • New Haven, Conn • Waterville, Maine • London

Copyright © 2010 by D-L Nelson.
Five Star Publishing, a part of Gale, Cengage Learning.

LIBRARY OF CONGRESS CATALOGING-IN-PUBLICATION DATA

Nelson, D. L. 1942–
    Family value : (392 Chestnut Street) / D-L Nelson. — 1st ed.
       p. cm.
    ISBN-13: 978-1-59414-873-6 (alk. paper)
    ISBN-10: 1-59414-873-2 (alk. paper)
       1. Family secrets—Fiction. 2. Domestic fiction. I. Title.
    PS3614.E4455F36 2010
    813'.6—dc22   2009050628

Published in 2010 in conjunction with Tekno Books.

Printed in Mexico
2 3 4 5 6 7 14 13 12 11 10

To Julia of the twenty pages

ACKNOWLEDGMENTS

This book had many people supplying technical information including several people at the Waltham District Court and the Massachusetts Environmental Protection Agency. William Jordan, a retired safety engineer, and Major Betty Israel of the Salvation Army were incredible in sharing facts. As for moral support there's Mary Ahern, Susan Tiberghien and the Geneva Writers Group and especially Sylvia Petter, my writing mate who was quick to praise and quicker to send me back for the eleventh and twelfth rewrite. And as always, there's my daughter Llara, who tells me to keep writing, because it is good for her inheritance. And to Gordon Aalborg for growling so productively.

CHAPTER 1

Mark sat up in bed. His mother screamed. And again. His father yelled. He couldn't make out the words. It didn't matter. It was always the same.

The crucifix on the opposite wall shone in the moonlight. His kid brother, curled up in a ball, slept in the twin bed under a torn spread with the print of a football player so faded that the name of the team was no longer identifiable. The brat could sleep through earthquakes.

Crash. What had his father thrown this time? Or maybe his mother hit the wall. Like last time when he slammed her against the china closet. For the next week they'd picked up pieces of glass.

Once Mark wanted to protect her. Now he hated her. This was her fault. If she'd obey his father, it wouldn't happen. Men were the head of the house. Not to be challenged. Not to be baited. Stupid bitch did both. What other choice did his father have but to haul off and belt her? Show her her proper place. She'd never learn.

He pulled the pillow over his head. As he fell back asleep, he vowed to change his life.

CHAPTER 2

Jay Marsh turned onto a deserted Route 128. By tomorrow the glistening fresh snow would be dirty, oily slush. "Most people are probably already where they're going." He whispered, not wanting to wake his son and daughter in the back seat. The twelve-year-old motor of the Japanese compact hummed, its pings covered by the children's nasal breathing.

Carol Marsh nodded as the familiar landscape flickered by: Lake Quanapowitt, the brown national park sign with a witch announcing the Salem exit, the Peabody Shopping Center. She turned the CD player on low. The sounds of "The Little Drummer Boy" murmured through the car.

Jay glanced at his wife's profile as she brushed her long, black hair back from her eyes, a gesture that was automatic and frequent. "What's up? You've been preoccupied since you got home last night."

"Work. Lacey Andrews skipped." She sighed. "While the kids hung up their stockings and argued about what snack to leave Santa, I kept worrying about where she was and what she was doing."

"What happened?"

"Foster mother found her high, maybe on crack. Yelled at her. She split."

As her voice trailed off, he patted her knee. Glancing at the approaching tidelands with swept sand and dead cat-o'-nine-tails, he thought back to when they were first married when she was a new probation officer. He'd kept offering solutions—all she wanted was an ear. He swallowed a comment about her not being able to save every kid walking into her office. Life had limits—just like he had to do real estate closings to finance his pro bono work. No harm in pushing limits as far as possible.

Dusk muted the road. His headlights caught the few flakes still falling. As they entered the rotary that led to Rockport, Carol opened her window and sniffed the sea air.

Seth woke. "We at Grammy's yet?"

"Not yet," Jay said. In the rearview mirror he saw the five-year-old reach for his Matchbox truck, which hadn't been out of his sight since he found it in the toe of his stocking that morning. The boy's eyes closed. Seven-year-old Paige didn't stir. Their red curls, so like Jay's, blended, making them appear as Siamese twins joined at the head.

Wooden houses behind picket fences covered with snow-frosted dead roses lined the road. The roofs decorated with colored bulbs and lighted candles shining from windows filled him with happiness at the holidays—a break in the routine, more time with the kids, peace on earth and all that stuff.

"How much luck do you think Laurel will have finding her birth mother?" Carol asked.

"Pardon?" When she repeated the question he said, "Depends. Records stay sealed in most places. Search agencies have good success rates, I hear."

"Except she and Tony can't afford agencies. Slow down a little."

When he touched the brakes lightly, the car skidded, but he regained control.

"Her support group says a lot of parents want to be found," she said.

"We've gone support group crazy. I expect one to be formed for women with broken fingernails."

Now I've done it, he thought, but his wife refrained from reminding him she'd considered Adult Children of Alcoholics her lifeline a few years back. He hadn't thought she needed it especially since she only half-followed the twelve-step program. Without turning, he felt her eyes staring at him. He knew her head was tilted as she did whenever she wanted to introduce a topic that she was sure he didn't want to pursue.

"Ever think of going with Laurel?"

Her tone kept him from taking it as a challenge, although he would have liked to. "Why would I?" Not only did he not want to do it, he had never considered the possibility. In fact, he was convinced that Laurel was heading into dangerous emotional territory. Keep the past in the past.

"Aren't you curious about your real mother?"

"Anna is my mother. Don't need any other. Parenting has nothing to do with egg and sperm. Being there. That's what's important." Like he was with Paige and Seth.

"But we've never talked about it. You always avoid the topic and . . ."

He reached for her knee again. "This is Christmas. Stop counseling. It's your day off."

"But . . ."

"Let it go. It happened almost forty years ago. Ancient history." He held an imaginary microphone to his mouth, slowing down to steer with only one hand. "Ladies and gentlemen, we've reached Bearskin Neck in Rockport, Massachusetts. Look to your right to see Motive No.1. Unlike summer when tourists roam the boutiques and art galleries shoulder to shoulder, you'll now see only empty streets."

The compact car passed the window where once a painting of a blue nude combing her hair in front of a mirror had been displayed for almost two decades. When the artist left, Jay missed it as he still missed Oleana-by-the-Sea, where he and his mother had eaten once a month for years. Although the new owners had created a charming place with good food, he felt the ghost of the old place creeping through the new décor and hadn't gone back.

Anna's white wooden house, just off the Neck, was surrounded by a porch. The backyard ran down to a small, private beach. Boulders formed a natural wall between the sand and water. The front of the house looked over a sloping lawn hidden under clumps of snow.

Several cars were parked in the driveway and along the sidewalk. Jay parked behind the last one. When he opened the door, the cold air woke the children. They rubbed their eyes and shook themselves into consciousness.

Anna must have been looking out her window because she came outside with a shawl wrapped over her shoulders. No one could mistake her for a little old lady despite her white hair pulled into a bun at the nape of her neck. She stood strong and straight, her dress to the floor, a medley of colors reminiscent of the hippy era. She was the type of woman that people of all ages stopped to look at. Although she was in her mid-seventies, her skin was clear with only a few laugh lines around the eyes.

"Darlings." She bent to hug Seth and Paige. "Merry Christmas."

"See my truck, Grammy," Seth said. Anna took it and made a few "vroom, vrooms" sweeping it through the air before returning it to his open palm.

"I'm glad you're here." She kissed her son and daughter-in-law. The movement was graceful, as one would expect from a runner or a yoga devotee both of which she was.

Inside there was the babble of people that Jay had expected: artists, writers, musicians, friends whom his mother had accumulated over the years. Her Christmas Day open house drew locals and people from as far away as New York City.

Jay never failed to marvel at her. When his father had walked out, she'd been quiet for three months. He'd thought she was broken. At fifteen, anxious to help her, he'd become the man of the house while maintaining a white fury at his father for finding another woman. She called that period her "deciding-what-to-do-next-time" which was to sell their Concord house, move to Rockport, start her own studio combining her own work and giving lessons and leading a life she proclaimed was the one she'd always been meant to live.

"My family," Anna said to the crowd as the Marshes shed coats and boots and began greeting people they recognized from other open houses or summer visits spent on the porch watching the waves.

A man with three strands of hair combed over his bald head came up and pumped Jay's hand. "Your mother outdid herself again."

Jay failed to recall his name. However he let himself be led to the table with a holly centerpiece. Flickering candles smelled of hot wax. Through the bay window a cold, gray layer of clouds hung over the sea, blocking the full moon and creating an eerie glow that promised more bad weather.

After everyone had left, Jay rushed back and forth dumping food-encrusted plates into the soaking sink as Carol ran water and detergent into the dishpan. Suds bubbled up to her elbows.

"It was fantastic this year, Anna. But then it is every year," she said.

"Didn't I do a great job? What fun, but I am sorry the dishwasher gave up the ghost yesterday." Anna opened a drawer and pulled out a dish towel. "New subject: how are Laurel and Tony?"

"Tony still can't find a teaching job. He's started picking up furniture on trash day and restoring it. It's more beautiful than when it was new," Carol said.

"Clever man, your tenant. Can he sell them?"

"He does. At flea markets. Laurel is still hyper about her job," Carol said.

"Any luck in finding her birth parents?" Anna asked.

"Not yet."

Jay backed through the swinging door, his hands holding a tray with eggnog cups which rattled when he set them down on the oak table.

Anna started to dry a dish, but put it back in the drainer. Her eyes scanned his. "I want to say something. Seriously."

"You're not sick?"

"Doctor says I should be annoying you when I'm a hundred. Laurel made me think of it. If you ever wanted to look for your real mother, it wouldn't hurt my feelings. I mean I . . ."

He looked from one woman to another. "You guys double teaming me?" When they shook their heads, he said, "Mom, you're more than enough mother for me."

"But aren't you ever curious?" the older woman asked.

"No. Table's clear. I'm going to play with the kids."

Carol and Anna looked at the door that swung shut after him then at each other.

"I know I told him from the very beginning he was adopted, but . . ." Anna shrugged.

"You know your son. Stubborn."

Anna nodded.

Carol said, "I just wish he'd share more about what he's feeling."

"In that, my dear, he's like most men."

CHAPTER 3

Anna dozed on propped bed pillows, her glasses slightly cockeyed, resting halfway down her nose. The paperback book on her chest rose and fell with each snore.

The phone jangled her awake. She fumbled for the receiver on the far side of the night table and knocked over the box of tissues.

"Mom, just wanted to let you know we made it home safe. Did I wake you?"

"I was reading."

"Right," he said. It was a family joke that for Anna a book was better than a sleeping pill. "We forgot to ask. Any chance you could babysit for us New Year's Eve. Our kids and the Di-Donato's."

Damn, she thought. Somewhere through the clouds of the past, she heard her mother nagging that damn wasn't ladylike. Being ladylike hadn't been much fun then and was less now.

"What are you planning?"

"Nothing firm. Some First Night stuff. Maybe the fireworks."

She imagined Boston's skyline bursting into strings of color. Now Christmas was over she needed to work to fill her gallery. That meant nonstop painting. Besides, it was good to sometimes not be available. "I'll pass this time."

"I guess it wouldn't be horrible to stay home," Jay said.

"In case you're trying, remember I don't do guilt trips," Anna said.

Jay laughed. "Lord knows, that's not news. Go back to sleep. Love ya."

"Love you too." As she stretched to hang up the phone, she hit the brown lamp. The ceramic base clattered against the oak night table, but she caught it before it toppled.

Her son kept telling her to get a portable phone. No damned way. Old-fashioned, he had the nerve to call her. One of the problems of being in her seventies was if she didn't like something new, everyone thought it was because of age. Pissed her off.

Aggravating how people kept talking into cell phones. Just last Sunday night at the Wayside Inn she was enjoying roast lamb and mint jelly. The fireplace's reflection shimmered in her wine. It had always been her favorite eating place with its thick, aged beams, wide floor boards and pre–American Revolution ambience. At least it was a pleasure until some ding-a-ling, pretending to be important, barked into his phone how he wanted to see the poor person on the other end in his office at 7:30 Monday morning come hell or high water. She and her friend could barely hear their own conversation.

Her friend had said, "If Emerson or Longfellow walked through now, they'd be upset."

"And it would have interrupted Bronson Alcott's pontifications," Anna had added. "Thoreau wouldn't have noticed."

"Why not?" her friend had asked.

"He couldn't have afforded to eat here." On her way out Anna stopped at the telephoner's table and said, "Thank God, I don't work for you. There's not enough money in the world to let myself be disturbed at home on a Sunday night."

The man's wife smiled. "I agree."

The man said nothing.

Nope, no cell for her. Even her regular phone represented too much of an intrusion. She always unplugged it before entering her studio.

Anna turned out the light and slid under the beige duvet. Sleep remained elusive. She thought about Jay's reaction to her suggestion that he search for his birth mother. So typical. Fairy tale endings, happily ever afters, that's what he wanted. Not that others didn't, but a mature man would deal with the glass slipper not fitting Cinderella's foot when it grew plump with age. If a dragon stormed her son's castle, he would think of it as a horse with a thyroid condition and a fever.

Reading. That would get her to sleep. She picked up her mystery. She loved them all: Spenser, V. I. Warshawski, Blanche White, Kinsey Milhone and those forensic doctors. This was a new character, Caz Flood by some English chappie. *Cuckoo.* All his books had bird titles, a good gimmick.

This night reading didn't act as a sedative. She'd slept just the other side of too much before the phone call. Her own fault for asking Jay to call. Two, three, four o'clock went by. At the end Caz figured out the same thing Anna had. She debated going to work, but her studio would be too cold, too dark.

She closed her eyes. Roger. She still thought of him too often. Dead from a massive heart attack three years ago. What would her son, who idealized her, think if he knew she'd had a lover for seventeen years? She chuckled. He'd drop his teeth then probably deny it. She gazed at the icicles, long and thick, hanging outside her window. No one had known, not even Ellen, Roger's wife.

A married lover had suited Anna just fine. Passion, but when it was over, he picked up his dirty socks and left. "Sex without the sox" as she liked to joke privately. Ellen was responsible for his clothes maintenance, not her. Anna wanted no man cluttering up her days. No one to demand what was for dinner when she didn't want to cook. No one to ask where a shirt in plain sight was. When her married friends complained about having to accommodate their spouses, she'd always felt a bit smug.

Besides passion there'd been friendship. They'd talked everyday: a phone call, a stolen cup of coffee. He chatted about his research, his students. She discussed her painting, her gallery, Jay and later Carol and then the grandbabies.

His hands—how she loved them. Big. Sticking out of the sweaters he preferred to suits and ties. Those hands had been so strong with long fingers that opened the jars whose lids she couldn't budge. Then he would say, "Never mind, you got it started." Ellen had buried him in his Irish knit sweater, with a tiny stain, those hands folded across his chest. Anna had touched those hands for one last time when it was her turn at the casket—so cold. Not like the hands that caressed her, bringing her so much satisfaction.

To make it worse Ellen had been her best friend. Sleeping with a best friend's husband wasn't spot on. Sometimes when the three of them went someplace she wondered how obtuse Ellen could be. Of course, they had been careful. Had she felt guilty? Not really. She wasn't joking when she said she didn't do guilt trips.

Roger once suggested leaving Ellen.

"Don't you dare," Anna had said. Another woman might not have been as generous to the wife. Or maybe that was pushing it.

"You can rationalize anything," he had once said. She'd been sitting on his lap. It was spring and the house was filled with jugs of yellow daffodils, gathered to help thin out the explosion of yellow over-running her garden borders. She almost needed sunglasses when she walked up the path to the front door.

"I'm thinking of starting a business," she'd said. "Rationalizations, Inc. If you want to do something or not for $5. I will give you all the reasons you should or shouldn't do it."

"Let's test it. Give me five reasons why we should make mad, passionate love," he'd said and she'd found eight without hesitation.

There'd been no one since him. Old women wearing flannel nightgowns and sports socks to bed were not in great demand, although Alan did make a pass at her tonight. Old goat. Probably couldn't get it up anyway. What do they say about old men? Tea on their ties, and pee on their flies. She'd kissed Alan's cheek and told him, "We've been friends for so long, we'd probably laugh at the wrong moment."

Fending off men, although rare these days, wasn't new to her. When first divorced, most of her friends' husbands had offered to fix things around her house including her sexual needs. "I'm sorry I can't because of my eyesight," was one of her brush-offs.

"Eyesight?"

"I might be blinded by your wedding ring." And she would take their arm, stand on tiptoe and whisper in their ear, "Although it is lovely to be asked."

Roger was different. She'd lusted in her heart long before he approached her. When her marriage had been failing, she never let on that the tall anthropologist, white haired and younger than her by five years, had rung her chimes. Even if the phrase was out of date, she still loved it. She'd refused his first few offers, but to her relief he kept asking. When he claimed Ellen didn't understand him, she told him "She probably understands you too well."

One night, shortly after she'd moved to Rockport, when Ellen was visiting her mother in Maine, he arrived on her door steps and asked, "Can I buy you a beer?"

"No, but you can buy me champagne." She'd grabbed a shawl and headed to his blue Volkswagen Beetle. To get in and out he had to fold his long body like a circus clown.

They'd driven to Stockbridge, stayed in a bed and breakfast

and made love four times. The smell of autumn leaves had come through the window along with the cold air. When she'd gotten out of bed to close it, the braided rug had felt rough on her bare feet. So many memories.

Her hand drifted to her breast, and as she stroked it, she pretended it was his hand. However, there was no way she could run her tongue over her nipples. Her fingertip traced the outline, around and around, making her wet. Obviously her body hadn't heard the rumor that juices dry out with old age.

Her free hand went to her thighs, the skin sagging despite taunt muscles. Taking a hunk of her blue flannel nightdress she twisted it and pressed it between her legs.

She'd learned to pleasure herself that way when she was a child. The mistake she made was to share the discovery with her mother, who told her if she continued she would lose the ability to urinate. Pee was another one of those unladylike words. For a month, Anna had refrained then decided to risk it, thus debunking the first of many myths. She pressed herself harder into the cloth rocking back and forth. Release. Then she snuggled under the covers and this time sleep came quickly.

CHAPTER 4

Crunch. Jay glanced at the floor. An army of red and green lentils were scattered over the gold linoleum pattern.

"Carol? Paige? Seth?"

No answer.

Crunching his way to the oak table, he put his briefcase next to the red Amaryllis just past full flower. He hung his parka, wet from melted snow, over a kitchen chair. His red curls were plastered to his forehead.

A grainy head of lettuce rested in the soapstone sink. Two bottles with ice chunks on their seals defrosted on the drain board. Hmmm—sauce made with home canned tomatoes.

"Carol? Paige? Seth?"

Why hadn't his wife left a note when she went out—not like her to break that unofficial family rule? What about the family in Boxboro last month where the wife was kidnapped from the kitchen? What if one of Carol's delinquents came seeking revenge?

Don't be stupid, he told himself. This is the type of neighborhood people talk about with nostalgia. He could borrow a cup of sugar, jumper cables or a lawn mower from anyone up and down the street. He couldn't remember anyone being mugged, much less murdered, on Chestnut Street. If his neighbors saw anything remotely strange, they'd have called 911. That is, if they noticed.

"I spend too much time in the ghetto or listening to my wife's tales of delinquents." Maybe it wasn't abnormal to worry about urban dangers, but he refused to fall victim to it. Caution was enough—checking back seats before getting in the car, not wearing good jewelry on the T. He laughed at himself. Who wore good jewelry?

"Carol? Paige? Seth?"

Only quiet.

He pushed through the swinging door leading to the living room. Seth's blocks salvaged from garage sales, made a wall around the Christmas tree. Needles hid the holly-patterned rug which Carol had hooked. Bending, he stuck his finger into the tree stand—dry. Brown-green needles floated into his hair. Better take it down New Year's Day and not wait till Twelfth Night.

Paige's dolls were on the coffee table. Their dresses and paraphernalia half hid Carol's open, spine-up book. Other toys were tossed helter-skelter. A half-finished knitting project was beside the easy chair. Carol's work folders were scattered around—everything normal. She must have been feeling guilty about loafing, even though she'd promised him she wasn't doing a lick of work until January 2nd. He entered the bedroom without knocking.

Relief. His wife and Laurel DiDonato, their upstairs tenant, sat Indian style, face-to-face on their patchwork quilt covering the bed. Carol wore a Northeastern University sweatshirt, the one with the bleach stains on the left shoulder, jeans and her fuzzy gray socks—cozy socks, she called them. Her dark hair was pulled back with combs. Since she wore no makeup, her freckles stood out against her white skin, the only trace of her Irish heritage. He looked more Irish than she did.

His neighbor wore a blue-striped business suit with her company badge on the pocket telling the world that she was a safety engineer at Jackson Products, Inc., a Prospect Engineering Subsidiary.

The women held mugs. A smell of mint wafted his way. They didn't notice him until Carol caught his reflection in the mirror over the dresser. She jumped up to kiss his cheek.

"Where are the kids?" He waved at Laurel as he hugged his wife.

"Tony took them to some First Night stuff," Laurel said. "Along with my brats."

"What were you guys talking about?" Jay asked.

"Work problems. Big, big ones," Laurel said. "I've decided my promotion before the buyout wasn't such a hot thing."

"But that was a while ago." He slipped his loosened tie over his head.

"New company mantra. Cut costs, cut costs. That's all I hear. I can't; not without violating safety regulations." She waved her hands as she talked. She claimed growing up in Boston's Italian North End made it impossible not to.

"It's like that all over," he said. He took off his suit jacket. "Cheer up. Worry about it next year."

The two women exchanged a look that said, "Men don't understand."

Jay caught the look. "Hey, I try my best." He disappeared into the bathroom to change into jeans and his red plaid flannel Maine backwoods shirt. As he listened to the women examine each thing Laurel's boss had said, looking for nuances, he shook his head. Coming out of the bathroom he asked, "What's going on in the kitchen? The floor talks back to me."

"While I was washing the lettuce, I knocked over the lentils. Then Laurel came in upset, so I just left everything."

"You two keep talking, I'll clean it up," he said.

"Now you know why I keep him," he heard his wife say as he shut the bedroom door.

Tony DiDonato stood at the foot of the staircase outside of

Jay's and Carol's apartment. "It's quiet upstairs. Bet they're asleep."

"Let's check. Kids plus quiet equals danger," Jay said.

The two couples tiptoed up the stairs to Tony and Laurel's apartment to find four small bodies asleep in sleeping bags on the floor in front of a flickering television screen.

Laurel popped out the *Shrek* DVD. "So much for them seeing midnight in."

Each adult found a child, not necessarily their own, and made sure they were covered, a thumb removed from a mouth, a stuffed animal in easy reach. Then the two couples filed downstairs.

The table in the dining room was full of dirty dishes. The women wanted to clear.

"It was a good pasta." Tony popped a wilted lettuce leaf from the salad bowl into his mouth.

"Coming from a North End Italian, that's a real compliment," Carol said. "How much longer till midnight?"

"Ten minutes." Jay retrieved a bottle of New York champagne from the fridge and four movie cartoon penguin-decorated jelly glasses. "We're high class all the way." He carried everything into the living room on a tray.

Tony walked to the window and opened the drapes. His dark features shone in the window as he cupped his hands to the side of his head cutting the reflection. "It's stopped snowing. I've heard Cambridge already used up its plowing budget for this winter."

"They didn't allocate enough. Probably thought global warming would make less snow," Laurel said. "This will wreak havoc with the salt runoff even if we don't salt near the Charles River."

"My wife—always the safety engineer." Tony turned to her. "Stop bringing your work home."

Carol came up behind Jay and circled his waist with her arms.

"He does too."

"I can't fight for truth, justice and the American way or leap off tall buildings in a single bound in only eight hours." Jay twisted the wire off the bottle. "How much longer?"

"Five minutes," Carol said. She turned on the television. A crowd mulled around Times Square.

Laurel went to stand next to Tony by the window. He guided her to a chair where he pulled her onto his lap.

Jay reached for the remote and clicked through the channels. One station recapped the year—a local cable station was at a First Night Concert. He clicked back to Times Square.

"I must be getting old, but I'm sure glad we're here and not there," Laurel said.

They all nodded as the countdown began. Jay handed out the glasses.

Five, four, three, two, one. Shouts of Happy New Year came from the television as each couple locked themselves in an embrace.

"Rabbit, rabbit," they all said in unison before wishing each other Happy New Years. Tony claimed that if the first words spoken each month were "rabbit, rabbit" they would have good luck for the month. None of them had found any correlation between saying it and later events, but it had become a tradition.

Carol lifted her glass. "A toast to each of us. Laurel, I hope you solve your job problems and find your birth parents. Tony, may you get a tenure track job at a university. Me? I want all my delinquents to go straight, and for my husband, I wish him all the happiness he brings me."

The glasses clinked and they drank. All of them were too polite to comment on the slightly sour taste of the champagne.

CHAPTER 5

The clock tower read 6:45 A.M. as Laurel DiDonato angled her car into a parking spot in the almost empty parking lot behind the building. Once she'd had an assigned space, but Walter Anderson, the new president, had decreed only top company executives merited reserved places.

The redbrick structure housing Jackson Products had undergone many incarnations in its century-and-a-half-and-then-some existence: a leather curing plant, cloth mill, sewing machine factory, something top secret during WWII, and lastly a watch factory before it had morphed into what it was now: a biochemical company.

Laurel retrieved her cell from her briefcase and punched in a single digit as she strode to the entrance. "Hi, Tony."

Silence.

"I'm sorry about this morning." As she talked, she spied an icy patch on the walkway. Dangerous.

"I knew you'd call," he said.

She swallowed a mouthful of anger, not because he found her predictable, but because she felt predictable. As she reached the front door, she tucked the phone under chin and picked up a red plastic sand-filled pail. She walked back to the ice to scatter the grains. "I yelled because I dreaded coming to work." Rubbing her foot on the patch, she was satisfied no one would slip.

"I know. And that frustrates you too." His voice was cold.

Resisting the desire to call him insufferable or hang up, she said, "Robbie has a 3:30 dentist appointment." She reached into her camel-hair coat for her badge and slid it through the machine that registered her time of entry. At the click of the lock she pushed her way into the reception area with its wide polished wooden floorboards, and red brick walls covered by large sepia pictures of the building from different eras.

"I remembered. What time will you be home?" he asked.

She returned the security guard's wave. "I'll call. I don't want another fight if I get delayed and supper is ruined."

His tone warmed. "I'll feed the kids early. Then we can eat, just the two of us whenever you get home. Hold hands. Maybe light a candle. Over and out."

She put the phone away. With her professional life breaking into pieces the last thing she felt like was a candlelight dinner. Poor Tony. It wasn't his fault she had no desire for sex these days. But what the hell: if his days started at 5 A.M. and if he were occupied every second until he collapsed into bed, he'd be less horny too. Not that he didn't do a lot around the house. And refinish the furniture. And apply for jobs. As she imagined him slowly drinking a cup of coffee between chores, his feet up on the hassock, anger bubbled up inside of her. Again!

The only time that was truly hers was when she looked for her mother. Even that had to be sandwiched between other stuff. How had things reached this state? Thank the Good Lord Jesus they could remember better periods. At least, she hoped he did, too.

Laurel covered the twenty yards to her office. Hanging up her coat on the rack next to her secretary's desk outside her door, she noticed a new photo of two little girls in Catholic school plaid skirts and navy blue sweaters. Folders, stacked in piles, were arranged by color: red, green, blue, yellow. No edges overlapped; no papers stuck out. Bookends braced several directories, their spines military straight on the bookcase behind her secretary's desk.

Inside Laurel's office galvanized pipes ran under the wooden ceiling. Sitting on the one extra chair she exchanged boots for pumps. Her heels clicked on the polyurethane floorboards as she walked behind her wooden desk circa 1935. The old man had refused to throw out anything which was remotely useable, although he never hesitated to invest in needed equipment. A real prudent New England Yankee, she thought. She wished, no—more than wished—yearned, that he still headed the company.

One brick wall was hidden by books, mostly environmental laws and regulations issued under the Environmental Protection Act and from the Massachusetts Department of Environmental Protection. The State was still fairly strict, but since 2000, the National Agency seemed to disappear into some sort of mist, making it harder for her to convince the new CEO that rules must be followed.

Her University of Maryland diploma hung askew on the opposite wall despite her secretary's daily straightening. Once she wanted a masters and had been scheduled to go under a tuition reimbursement plan the next fall, but that was one of the first perks cut after Prospect bought out Jackson. Probably for the best, she thought, not wanting to fall victim to sour grapes. Work kept her away from her family enough. I—no—make that when Tony found a teaching job, *they'd* really have scheduling problems if she added classes to her daily mix.

She wondered how the Marshes stayed so calm. Carol almost never complained about Jay while Laurel constantly bitched about Tony. She couldn't even remember the Marshes fighting. Maybe they did but were quieter about it.

Her computer beeped. The company logo appeared. She checked her E-mail: a safety conference announcement and business stuff. What she wanted was a message: "I'm your mother." Sometimes she wished she hadn't started this search with its roller coaster emotions.

Clicking on the message from the personnel office, she read a new snow policy: anyone out because of bad weather would be docked a day's pay, including salaried employees. Somewhere in her files she'd stashed an article about an employee who, during a storm, skidded into an oncoming plow, on his way to work for a company which threatened employees taking snow days with termination. He sued the company and collected almost a million. If the old man was still here she'd have sent him a copy. If the old man were still here the policy would never have been written.

Bringing up her agenda, she saw appointments scheduled with reps from two dumping companies. One she'd used for a year, the other was courting her business.

Her secretary popped her head around the door. "Happy New Year, Boss," Michelle said.

Laurel nodded then started costing out hoods for the fourth floor lab tables where technicians were inhaling unhealthy fumes. Afterwards she wrote a justification using scientific reports on health hazards and statistics for possible—she changed the word to probable—law suits. In the old days she would have gotten three bids, chosen one instead of fighting for every cent.

When Michelle ushered in the first vendor, Laurel glanced at her watch. Holy saints. 11:30. The morning had disappeared. They exchanged the usual comments about holidays and weather. When he was seated, she said, "Ok, we've got to get these prices down."

"My company might be raising them. We're buying more land in Missouri."

Laurel knew that was one of the few states that still accepted hazardous wastes. More costly shipping meant prices went up. "That's your problem." She knew it was hers too.

A crackle from the loud speaker reserved for building-wide announcements interrupted. "There will be a meeting of all employees in the cafeteria at 2:30 P.M. Attendance is obligatory." The accent was recognizable as Anderson's British secretary.

"I need to move 300 containers of hydrochloric acid and another 30 of methyl bromide," she said. She tapped her felt pen periodically against her desk pad doubling as a calendar. "And we'll have quarterly shipments of 30 each. I didn't know people were backlogging the stuff. And I've no idea why."

"I'll get you an estimate."

"Keep your pencil sharp."

"Come on Laurel, I can't. It needs special handling. Some towns are getting finicky about what they let go through."

She leaned across the desk. "There's lots of stuff a hell of a lot more dangerous."

"Still we need special containers, seals."

"Send me an info sheet." Before she could say more Michelle appeared at the door.

"Sorry Boss, Crisis. Line 2."

After listening to the caller Laurel said, "Oh hell, I'll be right there." As she stood up she said, "I've an appointment with your competition. Remember that when you quote." What a bitch I am, she thought, as he shook her hand. He's given me great service, and I can't treat him the way he deserves.

She ran to the far end of the building, which was undergoing repairs. When she arrived, she was panting. Her last few steps were maneuvering around piles of wood, sawhorses and tools. Light shone on dust in the air through six windows with new clear glass panes not like the smoked or leaded glass in other parts of the building.

Paul, the janitor, stood outside a door, his arms folded. Sheet rock, hacked and stacked, lay in jagged pieces around the corridor. "Strange one, Laurel. We found a closet hidden for God knows how long." He opened the door and stood aside. An unpleasant odor hit her nostrils.

"Reminds me of dissection day in Biology 101." What she saw was six 55-gallon barrels piled in two stacks. Shelves in the room were gray with dust. "How long has this been closed up?" She breathed through her mouth.

"Since I've been here. Ten years. False wall," Paul said.

"Let's get suited up." Ten minutes later, covered head to toe in yellow rubber, they looked ready for a moon walk.

"Ladder?" Her voice was muffled through the head gear.

He went around the corner to retrieve a six-footer which he rested against the wall between two stacks of barrels. "What do you think it is?"

She shrugged. He steadied the ladder as she clunked up it in her thick boots. As the safety engineer this was her job, not his, but it had taken a good year before he forgot chivalry in favor of job descriptions. With rubber gloves she couldn't loosen the lid. She motioned they should lower the top barrel to the ground.

Together they struggled with the weight. Paul took most of it muttering, "Careful. Careful."

They rolled the six barrels outside the closet, lining them in a row next to the discarded Sheetrock. With both hands she tried twisting the cover. Nothing budged. Without being asked Paul handed her a crowbar. With her gloved hand she pried the lid off then rushed to open the window.

Three carpenters coming back from lunch stopped. "Shit, it smells like a goddamned morgue."

She motioned them out of the room. The carpenters, holding their noses, didn't need to be told a second time.

Paul peeked into the barrel. His rubber gloved hand pulled out a dead starfish. All the barrels were filled with formaldehyde-preserved starfish. "Weird. Where did they come from?" he mouthed.

As she struggled out of her rubber suit, static electricity caused her wool skirt to stick to her body. "Who knows? I'll start the paperwork to get rid of them. However, those guys need another place to work until the smell disappears. And leave the windows open."

Laurel heard her coworkers' babble before she entered the cafeteria filled with fake hanging plants. The room could hold 300 people without anyone feeling crowded. After lunch the wooden tables had been stacked to one side. Orange plastic chairs were arranged in auditorium fashion. Frost on the window formed lacy patterns and let in enough light so that the overhead lamps did not need to be turned on. A portable stage had been rolled in front of the food service area. Two office chairs and a microphone on a stand were the only items on the stage.

Walter Anderson arrived with his Vice President Peter Sullivan. Walter had taken over as CEO six months ago after the buyout had gone through, but Peter had been with Jackson for over ten years. He used to dress casually as most employees did. Now he wore a blue suit, lavender shirt and a tie that brought the color combination together. Anderson looked as if a *GQ* photographer was expected for a fashion shoot. Laurel imagined him sleeping in perfectly creased pajamas and his gray-streaked hair unmussed.

Michelle stood up and pointed to a chair next to her. Laurel scooted in, narrowly missing a coworker's foot, as Anderson pulled the microphone off the stand and held it to his mouth.

His voice was deep with a television announcer's neutral accent. "Some people like to coat bad news. I believe it builds anxiety. This is a bad news announcement. To cut costs we will have to downsize by 50 people, or one in six of you. Those staying will have to work extra hours, but that should be the only restructuring necessary. I will wait until the end of the week in case of voluntary resignations or requests for early retirement." He looked around. "Questions?"

Fred, a forty-year-old accountant, raised his hand. "Will we be offered out-placement services?"

"Negative."

Michelle whispered to Laurel, "Four years ago when orders fell, Old Man Jackson gave us a choice of a layoff or a temporary salary cut. He halved his own salary until the crunch was over." Laurel had heard about it when she joined the company a year after the event.

Another woman said, "But sales are up and production costs are down."

A murmur grew as people looked at each other. When they looked up both Anderson and Sullivan had disappeared.

As the employees filed out of the cafeteria, Fred came up to Laurel. "That happened so fast I would swear I imagined it."

"Seems more like a group nightmare to me," she said.

Back at her desk, Laurel tried to concentrate as she filled out the forms necessary to accompany the barrels of starfish to a disposal site. The halls were quiet. People hid in their cubbies.

Michelle came in and closed the door. "Are we in danger?"

"I honestly don't know," Laurel said. She wondered how she and Tony could manage if she were let go. She didn't need to check her home budget. She knew. Terribly.

CHAPTER 6

"What are you staring at, you little bastard?"

"Nothing Pop." Mark scuttled past his father, who stood at the kitchen counter, and sat at the Formica table which was still sticky from last night's supper.

The older man added vodka to his coffee in the Store24 thermos. A few drops spilled. He wiped them up with his finger which he licked clean.

Mark, ignoring his father, filled his bowl with Cocoa Puffs. He added milk from the carton with the four missing children, their smiles waxed over. The liquid turned shit brown.

The snow had stopped. Damn school. When the storm had started after supper, he'd hoped for a day off. He didn't dare cut class. Last time he did, his father caught him. Beat the living shit out of him. Mark shoveled the food into his mouth hoping to get away before a battle could start.

He thought about Richard Yeats. Before the Christmas break as Mark was walking home, a car driven by the high school senior had pulled up next to him. "Hey, man get in," Yeats had said then peeled out leaving a strip of rubber behind him. They'd gone to Prospect Hill Park where Richard drove off the road. "I've been watching you."

Mark tried to sound tough, to out-macho the guy that no one but no one messed with. Not teachers, not the principal. No one. "So?"

"Ya ever think the world sucks?"

Bizarre question. He'd tried to figure out what this was all about. "Lotsa times. Can't do a fucking thing about it," Mark said.

"You're wrong," Richard ran his hand over his shaved scalp.

"Ya? Prove it."

Richard snorted. "Tough fucking little asshole, aren't you? I like that. Prove it." He snorted again and poked Mark's chest with his finger. It felt like a bullet, but Mark didn't flinch. "Here's my address. Show up on Sunday. 8 P.M. Don't be late." He opened the door.

Mark sauntered home, mimicking Richard's swagger. He wondered why from all the kids at school he'd been chosen. Too bad he didn't have friends to brag to. He'd go. Wouldn't miss it.

Mark's father slammed a piece of bread into the toaster bringing Mark back to the present. The bottom tray fell out scattering crumbs over the counter. "Goddamned nigger. Stole my fucking promotion from under my nose." The rest of the muttering was unclear.

Mark's mother came into the kitchen with his little brother on her hip. The brat kept rubbing his eyes. Sleepers coated his eyelashes. She plunked the boy into his high chair without speaking to her husband or Mark. The little boy's toe stuck out from the left foot of his pajamas. Finally, she looked at Mark. "You'll be late for school."

"I've time."

Slam! His father's hand came down on the table. The dishes rattled. "Don't sass your mother."

Mark grabbed his jacket from its peg. Some day, he thought, I'll show them all. Sooner than anyone would think. He and Richard against all the assholes of the world.

CHAPTER 7

"You're late," Doug Faraday said as Carol Marsh bombed through the probation office door. The smell of cold wool rose from her black coat. Three women in the open reception area ignored their keyboard to witness the latest act in this ongoing drama.

Carol put down her briefcase to check her wristwatch. "Just fifteen minutes, Boss." She brushed by him and headed into the coffee room.

Four men, two in their twenties and two in their forties, sat at a rectangular table. The younger officers wore jeans and sweaters. The older ones had creased pants and ties, although one wore a cardigan. They all drank coffee as they worked on folders.

A pinkish cardboard box, half filled with muffins, rested next to the coffee machine. "These for everyone?" Carol asked.

The oldest man said, "Doug brought 'em. Leave me a blueberry."

Moldy mugs filled the sink. Carol grimaced and reached for a sponge. A few minutes later at her own desk, she rearranged papers to find space for her mug and muffin. From both sides of the half wall she heard file drawers being opened and shut as people pulled reports for appointments or court.

Her phone rang. She reached over her own stack of papers to grab the receiver. "Marsh."

"Doug, here. Can you come see me?"

Her boss's office was at the far end of the space allotted by the District Court to the probation office. Although he was the only one with four walls, his space was the same size and as messy as hers. He sat there, his dark wavy hair hanging over his collar, too busy again to get to the barber. Nervous energy kept him stalk thin.

"You're going to bawl me out for being late?" Carol asked. She moved several folders, bulging with papers, from his chair so she could sit. She'd explained so often that she couldn't leave the kids before 7:30 at the Friends School, and then it was a matter of traffic whether she reached Waltham by 8:00, that both of them could recite it word by word.

"Not this time. How frustrated are you with the computer system?"

What a strange question. Better than a dressing down. As for the computer system, it was almost impossible to get anything out of it. Data entry was so cumbersome most people ignored it all together. "Very."

Doug ruffled through his mess. "I know it's here some-where . . . I just had it . . . uh . . . there it is." He handed her a folder. "We've received a grant to install a new one, one that makes, or so they claim, entry and retrieval simple even for computer phobics."

"Would that it were so."

"Trust me, it's so. We need someone to drive the project." He stared at her.

"And?"

"I want you to drive it."

"Why me?"

"Despite being late, you're one of my best officers. Your case load is only 95 kids. I know you like computers. Not like *them.*" He jerked his head towards his door. Carol knew that the people on each side of his office were near retirement age and so set in their ways that she half expected them to arrive by horse and buggy. She was sure it wasn't their age but their personalities that made them so, because Anna was older but much younger in her head.

"Gotta send you on some night courses," Doug said.

Carol winced. The project sounded like something she would love to do, but to give up more personal time? "Can I reduce my case load?"

"Possibly by maybe five or so . . . depends on volume."

"More money?"

He laughed. "It's a grant not a miracle. Think about it, I'd really like you to head this thing. I need to know fairly soon because they've assigned a programmer to us and the first meeting is next week." He shifted in his seat. "Any news on the Andrews kid?"

"I was about to make some phone calls when you called me. I'd hate to lose that one."

He ran his hand through his hair but it fell back as it had been, out of control. "I know."

Carol circled the block twice at the Cambridge Friends School, a long, low series of attached classrooms with murals of kids painted on the walls. When a van pulled out, she grabbed the space, banging her Toyota into the snow bank.

Once inside she headed for the room where children of working parents waited after classes. Paige stood behind a carton marked "Store," talking to a boy with a handmade police hat.

The after-school co-coordinator walked over. "While they were playing village, there was a robbery."

"I can't leave yet, I've gotta file a report," Paige whined.

"The cop has to leave too," a voice behind Carol said. She turned to see the cop's mother.

"Oh all right." Paige ran for her parka.

Carol found a flushed Seth sitting in a corner sucking his thumb. Bending down she touched his forehead. Don't be sick, she prayed. He always ran a fever when exhausted.

Carol parked in her driveway. The big brass house numbers 392 shone under the porch light. Bless Tony for turning it on each night. Less chance of stumbling in the dark, especially when carrying a sleeping Seth into the house. The boy was a dead weight. "Paige, bring my briefcase, please." She almost whispered to not disturb her sleeping son.

As she unlocked the front door to the entrance hall that separated the upstairs and downstairs apartments, the smell of garlic and onions cooking coming from her place welcomed her. She hadn't told Doug that she was late because she took the time to start a Pokey Pot. Time lost in the morning was won at night. What he didn't know wouldn't hurt her.

Robbie DiDonato opened his apartment door and sat at the top of the stairs looking down at her as she was about to open her door. He was already in his pajamas. "Can Seth come up and play?"

"Not tonight. Your mom home?"

"Nope. She called Daddy and told him she'd be late 'cause she had a hell of a day."

Tony loomed over his son. "Hell is an adult word. Don't use it. What time will your old man be home, Carol?"

Seth seemed to grow heavier in her arms. "Soon." She spoke softly.

"Ask him to come upstairs after he eats, please," Tony said as Robbie ducked between his legs back into his own apartment.

Inside her own place Carol plunked Seth on his twin bed. His bedspread was crumbled. Making beds was a desirable thing that might happen once or twice a week, usually on the weekends. Mornings were too rushed and it was more important to get teeth brushed and all required paraphernalia in their book bags than beds made.

The apartment was cold. Carol left her son long enough to shove up the thermostat and almost immediately the radiators thumped. When she got back to Seth's room, he was still asleep. She pried him out of his snowsuit and pushed his inanimate arms into his cowboy pajamas. As she slipped him under the covers, his eyes flickered and he groped for his blankie, sticking one of the saliva stiffened corners into his mouth.

The word "germs" flashed into Carol's head followed by "maybe that's why he's sick." Stop it, she told herself. It is impossible to control everything. Unhealthy thinking wanting too much control. Banish it. Now. Although controlling some things at this point would be nice.

As she entered the kitchen, she was surprised to see Jay spinning the lettuce dryer. "I didn't hear you come in," she said.

He stopped to hug his wife. "I came in the back and never got further than the kitchen."

She believed him. His coat was thrown over a kitchen chair. His briefcase was on the table next to the morning's newspaper. "Tony wants to see you. Probably wants you to go with him on a trash hunt, but that's just a guess."

Carol lay in bed under a patchwork quilt. The drapes were drawn against the wind whistling around the house. She wore a flannel nightgown that would have been perfect for any of Louisa May Alcott's little women, and was long enough to cover her cold feet. To her left was a stack of folders. She took one, made some notes and placed it on the larger pile to her right. Another day survived.

Jay came in and sat on the bed. His cheeks and nose were red. "We just got back."

She'd been right about what Tony had wanted. After her

husband had read Paige a story, he'd gone out with the upstairs neighbor in search of trashed furniture.

"Good hunting?"

"Great. He found a kid's desk, an end table and four chairs. I checked Seth. He still has a fever."

She put her hand on his cheek. "Youch, you're cold. How was your day?" This was the first time they had to talk. At dinner Paige kept them occupied with her talk about the village she and her school chums had set up, the robbery, their plans to set up a co-operative so everything was fair for everyone. Although that had been a teacher's idea, the kids had liked it.

"Lina took care of three filings and found me another pro bono case. Family being evicted from Blue Hill Ave."

"Subprime or nasty landlord?"

"Nasty landlord." As he talked, he undressed, throwing his jeans and sweater on the chair, then jumped under the covers letting in cold air. "And yours?" He propped himself up on one elbow, his head on his palm as she talked about the computer update project. "You going to do it?"

She held her ballpoint in her mouth as some people hold cigarettes while she shifted the folders to the floor beside the bed. "I can't handle courses at night."

"Find a day course. Negotiate," he said.

"Just like a lawyer." She switched off the lamp. "Best moment of the day."

He cupped her breast. "Let's make it even better."

CHAPTER 8

Tony DiDonato circled the end table he and Jay had retrieved the night before from Brattle Street. Amazing that people in that mansion threw it out. Usually the mucky mucks called antique dealers when they wanted to get rid of something. Well that mucky muck messed up.

He would love to spend just one night in one of those old historic homes with their Colonial-era columns and wood siding, which was more than he would ever be able to afford. He could just imagine what the owners had to pay for heating, never mind the mortgage.

He ran his hand along the tabletop: with the grain, against the grain. An abandoned child. Abused. Gouged. Unappreciated. Delicate lines. Almost French. Louis XVIish.

He felt like a monastery scribe faced with a piece of blank parchment. Wood in place of parchments. Sanders not brushes. Powdered ink replaced by varnishes. Words brought to art. Wood reborn.

A Gregorian chant played on the portable CD under a cloth protecting it from sawdust and grit. *Ave Ave Ave. Hallelujah. Media vita in morte sumus.* Life in death. He would rescue this table from death.

Other pieces: headboards, chairs, table and a desk in various stages of repair were placed around the sun-warmed room. The radiators were off despite below-freezing temperatures outside. Someone forgot to tell New England about global warming. As

43

soon as the sun set, he would have to turn the radiators on and could no longer rely on the sun to toast the room through the double-glazed windows.

Cocooned. Calm. Content. He sat on a wooden box as he stared at the table waiting for answers. *Ave Ave Ave. Hallelujah.*

The tabletop's paint splatters, burns and holes faded. In its place he saw a panorama of angels singing among curly cues.

He knew most of the refinishing techniques, as taught to him by his father. Under his tutelage Tony had learned woods and how to sand and refinish, all the time wishing he could work at McDonald's like other kids but knowing he was needed to support his father in his failing health. The old man wouldn't admit weakness, and Tony had to pretend he wanted to do this. Even today, he doubted that he had fooled his father, but Tony never regretted letting his father save face despite putting aside his personal desires.

He went to the bedroom. One wall was a floor-to-ceiling bookcase made with planks and bricks. Laurel's professional books. Her novels. His books on Old English, Middle English, Latin, language development, early church plays, Chaucer, poetry, texts about the Middle Ages, history, battles, the Catholic Church. The third shelf to the right was filled with texts on woodworking. The fourth contained a mishmash of subjects.

It was there, the book on Versailles that Laurel had given him when they were first married and dreamed of touring Europe. That was before kids and bills. As he flipped through the pages, he found what he was looking for. In his memory there was another book that he had picked up years ago in a used book store, but he wasn't sure that they still had it. As he ran his finger up and down the fourth shelf, he hoped it hadn't fallen victim to one of their attempts to bring order into the chaos of their lives by decluttering, not that it ever worked.

There it was. *Manning on Decoupage.* Taking it back to his work room, he began reading.

CHAPTER 9

The smell of coffee tugged at Jay Marsh's consciousness. He tucked the duvet around his neck. His left foot felt a cool spot—when did Carol leave? The low hum of children's cartoons and children's voices mixed with kitchen melodies—dishes clattering, the fridge's door shutting. He closed his eyes and let himself drift. Saturday mornings, a gift from the gods.

Carol, in her plaid bathrobe knotted at the waist, padded into the bedroom carrying a breakfast tray which she placed before him. A red headband kept her black hair from her eyes.

He took in the two dishes of pancakes and bacon, glasses of orange juice and cups of coffee and waited for her to crawl into bed before dribbling syrup onto the food. As he sipped her orange juice, thick with pulp, he glanced at the clock: 7:30.

She saw him do it. "I'm actively enjoying not dropping the kids at school."

He watched her blow on her coffee, fluttering the steam—one of her habits. Others? Rinsing out the bathroom sink by letting water flow into her cupped palm, tucking their night clothes under their pillows when she made the bed, and even when he made the bed and left them on the chair, fastening her hair with an elastic before doing the dishes. He imagined his mother saying, "Little acts build a family."

After they finished their breakfast, Jay put the tray on the floor, locked the door and climbed back into bed. "All quiet, but did I hear the DiDonato kids?"

She stretched. "Yup."

"What should be done today?" he asked.

"Cleaning, food shopping, dry cleaners."

"What has to be done?"

"Cleaning, food shopping, dry cleaners."

He unbuttoned her nightgown. "Let's forget the dry cleaning."

"As long as we're quiet," she said as he knew she would.

"We'll whisper our orgasms," he promised.

Saturday afternoon the Marshes and the DiDonatos watched as their children played along the Charles River. A few people skated despite the no skating signs. Unlike most years, the river had frozen over. The red-brick Harvard buildings contrasted sharply against the blue sky. Seth Marsh and Robbie DiDonato, rosy cheeked and white breathed, rolled snowballs to finish a fort started by others. Paige Marsh and Samantha DiDonato made what they said was a snow dog stating that snow men were boring, anyone could make a snowman. The resemblance to a dog took some imagination, but none of the grown-ups would contradict the girls.

"The river is getting safer each year," Laurel said. "Birds and fish . . ."

Tony grabbed her and pushed her into a snow drift. "Don't be a safety engineer today." He turned to the Marshes. "When I had my appendix out, she checked to see if the doors were fire proof. Didn't worry about my old bod."

Laurel brushed the snow from her parka. "That *was* worrying about your bod, dummy."

Carol flopped on an untrampled spot of snow, moving her arms and legs ninety degrees to make a snow angel then held her hand out to Tony who pulled her up.

Jay stamped his feet and blew on his hands. "What do you

say we head back?"

Snow barricaded the sidewalks. Eventually it would be shoveled into trucks and driven out of the city, but commercial streets were always cleared before residential areas.

The women walked ahead of the men who were pulling the kids on their sleds. They were so deep in conversation that the men could have said horrible things about them and they'd have never noticed.

"Laurel is almost calm," Tony said.

"Think she'll be downsized?" Jay asked.

"Faster Daddy," Paige said.

"If you want to go faster, you'll have to wait for a reindeer," Jay said and was rewarded with a giggle.

"Can't imagine it. But you know her. Worry, worry, worry." Tony scooped snow to form a ball and caught Laurel in the middle of her back. Her retaliatory snowball fell short of its mark.

Jay pulled his two kids from the claw-foot tub wrapping each in a bath sheet the same shade of blue as he'd painted the outside of the tub. Carol had stenciled the blue with white daisies with bright yellow centers. He handed Paige a nightdress pre-warmed on the radiator then held out Seth's pajama bottoms for him to step into. The child rested his hand on his father's shoulder to keep his balance.

The bathroom smelled of baby shampoo. Water glugged down the old drains. A black ring circled the inside of the tub. Steam on the mirror distorted the blue cornflowers on the wall paper he and Carol had hung with only minor battles. A corner was coming loose. I'll fix it tomorrow, he thought, or next week or next month. Why did life always seem so rushed with so many details?

For no logical reason, he remembered the day he met Carol.

She'd been crossing Boylston Street by the Harvard Co-op, her arms full of books. He'd swung around the corner on his bike and hit her. They'd been inseparable since his apology.

While he was still in law school, a Saturday night in was a disaster. There were girls to screw, beer to drink, studies to forget. If anyone had told him then that someday he would be thrilled to stay home on a Saturday to bathe two kids, he'd have called them nuts.

"Ready Partner?" he asked as he slipped the pajama top over Seth's head. He tucked the boy over his shoulder and said to Paige, "Pick out a book, Curly Top, while I read to your brother."

"*Green Eggs and Ham, Green Eggs and Ham,*" Seth chanted. Jay knew the book by heart. Seth tried to order green eggs once. Carol tried adding food coloring, but the eggs had turned a sickly gray.

Before Jay reached the fifth "Sam I am," Seth slept. Jay turned off the bow-legged cowboy lamp found while scavenging with Tony.

Paige waited for her father. They were on chapter four of *Summer at Buckhorn*, about a group of children on a farm. The book was another salvage on a Tony trip. The yellowed pages smelled musty. Each night sniffing them was part of the ritual. Paige told him she believed the characters came out of books when you read them. She worried that the old paper would be unpleasant and left the book open on her night table so the characters could romp over the words.

He wondered how he and Carol could produce two such different children. He had problems following the twists of Paige's imagination. Seth needed to know how everything worked in reality, not fantasy. However, he couldn't deny fathering either of them. Their red curls replicated his own.

He found Carol tying newspapers to be recycled, newspapers

that they hadn't even had time to read. He really should cancel some subscriptions to save some trees. A fire burned in the fireplace. The living room looked different. The coffee table, although not bare, had books and magazines neatly stacked. Toys were in the toy box.

This was a routine that Jay knew was more than Carol bringing order out of mess. Although she didn't talk about it much anymore, he was sure she was still haunted by memories of coming home from school and finding this same house in disorder and her mother passed out on the couch. By the time he had met Carol her father was dead, killed during a robbery intervention. As a result, the mortgage and her education had been paid for by the Police Association that cares for the families of officers killed in the line of duty.

She'd buried her mother only a few months after.

Other girls he'd dated lived with parents or shared an apartment. Carol was the only one he knew that owned a two-family house.

He'd suggested during the first year they lived together that they sell the house if her memories were too painful. She preferred living mortgage free and getting income from the second apartment. Instead they redecorated.

"We didn't get all the housework done," she said.

He recognized the tone she used whenever she wanted more order than was possible with two to four children playing and never enough time. He would banish her ghosts, send them back to a non-intrusive place.

"Or pick up the dry cleaning."

"But I bet the kids will remember playing in the snow more than a dust-free house and mommy and daddy in pristine suits." When she smiled, he added, "Besides a clean home is an oxymoron. Anything good on TV?"

"Changing the subject?"

"Yup."

She settled on the couch with her head on his lap as he channel surfed: click a movie, click CNN, click basketball, click a comedy. "You drive me nuts when you do that," she said. "I can't even get a feeling of what's on."

He smoothed her hair. Her skin was white, but it was always white. Red patches, windburn dotted her cheeks. "The man who controls the remote, rules the house," he said.

She grabbed it and clicked the TV off. "Same with women. Can we role play what I will say to Doug?"

"Why not? Nothing good on TV anyway."

A knock at the door caused both of them to look as Laurel stuck her head into the apartment. "You guys want to come up and play cards? I'm going crazy thinking about work."

"We don't want to leave the fire," Jay said. He got up and poked at the log. Its red inner glow showed through ashen bark. "So come down here."

"I'll get Tony and some wine," Laurel said.

CHAPTER 10

"We gotta fight back. Kill the Niggers and Jews. The world is controlled by goddamned Jews. Our heritage is America for the Americans, not all those foreigners." Richard Yeats pounded the table with his hand.

Six boys between fifteen and eighteen, including Mark, sat on the floor in Richard's basement playroom. Four of the kids' heads were shaved, including Richard's. A beer sign flashed neon bright behind the bar. Several rats ran circles in a cage. To the left of the bar was a case holding thirty rifles. Army-green lockers were stacked floor to ceiling next to the stairs. Although windows and a door leading to the backyard made up the other wall, the glass was boarded up.

Richard held his hands out. "We must protect ourselves. Protect our families. Protect our nation. No more of our lives lost in some God forsaken country we've never heard of before our dumb ass president sends us over there." He paused and looked at each boy. "We want to fight terrorists; we gotta fight 'em here. Lock up the country."

Mark sat spellbound listening to the words that were a variation of his father's. But this boy, who was only three years older than he was, was going to do something about the problems. Not just bitch. Not just get drunk and beat up on a woman and kids.

"My father is in Maine right now training his militia to fight when the time comes. I'm raising my own regiment of kids who think like me, kids who care. We want to make the future, not just follow stupid politicians who only want to line their own pockets."

Mark wondered what he could do.

"Join me," Richard said. "But I only want the hardest and the best. That's why I invited each of you to come here tonight." He went to the cage and took one of the rats by the tail, swung it around and dashed it against the wall several times until its gray fur was red. "Those who are with me grab a rat and kill it. Those sissies who aren't get the hell out of my sight."

One of the boys stood up and headed for the door. "See ya."

Richard flashed across the room, grabbed the kid and pinned him to the wall next to the door. "If you tell a living soul what happened here tonight, I'll kill you."

"Hey man, I'm cool."

Holding him by the collar with one hand, Richard opened the door with the other. He threw him into the backyard. "Get outta here, you sniveling coward."

A kid next to Mark walked to the cage. "I'm with you." He smashed his rat against a wall.

"Mark, you in?" Richard asked.

Mark reached into the cage, but instead of pulling the rat out by the tail, he picked it up by the neck. It felt almost silky. I'll show them, he thought. He twisted the neck until it snapped. He felt its last quiver before it lay still and warm in his hands. For the first time he realized he had the power of life and death.

CHAPTER 11

"It's like this, Doug," Carol said. Dressed in jeans and an oversized red sweater she looked more like a student than a probation officer.

"I'm listening." He sat opposite her in the coffee room. He looked at his watch and straightened his tie. She guessed he was due in court upstairs because he only wore suits on court days.

"I want to do the computer project."

"Good when do you . . ." Her raised hand stopped him. "Why do I hear a but?"

"Because there is one, actually two." She held up her forefinger. "The night courses. Can't do it. My family and all that. Second but." Her middle finger popped up next to the forefinger. "I've an idea."

He closed the door as someone approached. "I'm listening."

After shuffling through her briefcase, she found a folder with several papers. She handed him a sheet. "Here's my case load now: appointments, court time, visitations, etc."

He scanned it.

She gave him several other sheets. "Now here's the time I estimate it will take working with the programmer. Notice my ideas on the database on Sheet 4." She let him find it.

"Looks like you've got some good ideas and given it a lot of thought."

She hadn't found it that hard because it was mainly her wish list ingrained from years of frustrations at not being able to get at data she needed despite knowing it was in the miserable computer someplace.

"Thanks. The drawback is the night courses."

A frown ran across his face.

"Before you say no, look at this." She pulled out a brochure. "Here's a list of workshops with the info I need, all intensive, all during the day. If I took Mondays and Thursdays for four weeks, I'd have them all done. We've eleven people working here. If each takes two of my cases I could handle the remaining eighty. No sweat. And I could do some of the project work at home nights and still be with my kids."

He looked at the lists, rubbed his chin and nodded.

"Prices are less during the day. Fifteen percent."

"You've got a deal. Think you could make the classes without being late."

"They start at 9:30. In Cambridge, less driving."

As Carol entered her cubicle, the phone rang. She cradled it against her shoulder as she filtered through her phone messages. "Carol Marsh."

"It's Leo." His voice was graveled as if from too many cigarettes except he didn't smoke.

"What's up, Pal? What kid are we double whamming today?"

The normal response from the cop should have been, "You counsel, I coach," referring to his off hours time getting troubled kids into sports. Instead Carol heard only background noise. "Is it David?" She often made X-number of hours with Leo as part of her probation requirements. Usually after the first couple of times, the kid went on his own, but David had been fighting it. She heard Leo's intake of breath.

"Not David, this time. Sorry, Carol, bad news. Real bad. Lacy Andrews."

Before he could say "dead" she knew what was coming. She

sank into her chair, her hand covering her mouth. Lacy was fourteen. "Oh God, no." Her voice was part plea, part whimper. "What happened?"

"We busted a crack house on Prospect Street. She was in a room. Second floor. Probably dead a week. Listen. Her foster mother's away. I hate to ask, but can you identify the body?"

After Carol hung up the phone, she opened her top desk drawer to touch a photo of Paige and Seth taken during a picnic at Beaver Brook Park last Labor Day. The kids waded in a pool, their bodies golden, their hair wet and their eyes squinting against the late afternoon sun's glare.

Travis, the guy in the next cubicle, came in. He turned a chair to sit horse-saddle style. His thick neck and muscles showing under his shirt, made her think of wrestlers. "Do I hear a problem?" he asked.

Carol told him. "I know it's not a first time, but I never get used to losing one of my kids." She swallowed several times trying to control the pressure behind her eyes.

"It's tough."

"I gotta go identify the body. Leo should be here any minute to pick me up."

As if on cue, Leo walked in. At forty-five he was in top shape from spending so much time working out with the kids. Today he was in uniform and carried his hat with ear muffs. Carol grabbed her coat. "Travis, can you brief Doug, please?"

"Sure, and I'll reschedule your appointments."

The cruiser was parked with the engine running in front of the court house where the probation office was located. Leo opened the door and started to put his hand on top of Carol's head.

"Hey, I'm not under arrest," she said.

"Force of habit."

★　★　★　★　★

Inside the morgue the smell of formaldehyde hit Carol with memories she didn't want. At seventeen and three days she had identified her father's body in another morgue. Her mother had been too drunk to do it. The smell was the same.

"We can wait until your mother sobers up," the chief had said.

Her mother hadn't been sober for weeks, and Carol wanted to get it over with. Because she was a cop's kid, they'd laid the body on a table draping him with a sheet, rather than just pulling open the drawer. He looked asleep. When she stepped to the bottom of the table, she saw the other half of his head had been shot.

Her second experience was when her mother had frozen to death in a snowstorm, too drunk to find her way home. God, how she hated morgues.

Leo took her by the elbow. "You going to faint or anything?"

"I'm an old hand."

"Tough lady."

Not really, she thought.

The man on duty nodded to them. He chewed gum. "Ya here about the Andrews broad?"

Leo nodded. The man shoved a clipboard at them. Leo signed it and handed it to Carol. The man walked ahead and stopped at a bank of drawers. He opened the third from the left in the second row. Carol held her breath. Despite the cold, the stink from decomposing flesh mixed with the other odors.

Until that moment, she'd hoped Leo had been wrong, although she knew he wasn't because he'd seen Lacy from a distance talking with Carol. Leo was right. It was Lacy, but unlike the last time when she saw her, her hair was matted. Her skin was white, green and blue at the same time.

"Overdose?"

"Probably. No autopsy yet. Just another stupid bitch doing drugs," the attendant said.

"That kid never had a chance," Carol snapped. "She had the bad luck to be born to a rotten mother."

"Sterilize them all," the attendant said.

"All who?" Carol asked.

"Welfare mothers. Immigrant mothers if you can catch them."

Before she could answer, Leo propelled her out of the room, grabbed her coat and pushed her into the corridor. "I'll buy you lunch. Burgers."

Sleet stung their faces as they left the building to dash to the cruiser.

After they'd ordered into a clown's mouth at the drive-up window, he said, "Feel dumb talking to a plastic clown." They drove to the next window where the kid in the striped shirt shoved a bag at them.

Leo parked the cruiser in the far corner of the lot. "That guy at the morgue is an asshole." He divided the food, setting hers on the glove compartment tray which he had opened for her. "We busted three people, no dealers. No one's posted bail."

She picked up a French fry and fought gagging. She and Lacy had eaten here four weeks ago. Sitting inside at red plastic tables, Lacy talked about going back to school and had said she would be the first in her family to graduate. She'd bragged about her appointment with the principal to ask for re-admittance.

"What could I have done differently? Seen her more? Called more?" Carol unwrapped her fish sandwich and sat it down next to the uneaten fries. A mayonnaise-coated piece of lettuce fell on her jeans leaving a greasy splotch. She rubbed it with a napkin.

"Probably nothing. For every kid we save, we lose ten."

"Sometimes I think we should legalize drugs."

"Wouldn't work."

"What we're doing isn't working either." She started to cry. He handed her his napkin and looked out the sleet-coated window until she'd finished.

Carol skidded into her driveway. Sleet lashed her windshield. Lights shone from the upstairs and downstairs apartments. Entering the kitchen, the first thing she saw was her husband standing at the sink. Potato peelings were piled on a newspaper. Chopped onions, mushrooms and a bowl of beaten eggs were lined up on the counter.

She kissed him. "Twenty-five percent of that kiss is I love you, but the rest is thank God, you've started supper."

Glancing at his watch he said, "I just was starting to worry with the sleet and all."

"The roads sucked. I saw two accidents. You did pick up the kids?"

"Relax. They're in the living room with Mom."

"Anna's here?"

"They cancelled her adult education class."

Carol went into the living room. Her mother-in-law looked as elegant as ever in boots, a long skirt and boiled wool jacket. Her white hair was in a perfect bun. Paige and Seth flanked her as she read them a story. As soon as the kids spied Carol they bolted almost knocking her over with their hugs.

Anna got up and hugged her daughter-in-law. "Hope you don't mind that I sleep overnight."

"I'd mind you driving to Rockport in this weather a lot more. Your nightdress and toothbrush are where they always are."

"It's my turn to have Grammy sleep in my room," Seth said.

"No mine," said Paige.

After several mines and no mines, Carol ruled Anna would sleep in Paige's bed and Paige would sleep with Seth.

When the children groaned, Anna said, "Let's have a big groan and get it all out."

There was a loud groan.

"Is that the best you can do?" Anna asked.

The volume mounted.

"One more. Your most giantest groan ever," Anna said.

As the kids roared Carol and Anna covered their ears.

Jay came in with a fry pan in his hand. "What's the noise? Never mind, supper's ready."

As Carol wiped the table, Jay stacked plates in the dishwasher. "How'd it go with Doug?"

"He bought it." She rinsed the sponge. "But Lacy Andrews is dead." Without wanting to, she started to cry.

He put down the towel he was holding and gathered her into his arms. When he reached for the Kleenex, he realized the box was empty and pulled off a paper towel from its rack. Just like he would with the children he held it to her nose. "Blow."

She did.

"I knew you were distracted."

She did the small things that kept her from crying again: throwing the empty Kleenex box into the paper recycling bin, putting soap into the dishwasher, rearranging two dishes. As she did she told him everything. "I wanted to shake her awake. It's dumb."

"No, it's not."

Carol ran cold water into her cupped hands and splashed her face. Her white skin was badly splotched. "I know I can't control what others do, but hell, the kid was just fourteen. What a waste."

"I know." He reached for the tea kettle and took three mugs from the free standing cupboard, which had been in the back hall. As a child, she'd hated its black chipped paint. Her mother's bottles had been hidden behind the canned goods on the bottom shelf, and although she had wanted to empty them, she had never dared. She wanted to throw it out. Jay liked its lines. They made a deal. If, after Tony refinished it, she still didn't like it, they would get rid of it. Their tenant-neighbor had spent several weekends sanding the oak he'd discovered underneath. He claimed the cupboard had thanked him with each brush of varnish. What had been ugly was now beautiful.

Carol took it as a metaphor for how her adult life compared to her childhood. She touched the wood. Too bad all ugly things couldn't be transformed, the dead brought back to life, kids reformed with the stroke of a brush.

Taking the tea bag canister and hugging it to her chest, she thought of the AA prayer: God grant me the strength to change what I can, accept what I can't and have the wisdom to know the difference. For the first time since Leo's phone call, she felt centered.

Jay had put on a Rebecca Parris CD, and when Carol joined him in the living room he fluffed a pillow for her. "Sit down. I'll check the kids and Mom." He covered her with a crocheted afghan.

Jay found his mother, already in her own nightdress and a robe she'd borrowed from Carol, in Seth's room. Her white hair was in a long braid down the back of her neck. She shared the twin bed with Seth while Paige lay on the trundle that had been pulled out.

"And so Daddy's birth mother put him in my arms, and I fell in love with him," Anna said. "And then she gave me a stuffed rabbit and asked that I give it to him from her."

"Did the rabbit have a name?" Paige asked.

"He sure did. Funny Bunny, 'cause he had one eye off center

and was half green and half orange. Your Daddy slept with him for years."

"Where's Funny Bunny now?" Seth asked.

"I washed him once too often and he kinda disintegrated. We tried surgery, but eventually we just had to throw him out."

"I wish I could see him," Seth said.

Anna grabbed a piece of paper and quickly drew a picture. Paige popped up so each of them could study it.

"Time for sleep, brats," Jay said.

The children slithered under the covers. Jay turned the lamps off, but left the night light on. He kissed both heads, straddling the trundle to reach across to Seth.

Outside the room he said, "I can't believe you told the kids that story."

"Why not? It's part of you."

"Not really. It happened too long ago." He followed his mother into the living room where Carol had fallen asleep, her tea untouched. He was glad to be able to turn his attention to waking her enough for her to make her way into the bedroom so he wouldn't have to discuss it anymore.

CHAPTER 12

"Send a truck . . . tomorrow? Great . . . I'll get the paperwork ready." Laurel DiDonato spoke into the phone. After hanging up, she went to her secretary, who worked at her computer with such concentration that she never noticed her boss. Laurel waited until Michelle paused before speaking. "I need a hazardous waste manifest for shipment to Mississippi. Any left?"

Michelle pulled a form from her drawer and handed it to Laurel. "The hydrochloric acid? And methyl bromide?"

"Yeah. How do the figures look?" Laurel pointed to the spreadsheet on Michelle's screen.

"Bad. Real Bad. Costs are up. Fifteen percent," Michelle said. "Probably gas prices."

Sucking in her breath, Laurel used her finger to follow a row of numbers across the blocks. "Anderson will shit a brick."

Michelle shrugged. "Can't make up numbers."

"Not if we want to do this right." Laurel and the president had had too many fights over the costs of shipping hazardous waste to southern states. The last battle still pissed her off.

"Dump locally," he'd said leaning back slightly in his chair and looking up at her. He hadn't invited her to sit.

"I can't."

"That's the wrong answer." As always he kept his voice so low she needed to strain to hear him.

Although her stomach flip-flopped, Laurel had tried to be firm. "There aren't any waste sites in Massachusetts," she told him. As she tried to explain the Commonwealth's laws, he interrupted her, his face in a scowl. "Be creative, damn it." He'd spun around to look out on the river and kept his back to her.

Staring at his fifty-cent-piece-sized bald spot, she'd forced her anger down. Creative? How? The laws were specific. No leeway for creativity. Good thing, she thought, as long as men like Anderson, existed. Profit before people.

Laurel went to the file cabinet where a small carton of yellow metal plates marked with the company's ID number sat next to an empty vase. "I'll get Paul to stick these on the containers. Keep . . ."

Her office phone rang. As she reached for it, the view from the window distracted her. The middle of the river had thawed. Dark water ran over rocks and six ragged pillars, all that was left of a dock. Sun reflected off the broken windows of the factory on the bank opposite. Next to the building was a cemetery. She blinked. "Laurel DiDonato here."

"This is your pal Fred, formerly from accounting." In the cafeteria an hour before they'd been discussing last night's Celtic's game and office drivel. The line crackled, and she couldn't hear him.

"Can you repeat, please?"

"Sorry, I went under a bridge."

"Where are you?"

"On my way home. And I'm not sick. I was fired. They'll hit about thirty today: call 'em in, shove 'em out. Thought I'd warn you."

Laurel sank into a chair. "Jesus, Mary and Joseph." Who else? Her budget wouldn't stretch enough on unemployment.

"Don't know. This was no golden handshake. Gave me three v-days I had coming plus two weeks' severance. That's all. Said I was lucky that they wouldn't contest my unemployment because of a mistake I'd made. I don't even know what the bastards were talking about."

"Who said that?"

"John the Prick." He used the staff's nickname for the Human Resources Manager, an import from the parent company's parent company.

"Anything I can do?"

He laughed without humor. "Tell my wife."

Laurel had met his wife several times when there were still company picnics and dinners. "She'll be fine."

"At least she's working. Listen, I'll be back in touch." The phone went dead.

Laurel walked down three flights of stairs to look for the janitor. The middle floor was laboratory space where the scientists hovered over computers and test tubes trying to find products to make the company richer. The bottom floor was production and maintenance.

Unlike the scientists and production people in white lab coats, the janitor wore blue coveralls with a bib and pockets to hold nails and a loop for tools. Paul was on the floor in his office, his legs spread as he tried to piece a chair together. He looked up. "Sad day. I keep taking boxes to people I'll never see again."

"I know. I heard."

"You and I should be safe. We're the only ones who know our jobs." He wiped his hands on his overalls.

"You're probably right—especially you," she said. There wasn't a splinter in the building he didn't know about and wouldn't fix when its turn reached the top of his list. "I feel sorry for the others."

"Goes without saying. The old man would have a bird if he knew what they've done to his company." This was not a new conversation. Employees from before the sale repeated it over and over, usually when those who had just arrived from headquarters weren't around.

Laurel spoke the next line in the old employee ritual. "You can't rewrite the past."

She gave Paul the yellow metal plates. "Pick up is in the morning. I'd better get back."

She pushed the button by the elevator shaft. The elevator, an old-fashioned cage with a metal grill criss-crossing Xs, took forever. Old black cords, thick with grease, hung snake-like in the hole while the elevator eked its way up and down, the sound setting teeth on edge. Replacement plans had been cancelled after the company sale. Although she worried about its safety, by an unknown miracle, it had passed its last inspection. Creaking and shuddering it descended, appearing over her head, like a monster from a horror movie. Then it stuck halfway between the two floors. Stepping back she saw no feet or legs, thank God. No one was in it. This time. Maybe there was an elevator saint somewhere. She climbed the three flights back to her office.

Michelle was not at her desk. Maybe she'd taken an early lunch.

When Paul did not answer his phone, she e-mailed him about the elevator.

On her bookshelf she found the latest issue of *The Environmental Safety Journal* and turned to the help wanted section. Nothing interested her.

Michelle had left a copy of a standard from a technical committee that Laurel worked on with the National Fire Protection Association. Anderson had made it clear that the only reason he supported any of her committee work, was so she could veto anything that might impact their bottom line negatively. Picking up the standard she thumbed through it. For two years she'd argued to get certain restrictions added, that Anderson now want vetoed. She threw the standard against the wall.

Her stomach told her it was lunchtime. Problems only increased her appetite. If she and Tony ever got divorced, she knew her weight would balloon. They wouldn't divorce, however, because they were too Catholic and had been through too much together since junior high in the North End, Boston's Little Italy, to train new mates.

Although the cafeteria tables were full, the sound of conversation was muted. No laughter. Three of the four men who normally played bridge ate at their regular table, each in the same place as usual, but there were no cards, only whispering.

As she advanced in the salad bar line, she noticed that the tomatoes were the same pink as her daughter's salmon crayon. All the garlic, oil and oregano in the world wouldn't give them any flavor. What happened to real tomatoes? What happened to those case studies where companies worked together to solve problems? What happened to ethics? Probably they went to the same place as Prince Charming was hiding out.

The phone rang as Laurel walked by Michelle's still empty desk. Her screen saver showed a kitten asleep under a dog's ear. As soon as Laurel picked up she heard Paul say, "They're gone."

"What's gone?"

"The hydrochloric acid. All of it. Every container. And the bromide too."

Laurel cursed that the U.S. had dragged its feet on the international standards against using methyl bromide as a pesticide. Why couldn't they just have signed onto the Montreal Protocol forbidding its use?

"I'll be right down." She bolted. Her heels clattered on the metal stairs like gunfire. She swerved around the corner and into the storeroom where Paul stood. Behind the lead door where the containers had been were only dust-free circles contrasting with the dirty floor.

"This doesn't make any sense," they said at the same time.

"How can we lose something this toxic?"

"Are you sure you didn't send it out already?" At her glare, he added, "Sorry. Guess not."

"Well it can't be dumped here, because no one is vomiting. Maybe it would be better, because then we would know where it was."

Laurel took the stairs back to her office three at a time, rushed to her office to pick up the telephone, then set it down and went back to Michelle's desk. The photos of Michelle's children and their drawings were gone from the cork board. The desktop was empty except for the shut-off computer.

Which crisis call to make first? HR, although she thought of them as Human Remains.

"I'm sorry, but John is in a meeting and can't be disturbed," the HR secretary said.

Laurel stuck out her tongue at the phone. "Perhaps you can tell me if my secretary was downsized."

"Laurel, you know I can't comment on that."

"Let's say then, if I found her desk empty, all her personal belongings gone, I could make the assumption that she is no longer employed?"

"The official word comes from John," the secretary, one of the old employees, said. Then she whispered, "Boy do you have that right."

"Shit."

"Double it," said the secretary. "I'm sorry, someone is on the other line."

Laurel drummed her fingers on the wooden desktop. She bolted to Michelle's computer. The password known to both of them no longer worked. The files? Running to her own computer she brought up the copies that Michelle almost always sent to her. Saints be praised. She dialed the president.

Walter Anderson's secretary was less helpful than John the Prick's. She protected the president better than St. Peter protected the pearly gates.

"Please leave him a message that 300 containers of a very dangerous chemical have disappeared from the basement," she said.

By the time she finished work that day he still hadn't called back.

"Sit down, Laurel. You'll wear a hole in the tile," Tony said.

A garbage soup, made from leftovers, bubbled on the front burner. Once a week Tony dumped the contents of all the dribs and drabs of meals into an onion-flavored broth and processed it until it was smooth. Mostly it was wonderful. When it wasn't, he added curry, plain yoghurt or cream. Sometimes they called it Soup *L'immodizia*, thinking the Italian word for garbage made it sound gourmet, not budget.

Although no heat was under the pot, steam rose from the liquid. He had shut it off moments before when he saw his wife's agitation.

She pulled out the kitchen chair, rested on it a moment, then got up to pace. "One day. All that in one day. You've forgotten what it is like to work in the real world."

"Your next sentence should be, Honey, I'm sorry you've not found a job after trying so hard," he snapped.

Normally, she would have repeated his words, but she just waved her hand.

He glared. "I'm on your side, remember?"

"But where are they? They're toxic. It's not just the risk of losing my job, it's the danger."

Rather than point out she hadn't even heard him, he set the table with four mismatched soup plates, placing cloth napkins held in rings on the dishes. Samantha's had a chipped decal of a squirrel eating a nut. Robbie's had a horse, Laurel's was marked with an L, and his with a pinecone. "Look, the kids are hungry. Can you stop raging and do something constructive?"

She walked to the counter and threw his chopped carrots and celery in a bowl. Using a wooden spoon she scooped mayonnaise out of the jar and licked the spoon before running water into the empty bottle. Each action had either a slam or an imagined slam. "It would help if you were more understanding." Her voice was decibels louder than normal.

"It would also help if you kept work and home separate." His comment was louder than hers.

"When you were working on your useless Ph.D., I listened to your problems, including every dumb thing said by your dumb advisor. Why can't you listen to me?" She banged the wooden spoon so hard on the countertop that the head flew into the air leaving her holding the handle.

Robbie, already in his pajamas, came into the kitchen. His dark hair, wet from his bath, curled at the ends. "Why are you fighting?"

"We aren't fighting. We're discussing loudly. We're Italian." Tony spoke in a normal tone.

"True," Laurel said as she ladled the soup into the bowls.

Picking up her son, she smelled his cleanliness, so different from the sweaty little boy shoved into the bath twenty minutes ago. She put him down, tapped him on the rear and said, "Go get Samantha. She's downstairs with Paige."

"Are you feeling any calmer?" Tony asked as Laurel put the last dried dish in the cupboard. The door was clear glass and the overhead light caught the colors of glasses from jelly and mustard containers. Leftover soup cooled in a former tomato juice bottle. As a safety engineer Laurel would not allow her food to be put in plastic containers or touch anything chemical.

She hung the dish towel on its peg. "No. While you put the kids to bed, I talked to Michelle. She's really in shock. Scared. So am I." She reached out for her husband.

He surrounded her with his arms. "We've been through worse."

Snuggling against his chest was like water on fire: all the angry words she'd thought about in the last hour sputtered into nothingness. "I'm not trying to set records," she said relieved that she wasn't good at holding grudges, even when she tried.

He stroked her hair. "I'm going on a trash safari."

Although she wanted him to stay with her, she knew he wouldn't want to go over everything again. He hated repetition. Also, he needed to find more stuff to remake for the flea market at the end of the month. Jesus, Mary and Joseph, sometimes she hated being an adult.

After he had gone, she sat at the table wishing she smoked so she could keep her hands busy. Instead, she took a packet of chocolate cookies and went into their bedroom.

The room was so crowded she needed to slither sideways between the double bed and the dresser, which Tony had painted with a faux marble. No one could have told the difference unless they touched it. At the foot of their bed her computer sat on a board supported by two sawhorses. A yellow plastic laundry backer, filled with clothes needing a button or a seam stitched up, was partially hidden underneath. Some things Tony refused to do: ironing, putting away clean clothes and vacuuming. Probably the kids would outgrow the clothes before she got them mended.

In all the years that they had lived at 392 Chestnut Street, they had never found a good utilization of the rooms. At first they had slept in the big bedroom, which the kids now shared, having been moved from the middle-sized one that Tony appropriated as a workroom. Although Laurel had tried to keep her computer in there, varnish and paint smells had driven her out.

At some point she would need to separate her children's sleeping quarters. A boy and girl shouldn't share a room after a certain age. The family could always move. Nah. Leaving the Marshes wasn't worth an extra room.

The screen grew light blue. She brought up the Web and waited for the navigation wheel to appear. Dragging her mouse, she pointed the bookmark to an address where birth mothers searched for children given up years before. Four new entries popped up: three looked for sons and one for a daughter born five years after Laurel. Someday, she thought. Someday, maybe my real mother will look for me.

She hit a hyperlink to a site where children searched for birth parents. The screen showed a newspaper-like page with the headline "MOM I WOULD LOVE TO MEET YOU." Underneath was Laurel's photo taken as a newborn. Although she could have recited it verbatim, she read what she wrote six months before. "I was born in Baton Rouge General Hospital, Baton Rouge LA, July 24, 1974. My mother used to be a college student of Italian descent. I know nothing about my father. St. Anne's Catholic Parish arranged the adoption. If you are my mother or father, I want to meet you. You've two beautiful grandchildren. E-mail: Laureldd2020@hotmail.com.

No one had responded. What if her mother was of the generation that had not embraced computers?

Everyone in her support group had their own page. They'd had a Web party one night: entering photos, trying to find words to reach across decades. None had located their birth mothers, but they read stories of people who had.

Clicking back to the E-mail page, she sent Walter Anderson a message. "Please respond. We've a major problem. A large quantity of a highly toxic subject has disappeared." She paused. What will get him to answer her? "We could be liable for heavy damages." That would work better than talking about health and environmental damages. "Before I alert the Department of Environmental Protection, we should meet." Maybe the DEP threat would work. She wasn't sure.

CHAPTER 13

Mark opened his bedroom door. No lights. No television. Quiet. His father's snores filled the hallway drifting into the boy's bedroom across the hall. Mark pressed the door shut, letting it click, then tiptoed to the window. As he opened it, he listened. Nothing.

Wearing his backpack, he stepped onto the porch roof, lowered himself over the edge, shimmied down one of the two columns flanking the front door to stand on the porch rail. From there he jumped over the low cut bushes. The full moon, although hidden behind clouds, left a silver round glow in the middle of the sky. Looking back, he saw no light in his parents' window.

Running down the street, he spied Richard leaning next to his black American brand car. No Nip car for his squadron leader.

"You're late." Richard blew on his hands.

"I had to wait until my parents fell asleep."

"This is war man. You do as you're told."

"Ok," Mark said.

"What was that, Private?"

"Yes, Sir."

"Better."

They got into the car. Richard drove up to the gates of the cemetery marked with strange looking letters. "Look, those mother fuckers don't even use an American alphabet." He snorted.

Mark put a black cap over his almost shaved head. He hadn't dared cut off all his hair.

"Rendezvous at Winslow's at exactly midnight. Synchronize watches," Richard said. Mark held out his watch to compare the two time pieces.

"Jesus, a Swatch. Made by some faggot Ey-talian for a Swiss Jew banker," Richard said. "Get a Timex."

"Yes Sir."

Richard leaned over Mark and opened the passenger door. "You know what you have to do."

As Richard drove away, Mark stood at the cemetery entrance. The iron rails were vertical and too close to wedge even his skinny body through. His backpack, which he threw over the top, landed with a thud. How in a flying fuck was he going to get in? He couldn't fail his first mission.

He saw a pine tree on the street side with boughs reaching over the eight-foot brick wall surrounding the cemetery. He jumped, caught the lowest branch which cracked, dumping him on the sidewalk.

Fuck! A car. As he ducked behind the tree, the headlights shone on a garbage can knocked over by the wind or a dog. When the tail lights disappeared he rolled it to the tree. Its hard black plastic held his weight long enough for him to grab a higher, stronger branch. Bark and twigs scratched his face and pitch made his hands sticky as he climbed higher.

He tested his weight on the branch grazing the top of the cemetery wall. Too fucking weak. The higher ones were thicker, but he would have a longer fucking fall. No other goddamn choice but to try the lower branch. Inching along while holding onto the branch above, he thought step . . . step . . . step . . . step each time he put his foot down.

Crack!

His shoulder hit the inside wall as he fell, landing on his right hip. He staggered to his feet. He was in. He rested against a gravestone. Spooky.

Retrieving his backpack, he fumbled for the small flashlight he'd bought at the hardware store the same day. He found the spray can. As he shook it, the little ball rattled. At home the sound was barely audible. In the stillness it seemed to have a microphone broadcasting off the gravestones.

When Mark pressed the muzzle, his hand grew wet. His fingers smelled like paint. Damn. Wrong direction. He used the flashlight to find the pinprick-sized hole. He turned the nozzle so it was a few inches from a gray marble stone. With a few hisses the letters in the name Markowitz disappeared under a swastika.

Damp and cold were forgotten. Strength surged through his body. Ya, he was doing something. His commander would be proud of him. He was avenging the slights his father had suffered.

The next stone bore the name Rosen. Shaking the can again, he wrote "Death to Kikes."

Stone by stone he vented his hate in paint, no two the same. Then the mother fucking can jammed. He should have bought two. He tossed it in the air as far as he could. It pinged off a headstone.

He climbed over the cemetery wall using the stone wall of an above-ground tomb. Waiting outside was a cop car. Two cops sat inside, drinking coffee from paper cups. They saw him. He ran, but not fast enough.

The bricks felt cold and rough against his face as one cop shoved him against the wall. His hand bore through Mark's back as the other patted him down. "He's clean. What were you doing in the cemetery, son?"

"I wasn't in the cemetery."

The bigger cop shone his flashlight through the iron spikes of the gate. "Someone's defaced the stones." He turned the light back onto Mark and grabbed his right hand. "Looks like fresh paint on you."

Mark felt himself whirled around and handcuffed. The cold metal cut into his skin. The younger cop covered his head with his gloved hand as he shoved him into the cop car. A wire mesh separated him from the cops in the front seat. He was trapped. God. His old man would fucking kill him. He'd be a bloody pulp.

As the cruiser drove by Winslow's he saw Richard's Ford. Fuck. He'd failed his first mission.

Chapter 14

"We need to talk about the V-word," Jay Marsh said as he pressed a fresh-cut orange onto the yellow plastic squeezer. Juice dribbled down the egg shaped center, perfuming the kitchen.

Carol sat at the table, surrounded by folders and multi-colored felt tip pens. Sun streamed in the window, giving her a halo. She capped a blue pen. "I hate all the letter word this, letter word that: F-word, N-word, V-word. It's overdone."

Using a spoon, he fished out three seeds before pouring the juice into a glass. He handed it to her. "You're avoiding the topic."

"No, I'm not."

"Yes you are. Whenever I bring it up, you change the subject or go off on a tangent." Leaning against the sink, he watched his wife pick up a flat circle plastic container. She pushed a pill from one of the holes and swallowed it with the juice like a drunk with his first whiskey of the day.

He remembered seeing a commercial in a reprise of some of the great television ads. Mother Nature being furious when someone told her they replaced her butter with margarine, and she hadn't noticed, zapped the perpetrator and told the camera, "It's not nice to fool Mother Nature." Carol had been fooling Mother Nature since their diaphragm failure named Seth arrived.

"I've lots to do. New cases next week, plus those damned

computer classes," she said.

"Wasn't Doug reducing your work load?" He grimaced at letting himself be distracted.

"He did, till Dave had a heart attack. We've split his cases. I told you."

She closed one file and opened another.

"You told me about the heart attack, not the case load," he said.

Paige and Seth burst into the kitchen. "Can we make valentines now?"

"Yup." As Jay got out paper doilies, red construction paper, glue and stickers of animals, hearts, hamburgers and flowers from the top drawer, Carol piled her folders on the sideboard.

"Don't think this conversation is over, darling wife. Just postponed." He slapped her bottom. "You've been on the pill too long."

Carol stuck out her tongue.

"That's not polite, Mommy," Seth said.

Jay watched his daughter rub her eyes. She looks pale, he thought. I hope she isn't coming down with a bug—and if so may it only last today.

Monday morning, still in robe and slippers, Jay turned on his computer. In the background Matt Lauer promised that Al Roker would talk about the Northeast's unseasonable warm spell. "This is the *Today Show* and in the next half hour we will talk with Jon Stewart, and Suze Orman will discuss your finances. Martha Stewart will demonstrate how to make a Valentine cake." When the doorbell rang, Jay shut off the set.

A good-looking black woman, almost as tall as he was, stood on the top step. A small child wrapped in a blanket, rested on her shoulder. "Hi, Boss."

"Come in, Lina. How's Syeeda?" he asked.

"More or less better. Temp under 100°. Paige?" She put her daughter on the couch and began unwrapping her; she neither co-operated nor fought. Under the blanket and coat, she wore pajamas.

As soon as her mother finished, she put her thumb in her mouth and closed her eyes. Her face had scabs.

"Paige's spots are popping out. Now I'm waiting for Seth to get them the day Paige goes back to school." He sighed. "I suppose it would be too much to ask to have all three children get chicken pox together."

"Dream on, Boss."

"I've already pulled out Paige's trundle bed. Put Syeeda there."

As he waited for his paralegal, Jay looked out the window. The lilac tree had buds. False spring. Those buds would get schmuckled when the temperature dropped again.

Carol ran into the probation officer, her coat and suit jacket open. She could imagine Anna saying this was perfect flu-making weather: a couple days warm, a couple days cold. Anna. Her birthday was coming up. Carol had no idea what to get her, or when she'd have a chance to look.

"You're late," Doug said as Carol walked into the coffee room. "Even by your standards." The wall clock read 9:25. He folded his arms. "Got a new excuse?"

The odor of yesterday's coffee grounds, old pizza and God knows what hovered in the air.

"Paige has chicken pox. I had to drop her Valentines and cookies at school, accident on Route 2. How does that sound?"

"Not bad. Something new in the series. Valentines. Go pick up Dave's cases. You were due in court an hour ago. Travis covered for you." He shook his head. "What did I do, Lord? I have people covering for my people covering people." He raised his hands towards heaven, supplicating an unknown deity who made no comment.

Carol took off at a run. The old clock at the top of the stairs showed 9:35. It reminded her of the old clocks in her grade school. Clocks weren't tyrants then.

At the top of the stairs Travis, her colleague, signaled her. "Late again."

"Have you tried respecting your elders?" she asked taking three folders from him.

"I did by covering for you during three hearings. And now I'm giving you three spanking new delinquents, all first offenders, and spanking might be the right word." He pointed to a girl with black spiked hair next to a tired-looking woman and a boy, who sat between a couple, on a wooden bench outside the juvenile court hearing room. Their faces were immobile. No one talked. No one even moved.

Next to the bench was a room. Through the glass door, Carol saw a slight boy with an almost shaved head. Although she could hear nothing, the body language was unmistakable. Travis pointed. "That one looks like trouble."

Carol stopped at the bench. "Thomas Locarnini?" The boy with the suit too small for him raised his hand. The woman with him pulled a tattered tissue from her purse to blow her nose.

"Put your hand down, you're not in school." Carol kept her eye on the drama going on behind the glass.

"Susan Ames?"

"That's her," the woman said. She pointed her thumb at the girl with gelled spiked hair.

"I'll be back in a few minutes. Please wait."

As she opened the door, the man pulled his hand back to hit the boy. Carol grabbed his sleeve. A table, two chairs and three humans almost filled the space. Had the man wanted to deck her, she wouldn't have had room to fall.

"That's enough!" Keep cool, she told herself as the smell of alcohol hit her nostrils. Never could she smell it without her stomach knotting. Separate past from present. "I'm Carol Marsh, Mark's probation officer." The man narrowed his eyes to slits. She wasn't sure if he were glaring or trying to focus. "If I have to call security, I will. Are you Mr. Hanson?"

"Ya, I'm the father of this stupid little turd." His words were slurred.

Within a second Carol took in Mark's face. It was as if he were somewhere else. She made mental notes of what to write in his file later. Diffuse this situation. Fast. "Wait outside, Sir."

The man looked from his son to her and back. He went to the boy and shook his fist then pointing a finger almost into his nostril. "You do what this woman says, you hear, you little bastard?" The glass rattled as he slammed the door.

She sat at the table. Each probation officer had his or her technique for starting a case. Carol preferred silence and used the first few minutes to look through Mark's folder. The information was sketchy: Caught desecrating a Jewish graveyard, hands paint covered, matched paint on graves, no prior arrests, grades average to above average, school attendance okay, public defender assigned. Carol knew him. Lazy. When she finished, she closed the file, folded her hands and stared at Mark. He refused to meet her eyes. The minutes ticked by, each second clicking and echoing in the room.

His eyes darted past hers. He sat ramrod straight without his back touching the wooden chair slats. Turning around, she saw the father hovering outside. She got up and went to him. "It'll help if you go get a cup of coffee. There's a place across the street."

The man opened his mouth, said nothing and turned on his heel. She returned to the room.

More silence. OK, she thought, new technique. Direct approach. "Why did you do it?"

"My name is Private Mark Hanson. Serial number 0028A. Under the Geneva Conventions that's all I've got to tell you."

"If this were war, you'd be right. This isn't war."

He shrugged. "My name is Private Mark Hanson. Serial number 0028A."

"Mark, let me tell you something. I can't lock you up, because there are no reform schools in the Commonwealth, but I can send you for a psychiatric evaluation." She paused trying to think of her next words. "I don't want to do that. But we're assigned to each other, and I hold power over your future."

Good, she thought, as his eyes flickered towards hers. In that second she felt something, a signal, an instinct, something indefinable. She'd felt it before working with some kids, although she'd missed something with Lacy Andrews. When she denied those feelings, she always regretted it. "Take off your sweater and shirt."

"My name is . . ."

She leaned across the table and bunched the wool of his sweater in her hand. He winced. "I said strip. To the waist. When I get back you'll have no sweater, no shirt and no undershirt. Do you read me?"

Since he was so enamored of rank and serial number, she'd show him raw authority. As she left, she slammed the door.

The two families waiting on the bench looked at her. She flipped through their files before making appointments later in the day at her office. If they were unhappy about a second trip, no one said anything. After they left, she rested her head against the tile wall and exhaled.

Back in the room, Mark stood with his arms across his chest, like a woman trying to hide her breasts. Each rib could be counted. How vulnerable he looks, she thought, like Seth just out of his bath. "Turn around."

"My name is . . ."

She pretended to be a drill sergeant barking orders. "Turn around." As he did, she barely controlled a gasp. His back was a map of red strips, some with pus. But not all were new. Scars, long healed, reopened and re-healed, were written between new wounds. Small circles that could only have been made by cigarettes dotted the stripes. Fighting to keep any tremor from her voice, she said, "Get dressed."

The boy grabbed his shirt, his mouth zippered, his eyes shut, but a few tears escaped. He pulled his sweater over his head. His voice shook when he said, "My name is Mark . . ."

". . . Hanson. Serial number 0028A. I know. Who did this to you?" She ignored the lip quivers.

He shook his head.

"Sit. I'll be back in a few minutes."

She took the stairs to Judge Horne's chambers two at a time. Outside she paused to rummage through her bag. She pulled out mints, lipsticks, tissues until she found her phone. She punched in a number that bip-bipped until she got a ring. Eventually a woman answered.

"Hi June. This is Carol Marsh."

"How are you?" The question was genuine, not routine politeness.

"Fine, how many kids do you have at this moment?"

"Four. I'm afraid to ask but why?"

"Can you handle another?"

"You always do this to me, Carol. You know four's a full house. Then you try to sweet talk me into five or six."

"It's just one," Carol said. "He's even skinny. Won't take up much room. His back is a mass of scars."

When June sighed and asked for more information, Carol knew she had a chance. She outlined the problems, abused kid, alkie father, first offence, salvageable. She didn't mention the crime.

June was silent.

"Come on, the kid needs someone like you." And Carol didn't add that there were so few foster homes that would provide what June provided.

More silence.

Carol let it ride.

Just as she was about to speak, June said, "I'm not saying no, I'm just wondering how I can work him into the current group. A rough bunch. Just got 'em broken in, so to speak. A new one could mess it all up."

More silence.

"Ok, Ok, but this is the last time I'll let you do this to me," June said.

Carol knocked on the judge's door. When she entered the first thing she saw were walls of law books absorbing what little light the one window let in. A secretary, a woman in her early fifties, with hair so tightly permed it ressembled little metal springs, banged on an old HP keyboard so used the letters had worn away. When she saw Carol, her face broke into a smile.

"Hi Ellen. Semi-emergency. I need an appointment with the judge. First second he has free." Before Ellen could reach for the agenda, the judge strode in, his black robe open. The bailiff followed.

"Well Carol, what hopeless case are you pleading for today?" His smile was warm. Probation officers called him Macho Marshmallow because of his thick white hair, white Daliesque mustache and pro-kid stance. Unlike some judges, who became more hardened with each case, Judge Horne got wiser. He could be found at the local Y shooting baskets, teaching, wrestling or even cruising streets to find a runaway.

"Case you heard this morning. Mark Hanson."

The judge nodded. "Defamation of property. Newspapers doing anti-Semitic editorials. Scrawny kid. Father looks like a bad apple."

Carol could have given the judge any name of a case he'd heard years before, and he'd rattle the main facts as he'd just done on the Hanson case. "He's been whipped. Badly, and a lot. June Finnegan will take him. There's a younger brother at home. I'll get a CHINS out on them."

"Give me proof," the judge said. He leaned toward her. "You know I can't just wrench the boys out of their home."

"Look at Hanson's back," she said.

"Where is he?" After Carol told him, Judge Horne asked the bailiff to fetch him. The man returned, dragging Mark by the arm. The kid wrenched free and stood in the corner, almost pouting.

"No one will hurt you, son, but Ms. Marsh has made some disturbing observations. I'd like to see your back."

Mark hesitated before pulling up his shirt.

The judge's mustache twitched. He ran his hand through his hair and sighed. "Take him to Waltham Hospital and get him cleaned up." He walked over. "A couple of those look infected. Get him photographed. I'll change the order to Finnegan's custody and sign a CHINS. If ever there was child in need of service . . ." he shook his head. "There's too damned many kids in need."

Carol sent the kid with the bailiff to search for Mark's father. He wasn't anywhere in the building. She went across the street to the coffee shop. The clerk behind the counter greeted her. "Hey, this isn't your donut day."

"I've another mission. Did you see a man wearing a black raincoat smelling like a brewery?"

The clerk shook his head. "Want a dozen donuts to go?"

"Later, maybe." The air was cool when she left, and she

wrapped her scarf around her neck one extra time as she walked toward to the center until she came to Frank's pub. This wasn't a yuppie bar with hanging plants. This was a saloon, a place for hard drinkers, who lined up in the street before opening. The smell of alcohol and sour rags hung heavily in the air. She fought an urge to vomit.

Mark's father's head was resting on a wooden, pock-marked slab with hundreds of circles from too many wet glasses marring the surface. Carol stomped over and shook him. "Mr. Hanson. Mr. Hanson!"

He slurred something. She looked at the bartender who shrugged.

On way back to the court house she fought an urge to cry, not just for Mark but for herself.

Seth carried two plastic bags of valentines into his house. One was his; the other was his sister's.

"Hi, Sport," Jay said. He turned away from his computer. Lina put down her yellow legal pad. Her printing was as neat as typeset.

Seth waved to Lina and climbed on his father's lap to show him the valentines. "I got this from April. She's stupid," he said.

Carol walked in. "How's Paige and Syeeda?"

"Asleep. Work is limited with cranky, sick awake kids," Jay said.

"Tell me about it," Carol said.

Lina shoved her legal pad into her briefcase. "I'm outta here."

"Do you want to stay over?" Carol asked. "There's the trundle in Seth's room or the couch."

"Nah. My mom's coming in from Atlanta tonight. She can baby sit tomorrow. Besides, Syeeda is better in her own bed. Office or here tomorrow, Boss?"

"Carol, can you stay home tomorrow?" Jay asked.

"Surely you jest." Carol sat down to take off her boots.

Jay turned to Lina. "Call me from the office in the morning. I'll give you a list of stuff I need. Now, if I have to go to court, how would you feel about staying with Paige?"

"Other duties as assigned, that's my job description," Lina said. She went out to warm up the car before bundling up her daughter.

From where Jay lay in bed propped up with the *New England Law Journal* he could watch Carol rub cleansing cream on her face. He knew it smelled like peaches.

She tilted her head to the left then right. She dragged her jaw down.

"You don't look old," he called.

"Either you or the mirror is lying. I'll pretend it's the mirror."

He watched her undress—he appreciated that she had filled out from the skinny kid he had knocked over with his bike. A few stretch marks on her tummy—slightly pouchy no matter how hard she tried to pull it in. "Want to watch TV?"

She pulled the blue flannel nightgown over her head. "Go ahead, but I'm going to sleep."

"Since you're half asleep, let's talk about the vasectomy."

She put the pillow over her head. He picked it off. "What's your biggest objection?"

Sitting up in bed, she took the pillow from him and hugged it to her stomach. "I won't be able to have any more children."

He frowned. "You said we only wanted two."

"But I want the choice."

"You know that's irrational." He held out his arm, and she slid into it.

"Of course, I do, but I promise to think about it."

He shut off the lamp. Within seconds he heard her breath

slow down and followed her into sleep, the idea of television, law journals and vasectomies forgotten.

Chapter 15

Tony DiDonato watched his children scamper into the school yard. When the bell trilled, Robbie and Samantha disappeared into a crowd of jeans and hooded jackets moving as one into the building.

The day was his until he picked them up after three. Although maybe not, if Jay needed a sitter. Tony was so used to having the house to himself during the week, that footsteps and muted voices from below discombulated him. Any contemplative monk thrown into society would have felt the same. But then contemplative monks wouldn't be taking their children to school and delaying going home. Well, he had much to do there regardless of what was going on downstairs.

Shoving his hands into his pockets, he ambled down Mass Ave. toward Chestnut Street. He could see his breath unlike during last week's false spring. The bookstore that he so loved caught his eye. It wasn't part of a chain, another thing he liked about it. One window was used books, the other new. Through the glass door he could see the empty play area for children bored by their browsing parents.

Except for a clerk, shelving a new shipment from a cardboard carton, the store was deserted. She climbed up and down a wooden stepladder, shoving titles into various places. Her navy blue panty hose outlined good legs. Denim skirt. Good hips, nice ass.

He headed for the literature section. If this were 1300, and he'd wanted a book he'd have had to take a manuscript to a copyist. Wait days. Weeks. Running his finger down the titles he decided there was nothing he wanted to read. That lie lasted a second. Lots of these books he would like to read, but not one of them was in the budget, unless, unless he justified it as an investment.

In the handyman and crafts section he thumbed through a few books to see if there was a new finishing technique that he might have missed. Nothing. After all his father's training, maybe he should write the how-to books, not buy them.

Libraries. That was where he found all their reading material. The kids'. And Laurel's. When she had time to read that is, which was almost never. Sometimes when his wife came home he felt as if a succubus had entered the room draining his life forces. Not fair. Fair. Semi-fair. They'd been together since high school more or less. This was a less time. It would pass.

Several newspapers covered the counter near the cash register: *The Chronicle for Higher Education.* Now that was an investment. He counted out correct change. "I left money on the cash register," he called to the clerk perched on the ladder and held up the paper.

"Thanks," she said. Blond ringlets fell to her shoulder. The type of woman who drove Plantagenet kings wild. A fair Rosamund with cheeks like cherries and skin like snow. Blue eyed. Small boned. Just the opposite of Laurel. His hormones told him this would make a good fantasy later. Later, the hell with later. Fantasy was all he had. His wife was so wound up that whenever he touched her she jumped. When was the last time they had sex? New Year's Eve.

He passed a coffee shop, also privately owned. Cracked tables. He was tempted to buy the bookstore clerk a cup of coffee. He hadn't cheated on Laurel since grad school. During his masters. Then only twice. The last thing their marriage needed was for him to have an affair. But Laurel wouldn't know. Maybe just a nice chat with the fair Rosamond. Courtly love, like knights of old. Worship from afar. A token exchanged. Instead of a handkerchief, a cup of coffee. He entered the shop.

As he waited at the counter for the coffee, he scanned the want ads in *The Chronicle*. The Universities of Maine and Ohio were both looking for tenure track medieval scholars. That was him all right. Maine would be a great place to live, but he wasn't so sure about Ohio. Clark University was looking for a temporary instructor for the summer. About forty-five miles away. Might lead to something.

The paper cup did not totally protect his hands from the heat. He switched the cup back and forth as he headed back to the book store. Gloves. He should have worn gloves. *The Chronicle* he tucked under his arm. The bell over the book store door tinkled as he entered.

The woman, more a girl, maybe a college student, sat on the top rung of the ladder talking into her cell while chomping a piece of gum. "I'll meet you at Leo's after work. Love ya, honey." She snapped the phone shut. "Can I help you, Sir?"

"Did I leave a pair of gloves?" Women inspiring medieval knights to great acts of bravery and courtly love never chewed gum.

She shook her head.

"Not your fault." Later he sat on a bench at the edge of Cambridge corner. He twisted off the plastic cap and sipped. Too weak, not like espresso or ristretto that he made at home. He poured it on the grass and threw the cup into an overflowing trash barrel behind the bench.

Fate had stepped in. Better he respond to want ads than hormones. She was too young for him. Then an image of a fox jumping towards a bunch of grapes flashed through his mind.

Upstairs, his table waited to be sanded by hand, letting the rough paper move with the grain and checking every few strokes to feel if he got it right. He alternated between wanting to apologize to it for hurting it and accepting its thanks for saving it. Each day, he saved the table for his last project in the hope he could feel victorious about something, no matter how small.

Maybe he should work on his CV first. Nah. The faster they went out, the faster the rejections came in. Later. For a second he pictured Chaucer in a room with thick stone walls tapping out the *Wife of Bath's* tale on a computer and himself doing his CV with a quill pen.

CHAPTER 16

"Thanks for the ride." Laurel jumped out of Carol's double-parked car in front of Jackson Products. She wondered how come Carol understood how she felt—as if a rope wrapped itself around her stomach each morning before she entered the plant. When she tried to tell Tony, her words bounced off him, like one of the kid's soft sponge balls against a wall. Although she knew she'd been talking to a man without a job, she just wanted him to visualize her point of view. It shouldn't be a big deal, except it was.

Work shouldn't be like this. However, as family breadwinner, she had no choice. Breadwinner, rent winner, clothes winner, heat winner and now a new muffler winner. She'd ridden to work with Carol so Tony could replace the muffler. Much nicer to chat with her best friend about kids and the latest episode of their favorite television series than worry about pollutants, which was what she'd have done had she driven in alone. No longer could she avoid thinking about the 300 missing containers.

She slid her card in the box by the front door. It clicked open. The tower clock struck nine, two hours later than she usually arrived. Co-workers passed with barely a nod. Nothing like the old days. The empty spot where her secretary's desk stood reminded her to write Michelle a recommendation.

She called Anderson's office as she had done for the last ten days and like the last ten days his secretary put her off.

She called Paul. No answer. Every time someone didn't pick up the phone, she wondered if they'd been fired. When she looked up, Paul was outside her door waiting for her to hang up.

"I changed the safe room locks." He handed her a key. "Only two copies. Yours and mine, Baby. Can't be duplicated." He moved her briefcase from her guest chair and sat. "Any word from Anderson."

"Can't get by his witch-bitch."

"E-mail?"

"Lots. All marked urgent and company confidential. Nothing."

"Laurel, this stuff is dangerous. If it stays in the barrels, fine. But what if it gets into the water? The air?"

Laurel remembered the Tyngsboro condo complex a few years ago where pollutants had leaked into the water source. No one could shower, wash or cook with the water. Owners were stuck with unsalable, unlivable property. Or the case in Woburn where toxic waste had led to birth defects and a high number of cancers. She didn't have to look any further than her own company to find dangerous chemicals. The labs downstairs were full of potential health hazards.

"No marks on the containers, so they can't be identified as ours."

"Only if the thief put them on himself." Paul glowered.

"You're thinking that I believe that relieves Jackson Products of responsibility."

"Not at all. What I was thinking was that someone had done something criminal." He left.

Drumming her desk with her fingers, she wrestled with her choice. She paced the narrow floor space, sat down, looked out the window, stood up, sat down. Turning on her computer, she stared at the company logo without really seeing it. Once more she tried Anderson's extension.

"He's in a meeting," the witch-bitch secretary said.

"Is this a recording?" Laurel asked.

"Pardon?"

"You always say the same thing," Laurel said.

"Mr. Anderson is a busy man." The secretary's tone was the same Laurel used when explaining something to her kids such as why you can't leave the water in the tub running because it will flood the bathroom.

When they hung up, she wondered how men like Anderson, men who contributed to the bad health of people and the world, could sleep at night. Probably quite well, if the bottom line looked good.

Her computer screen showed the company logo and slogan: Helping people lead healthier lives. "Right," she said to herself. Supporting her family weighed heavily. But what if some engineer knew something that was dangerous to her kids and did nothing? She rummaged through her coat pocket for her cell. Then she remembered it was in her car. How much damage could one more day do? A lot if another day caused her to change her mind.

Laurel waited until 1:15 before escaping for lunch. The Watch City Restaurant in the other part of the building was too close. Outside she turned left and walked to the city center. The breeze nibbled at her face and whipped hair into her eyes.

On the corner of Main Street a sub shop had a phone booth. Less and less of those around these days. Each of the eight tables had been painted by a Brandeis University student. A refrigerator of soft drinks stood next to the counter behind which a man and woman filled orders that moved the line in seconds.

"What'll it be today?" the woman asked.

"Regular cold cut, the works, except for onions," she said.

Moving in fast forward, the woman slit the bread, slapped on several types of meat, followed by rounds of translucent cheese. With assembly line efficiency she added chopped tomatoes, hot peppers and pickles. Everything went on a paper plate with shell-like edges. As the finishing touch, she scooped chips from a can decorated with an owl.

Laurel swallowed a wave of jealousy because this woman didn't have to face moral dilemmas over slices of provolone. Maybe her feet hurt at the end of the day, but her soul was free.

Laurel gulped her meal with frequent glances at her watch. As the sub shop emptied, she eyed the public telephone. Twice she got up to use it, sat down then went back to the booth. Do it. Now. She picked up the receiver. If they gave medals in hemming and hawing, she'd take the gold. Sighing she dropped coins in the slot and dialed the Department of Environmental Protection. "Matt Rossi, please. This is Laurel DiDonato."

"I'll check, but he may still be at lunch," a woman's voice said.

Laurel doubted it. Her old college buddy seldom went to lunch. She imagined him carrying a food-laden tray from the food court below and eating at his desk while he worked.

The phone clicked. "Hi, Laurel, no time no hear. How's my ersatz sister?" His mouth sounded full.

"What are you eating ersatz brother?" she asked.

"Taco. How's it hanging?"

She told him.

"Shit! Any ideas?"

"Nothing I can prove. It might be my management," she said.

"Not like when the old man was there. You guys were first class all the way," Rossi said. "What can I do? Call an audit? Ask the AG to raid?"

"I'm not sure."

"Gotcha. Your job in danger?"

"It might be history, if I got caught talking to you."

"Let me check your home phone. I'll get one of the AG's Strike Force to call you there."

"Without a search warrant, the president will never let them in." Oh God, why had she started this? Jesus, Mary and Joseph. She pictured her family pushing all their belongings in shopping carts and sleeping in doorways. No, Carol and Jay wouldn't let that happen. "Matt, I'm scared." She could say that to him. They'd spent too much time studying for exams with Laurel saying she'd never pass, and he reassuring that she would and then laughing at her when she aced the test.

"Relax. This can be kept confidential. You can go in judge's chambers. And we can set you up as a confidential witness, especially since you've worked so well with us before."

"What does that mean?"

"The inspector takes your testimony. Presents it to the judge. You'll have to see the judge anyway to confirm."

She heard a crunch as he bit his taco. "Anything else?"

"Xerox as much paper work as possible. In case they tamper with the evidence."

"I'll do it before the weekend," she said.

"Good girl. Now onto pleasanter things. Did I tell you I went back to our old stomping ground?" She had to add more coins to learn what had changed at the University of Maryland. When she hung up, she looked at her watch. That was brave, she thought, but as she put on her coat she changed her mind, That was really, really stupid.

Back in the office Laurel headed for the basement, where she wanted to tell Paul what she'd done. She imagined him stretched out on a rack with Anderson torturing him. Better he stay innocent.

She picked up a screw driver from his work bench and rolled it in her hands. "Paul, I came from a very Catholic family. There's right. There's wrong. Abraham Lincoln walking miles to return a nickel, George Washington confessing to cutting down a cherry tree and Luigi Mangioni hiding Jews from Hitler."

"Well the first are probably not true, but who's this Mangioni?"

"My uncle. He was shot. After the war, my dad's family migrated to the States. But he always told me to do what I believed was right. He said if you didn't there was no hope for anyone."

Paul took the tool from her. "I don't have the foggiest idea what you're talking about."

Back in her office she checked her E-mail. Anderson told her he could see her from 4:13 to 4:21. He always chose off minutes with no room for lateness. Her watch read 4:10. She took off at a run.

Anderson's witch-bitch guarded his door. She imagined handing her a glass of water that would freeze when she took it.

The outer office had been refurnished with antiques and oriental rugs after Prospect bought it. The old man had used stuff that had come with the building when he'd bought it. "Go in," the secretary said without looking up.

Anderson sat behind a desk that belonged in a European château. He was talking into a Dictaphone, probably one of the last executives in the world not to use a computer. His guest chairs had spindly legs that made anyone with a few extra pounds uneasy about sitting in them. He put the microphone back in its holder and ruffled some papers.

"I've had some disturbing E-mails from you about a missing chemical." He folded his hands.

"Chemicals. Hydrochloric acid. Methyl bromide."

"It must be your imagination. We never had that chemical on the premises." He picked up the microphone. "I've a lot to do."

"I'm not mistaken."

"You're not listening. If I say you're mistaken, you're mistaken. Now that you understand, I'm pleased to tell you its 4:19 and we've concluded our meeting early. There's no need to discuss this again."

She swallowed several times. "They're dangerous chemicals. You should know that in March 2008 in Mecca, California . . ."

Anderson hit the palm of his hand with the microphone several times. "Then isn't it good we never had any." It was not a question.

"Mr. Anderson."

He turned his back.

"Mr. Anderson." Her voice was louder. "The containers were not the right ones. That's a strong corrosive and . . ."

Without looking around he said, "Good bye, Laurel."

"I replaced the muffler myself," Tony said. The kids were asleep. He sat on the couch with Laurel stretched out and her head in his lap. He stroked her forehead.

When he took his hand away, she brought it back. "Don't stop. Feels good." Riding home with Carol had helped. She'd vented so much that by the time she told Tony how her day was she was calm.

"I'm sorry you had such a shit day," he said.

She shoved her tingle of worry down. No need to spook him too.

Samantha came out of the bedroom, her blanket dragging behind. "I'm going to throw up."

Laurel grabbed her daughter, and they just made the toilet. Afterwards she gave the child a glass of water to rinse her mouth and wiped her face with a cloth. "Better?"

The little girl held up her arms to be carried back to bed.

"I'll put a wastepaper basket next to you, if you have to throw up again," Laurel said.

"Robbie says that's yucky."

"Your brother's asleep. He won't know." She laid the little girl on the bed, and rubbed her temples until she fell asleep. Then she tiptoed back to the living room.

"She OK?" Tony asked. He polished a lock for a desk. The smell of metallic fluid hung in the air.

Laurel wrinkled her nose and flopped onto the couch. An afghan of multi-colored crocheted squares was draped across the back. She pulled it over her legs and picked up *Business Week,* opened it to a story about women deserting corporate life to start their own companies. "She's probably coming down with chicken pox like Paige. Maybe we should warn your mother we won't be there for Sunday dinner."

Tony held the cloth against the opening of the can and tipped it. "It's early. Sam might just have a tummy upset."

Laurel wouldn't mind missing one Sunday dinner surrounded by cherubs holding lamps in her mother-in-law's house. The obligatory nature bothered her more than the event. Still, her mother-in-law had promised home-made raviolis. "We'll wait to see if spots come out."

He sat beside her and draped his arm over her shoulder so he could manipulate her nipple. " 'bout ready for bed?"

"I'm ready to go to sleep."

"I know a great sleeping pill." He nuzzled her ear.

She pushed him away. "Not in the mood."

He retracted his arm so fast it was like her breast had become a flame. "Will you ever be again?"

"Who knows?" She went into the bedroom. When the alarm went off the next morning, his side of the bed was empty and unmessed. After throwing her robe over her shoulders, she went in search of him.

He'd slept on the couch, still dressed, his knees hanging over the edge. The shadow on his face from not shaving diminished his angelic look, but Laurel still marveled at how handsome he was . . . better even than George Clooney.

His eyes flew open. "What time is it?"

"Five A.M. I know I have to get ready for work, but how 'bout a quickie, big boy?"

"Thought you'd never ask, Ma'am. Just let me brush my teeth."

Quickie was the right word. Laurel did all the things she knew he loved, taking his prick in her mouth, handling his balls and then mounting him. Part of her mind was on Samantha, part on the day ahead.

He came quickly. She didn't come at all, but she'd never faked an orgasm and promised him she never would.

"I don't know whether to thank you or ask why bother," he said.

"I think 'thank you' would be better," she said, although the words never look a gift fuck in the mouth ran through her mind. He didn't like her to be crude.

"Slam, bam, thank you Ma'am," he said, but his tone was playful.

She headed for the bathroom, but poked her head back into the bedroom. "Cute."

CHAPTER 17

Private Mark Hanson, serial number 0028A, sat on the edge of the bed thinking about the woman who had said, "Call me Aunt June," as she pointed out which drawers were his. She looked like a push over.

There were two sets of bunk beds in the room and two in the next. The other kids here were dorks. Petty crimes. Dope, shop lifting, stuff like that. None gave a flying fuck what happened to the USA. Just about themselves.

One of the niggers had said this was one of the better foster homes he'd been in. His opinion should count? No way, man. All the kids had horror stories about foster homes. Mark guessed it was routine to tell the new guy. He had his own horror stories too but kept them to himself. Soldiers kept quiet.

A piece of paper labeled "House Rules" was pasted on the closet door. Homework was to be checked before watching television, shower once a day, chores were required, curfew was 6 P.M. unless there was a school activity.

The house was full of lists: directions on how to leave the kitchen and bathroom and a sign-up list for chores which also had lists on how to do each one. How much information did it take to clean a toilet? Those assholes actually volunteered. A sign-out sheet of where you were going and what time you'd be back was next to the telephone by the front door. Fucking boring.

He wondered when he would get a chance to report to his

commander. He'd made one quick call while waiting for his father to take him to court. All he'd gotten was the answering machine, but he'd said, "0028A here. Intercepted by police. On the way to court. Will contact when I can." He hated fucking answering machines.

June came in with a pile of clean linen. "I want to check your homework before television."

The dorks had already shown her their stupid papers. He heard the sound of a Celtics game coming from the Wreck Room, which was what June called the living room. He smelled popcorn.

"I don't want to."

"Suit yourself. Kevin is shooting great tonight."

He debated going down anyway. How could she stop him? As soon as he stepped over the threshold, she was there.

"Homework?"

He tried to brush by her. Within a second she had him up against the wall with one arm around his back. "I guess no one told you I was an MP in the Marines. Black belt, too. No homework, no television, no leave the room."

What a strong bitch. She had a pair of balls. A cheer went up from the boys downstairs. Mark looked at his school books and wondered how he would be able to get a hold of his commander.

CHAPTER 18

Letters raced across Jay Marsh's computer screen. His typing had been clocked at one hundred words a minute. A knock broke his rhythm. When he smelled cigar smoke he knew without looking it was Bobby Reardon, one of the two lawyers with whom he shared office space, law library, coffee machine, copier, receptionist and postage meter.

Jay opened his window. The unseasonably spring-like air couldn't wash away the stench. "Put that damned thing out, please."

Bobby dunked the cigar stub in a coffee cup. It hissed. "You need an ash tray."

Jay didn't bother answering that smoking in offices was against the law. Both Barbara and Bobby made it a useless battle. They agreed on the Celtics, Red Sox and Patriots, nothing more.

"You're a fool to donate so many billable hours," Bobby would say.

"I want to make society better."

"And I want to make my bank account better."

Had Bobby been trained by Anna to shovel an elderly neighbor's walk without payment as Christian charity, he might have thought differently. Neither had any compunctions about charging the maximum to a doctor or stock broker.

"I want to kill the Battleaxe." Bobby ran his hand over his emerging scalp as he referred to the receptionist. The nickname held no affection.

Jay pressed "save" on the computer. "What's Barbara done now?"

"Called my client a scum bag."

"Is he?"

"Of course. Bank fraud guy. This is a new level of rudeness even for her. I mean usually she's only nasty to my petty crooks."

"If we fired her, she'd refuse to go or sue, and no one is as efficient."

Bobby took a new cigar from his pocket and licked the end. "At least ask Lina to talk to her. If she'll listen to anyone it's Lina. Catch ya later."

Alone again, Jay hit the print icon. The printer hummed before spitting out the paper. Whenever he worked through some intricacy or won a case for some poor individual against the big, bad world, he congratulated himself that he hadn't joined some high-powered firm. Less money—definitely. Less pressure—more important. Freedom—most important, priceless as the credit card ad said.

Lina opened his door without knocking. The beads at the end of her cornrowing halfway down her back tinkled. "Hey, Boss, when you get through shmoozing with that paper, your stepmother is here. And don't shoot the messenger."

"Shit," he said as Lina mouthed "shit" along with him.

"Why did you tell her I was here?"

"Because you are," she said. She exaggerated such an innocent look, he had to smile.

"Let's go see her."

"What's this 'let's us' shit, white man?"

"If I weren't afraid you'd sue me for sexual harassment, I'd slap your butt."

As she let him pass through the door, she said, "No law suit. I'd just deck you."

He hung back. "While I talk to my stepmother, can you ask Barbara to be nicer to people."

Lina headed back to her own office as Jay went to reception. "You think I'm suicidal?"

Jennifer Marsh waited on the beige leather couch with her back to the window where the lawyers' names were written in black-bordered gold paint. A woman, pushing a stroller, could be seen through the window. The office was half in a residential, half in a small business area bordering Harvard Square.

The blue of Jennifer's plaid kilt matched her boiled wool jacket. Navy flats led to excellent legs. Jay assumed she wore them because she was the same height as his father.

Battleaxe Barbara sitting at the reception desk, her fingers flying over the keyboard ignored them. Her typing speed exceeded Jay's.

"Jennifer, what a surprise." Jay couldn't remember the last time they'd spoken, but it wasn't long enough. Her once long black hair grazed her chin. Grey streaked her temples. He would have thought she was too vain to let the grey show. When he'd met her after his parents' divorce, he thought she would have been one of his father's law students—he'd guessed right. Probably she was nicer than he was willing to admit however; and he refused to release the image of her as the other woman, the home wrecker. Nor did he accept Anna's claim that her own marriage to his father had ended long before the separation.

Jennifer stood in one smooth motion. Most people propelled themselves from the soft cushions. "Can we go into your office?" He'd forgotten how much she sounded like Jackie Kennedy, a whispery little cotton batten voice.

Battleaxe Barbara spoke without looking at anyone. A cigarette dangled from her lips despite the no smoking sign above her desk. "I suppose you want coffee."

"Please, two sugars, milk," Jennifer said.

"Only have Cremora." Jay knew that Barbara had bought cream that morning but why she was lying was beyond him.

"That will be fine," Jennifer said.

"One for you too?" Barbara glared at Jay.

"Yes, like always."

"Can't remember how you take it," Barbara said. She ground the cigarette to smithereens in the ashtray, sprinkling the desk with ash.

"Black." He was half delighted she would serve him coffee, and half afraid she'd spit in it. What could Jennifer have said to her to make her offer?

In his office, he directed his stepmother to the round conference table, discarding the idea of using his desk as a barrier. Twenty years was too long to carry a grudge. That was his opinion—intellectually. Resentment battered his emotions as she slithered into her seat.

He leaned against the front of his desk rather than sit at the table. "Why are you here?"

"I want you to visit your father."

As he watched her, he remembered a dream he'd had after his father's remarriage. Even after twenty years, each detail was as fresh as when he was dreaming it.

Jennifer Holbein Marsh and Louis Marsh were on trial against Jay and Anna Marsh. Husband/father and lover vs. wife and son. Charge? Desertion.

Jennifer had taken the stand, raised her hand and swore to tell the whole truth, but from his place behind the defendant's table he saw her fingers crossed and her hand hovering above the Bible without touching it.

"And did you with malice and forethought lead Louis Marsh away from his wife and son?" Perry Mason was representing him and Anna.

"He was my mentor. We couldn't help ourselves," Jennifer looked at her lap. "I'm quitting the law to devote myself just to him. I'll be orderly and logical, not flighty like his wife."

"Stick to the question," Perry demanded. "Don't you know you're depriving the son of someone to play baseball with?"

Jennifer looked chastened. "He never played baseball with his son. He never paid much attention to him at all. It was Anna who wanted to adopt Jay, not my Louis."

"I object," Jay jumped up.

"Objection overruled," the judge said. The judge was Johnny Carson.

"Jay, Jay. Are you all right?"

Her whispery voice cut through his fog. "Sorry, Jennifer, I doubt if my father has much to say to me, or me to him."

"I know he hasn't contacted you for years." She looked directly at him. "He talks about you. He knows about Paige and Seth."

"There's an invention called a telephone and another called E-mail." He sat at the table.

Jennifer started to reach out to touch him, but at the look on his face, stopped her hand midair. "Louis said if you'd sent birth announcements he'd have called. He was afraid you'd hang up."

Jay had trouble imagining Louis Marsh afraid of anything. Funny—he never thought of Anna as anything but his real mother, but thought of Louis as his adopted father. And this woman, he realized with sudden clarity, wasn't his stepmother— she was his adoptive father's trophy wife, the reason Louis Marsh had abandoned his family!

Other memories bombarded him. At Seth's age, he and Anna played cowboy, creating a teepee by throwing a sheet over a card table. They pretended the luncheon bologna was buffalo meat. Each night it had to be all put away to not disturb his father, who had lots to do as an important Harvard Law Professor.

"He was so happy you became an attorney. If you're so against him, why did you choose his profession?" Jennifer interrupted his memories.

"Fair question."

"Do I get a fair answer? If you hated him so much, I'd have thought you'd have entered another field. Or not gone to Harvard."

"I wanted to help others. Harvard was the best school. Not doing either would have been to cut off my own nose to spite my father's face." Jay remembered how hard it had been to not walk down a certain corridor when his father was walking along, followed by adoring students, of ducking into a classroom rather than have to speak to him. Fortunately he was able to get other professors for his courses.

"Whenever he saw you, he told me. Jay, he's sick. Cancer. He won't live much longer. If you don't want to see him for his sake, do it for yourself." This time she touched his hand.

He pulled it away. "I don't see how it can possibly be for me."

"You may not want to accept advice from me, but I've lost both my parents. My Dad and I were buddies. When he died, I was devastated, but I healed quickly. In contrast, I didn't get along well with my mother. When she died, we were barely speaking. Some stupid fight about my not calling her when we got back from a holiday."

He wanted to say—ask me if I care?—but politeness overruled.

Jennifer continued in her breathy voice. It wasn't the voice of a lawyer who would present court cases. "Courtesan" was a better word for someone who looked up from the corner of her eyes and whispered. "She knew we were home, but I had . . . but I had to be the one to call first. That type of thing drove me crazy, although it doesn't seem all that important now. It took me longer to get over her death."

"Why are you telling me this?" he asked.

"Dad and I had no unfinished issues. Mother and I did. There's lots of unfinished business between Louis and you. Do nothing and after he's gone, you'll have to live with it. Better to act now." She stood. "Louis doesn't know I'm here. If you do come, don't tell him. Please."

She opened the door as Barbara came in with two cups of coffee on a stained tray. "Thank you." Jennifer drank half and put the cup back on the tray. "All I ask is that you think about it."

After she'd left, he sat looking at the coffee. He debated calling Anna. Although he tried to tell himself he shouldn't, because it would hurt her, he knew his mother would echo what Jennifer said. When Lina found him a half hour later, his cup was still full.

Cars spilled out of the Marsh driveway into the street. When Jay saw them, he remembered Laurel was hosting her searching-for-birth-parents support group.

As he opened the front door, noises from the kitchen told him Carol was home. She'd planned to arrive early to relieve Tony who'd ended up caring for the children in various stages of chicken pox. Jay was greeted by four pajamaed bodies. Their faces had scabs. When Seth reached to scratch, Jay pulled his hand away.

"I know. It'll leave a scar. It could be cool, like some super hero," Seth said.

Jay hoisted his son onto his hip. "Let's find your mother."

Carol was working at the kitchen table. She angled her cheek so Jay could brush it with his lips. "We've got all four kids all night."

"What can I do?"

"Get them into bed and read a story." She grabbed his necktie to pull him down for a real kiss. When she released him she added, "You've got time to get into something comfortable."

The house was quiet. About a half hour before they'd heard footsteps thumping down the stairs and cars starting. Someone had beeped. All four children slept through it.

Carol sat on the couch adding notes to folders, while Jay worked on the computer. The score of *Les Miserables* was on the CD player. Jean Valjean sang about the kindness of a bishop. A scratch was heard at the door.

Laurel stuck her head in. Tony could be seen behind her. "We've come for our kids."

"Take any two. Or leave 'em until morning," Jay said.

"Want something to drink. Herb tea?" Carol asked.

"No, it's been a bitch of a day, and I just want to crawl into bed. By the way, it's snowing hard, and they're predicting a bad one."

"Maybe there'll be no work tomorrow," Carol said.

"I wish," Laurel said, "except with the new policy, I won't get paid." The door clicked behind her and her footsteps up the stairs were muffled.

Carol placed folders in different sections of her briefcase. The slots were marked: court, filing, appointments. When she finished, she turned to Jay. "You OK? You seem, I don't know . . . funny."

"Jennifer came by." He repeated the conversation. As he talked, he paced.

Carol watched. "She really upset you."

He shook his head. "I just think she had a hell of a nerve."

As she capped her pen, she said, "It's all right to be upset."

He stopped pacing long enough to shut down the computer, and then put the CD back in its box. "I wish they didn't over-package these things. Bad for the environment. God. I'm beginning to sound like Laurel." He gathered his papers and arranged them in his briefcase. "I'm turning in."

She watched. "It's called avoidance."

"You're right. Coming to bed?"

"I should empty the dishwasher."

"Leave it 'till tomorrow." As he held out his hand she took it.

The clock radio woke the Marshes. The WERS student announcer said, "This is the blizzard of the century. Not since 1978 has so much snow fallen so fast. The East Coast is zonked in from Washington, D.C. to the Canadian border. This storm will break all records for March if not forever."

Carol rolled over and shook Jay. "Sounds like a day off to me."

The wind whipped around the house. He slipped out of bed to open the drapes. The windows were white with blown snow. Using the remote, he flicked on the television. A camera pointed at Storrow Drive outside the television studio showed a road normally clogged by traffic. Today, it looked like a snow-swept field. The announcer, dressed in a parka, his hood lined with fur and covered with white, peered into the camera. The wind's whistle whooshed into the microphone, distorting and muffling his words. "Everyone is instructed to stay home. The Governor has called an emergency. We've had almost a foot of snow and at least another eight inches is expected before it ends tomorrow."

Carol puffed her pillow and pulled her duvet to her neck. Jay got back in bed and snuggled next to her. The phone rang. It was Jay who rolled over to answer.

"It's me," Anna said.

"Mom, where are you?"

"Gloucester High School. They evacuated everyone along the coast. I just wanted you to know I'm safe."

"The house?"

"Waves were up to the porch when the police came. The way it's situated I think it will hold. It did in '78, but Motive No. 1 has been swept away and . . ." The phone went dead.

"Anna's OK?" Carol asked.

"She should be. She's in the high school," he said.

They stayed in bed watching the news, flipping channels until he shut it off. "Let's talk vasectomy. We've no place to go all day or maybe tomorrow."

"Why spoil a day off?" She rested her head on his chest, the flannel of his pajama top feeling soft against her cheek.

"It's never a good time for you. I just think it's my turn to take responsibility for birth control."

"But, it's so permanent. What if something happens to Seth or Paige?"

Both of them felt her tremble. "Adopt. There's enough unwanted kids."

"Tired arguments."

"But true. You don't really want another baby?"

She turned so they nestled like spoons in a silver drawer. "I want my options open."

"We could freeze some of my sperm."

"Kidsickles." She giggled. The clock ticked. Wind shook the casement. "Total sexual freedom would be nice. Never to worry if my period was late." She spoke so softly he wasn't sure she'd heard.

"Is that a yes?"

"A definite maybe." Because of her position she couldn't see his smile. In the past her definite maybes had mostly become definite yeses.

Chapter 19

Tony stepped from the dark subway into Haymarket Square. Blinding sun. Snow higher than dump trucks. Squinting even with sunglasses. Wind gusts picked at his skin. Thank God for beards and aviator caps with ear flaps. No horns blared, no car engines mumbled, no screeching breaks. Traffic was forbidden. The state of emergency continued while the National Guard cleaned up from the storm.

Without the normal noises he heard his own heart. He'd never been in such a quiet place. It must be like this walking in the woods or a meadow, but even there, there would be bird song, surely, or some type of noise. He walked into the North End, so different since the overhead expressway had come down.

He knew the North End like he knew his own body. He and Laurel had grown up here. This looked like a different land. Brick sidewalks shoveled in narrow paths with just enough space for a single file, if people were out on the streets. They weren't.

The bottom of a Resident Parking Only sign rested on top of a snowdrift. He assumed a car was buried underneath. Shops were closed. Shelves had been plundered of bread and milk like the last day of a liquidation sale.

The store window where strings of fresh pasta normally hung was empty. Mikey, the owner, Tony's high school buddy and Laurel's cousin, could be seen working in the back. He lived over the shop.

As Tony opened the door, bells on a rope jingled. He heard

pasta dough slap against a marble slab and saw puffs of flour rise. "How's it going?" he called out.

"We're alive." Mikey emerged wiping his floury hands on his apron. "And in your country?"

"Cambridge is across the river. It's part of Massachusetts and the U.S. of A."

"Might as well be another country." He pointed to the mass of dough on the table. "First and last batch. Outta eggs."

"Radio announced some delivery trucks should get through in the morning," Tony said.

Mikey picked up a marble rolling pin and attacked the dough: two rolls out, two in, two left, two right. "Get us some espresso, Man." He pointed with his chin to the machine on the counter next to a stainless steel sink.

Tony filled the top with water and coffee grounds then set two demitasses under the miniature spouts. Within minutes the machine hissed and snorted and spilled out black streams.

"So why are you slumming over here?" Mikey took the cup. He blew on it and downed the liquid in a single swallow before twisting the dough and resuming his up-down-left-right pattern.

Tony watched. "Checking on Mama."

"How's Laurel?" Mikey's eyes stayed on the dough.

"Taking care of the kids. They've got chicken pox."

"Ya, one of mine has it too." Mikey rubbed his nose with the back of his hand, and then cut the dough into two large squares. He dabbed ricotta laced with spinach in soldier-precise rows on one, covered it with the other piece and then sliced them into neat squares.

"Why don't you and the wife come over some time?" Tony asked. "We always visit you guys."

"Yah, we will." Mikey's tone was polite, not affirming.

"Better get going."

Tony's mother lived four doors down from Mikey's pasta

shop. The apartment where Tony had grown up was over a bakery. The Venetian blinds were drawn on the shop windows. A sign on the door was written in Italian and English. "Closed until we get the next flour delivery." Tony let himself into the hall with his key. It was dark. He remembered coming home from school and inhaling the hot yeast smell of fresh baked bread. It seemed strange without it.

As soon as he opened the door he was hit with the odor of frying onions. Sounds of the *Magic Flute* floated down the stairs. Mama always had an opera playing. Tony remembered as he and his sisters ran wild, Mama sitting in the middle of the confusion reading a score, running her fingers over black notes on five-lined bars as the Met broadcast on Saturday afternoons. Putting five kids through Catholic School, took all Papa's earnings. The year after Tony graduated, his father bought her a record player. Two months later he was dead. She still used it, although her children had offered to buy her a CD player. "What would I do with the records?" she would ask about those that she had scrimped to buy until she had one of each major opera.

"Mama? You there?"

She came from the kitchen wearing the apron she always wore except when she sat down at the dinner table. She was almost as tall as her son. A few strands of black hair escaped her chignon. "And where would I be?" Her Italian accent had almost disappeared from hours practicing English sounds in the morning with the *Today* show. She shoved a wooden spoon at him. "Taste."

He blew on the red gravy before putting it in his mouth. "Hmm. You've outdone yourself."

"You always say that."

"That's 'cause you cook better and better." He followed her back into the kitchen, where the gravy simmered on the stove.

"I just came by to see if there's anything you need."

"Your sisters' husbands have done that already. They live nearby, you know."

"And I live twenty minutes away." His moving out of the North End ten years before was an act of family treachery with comments from his sisters about breaking his mother's heart. His brother-in-laws never failed to make jokes about the unemployed Doctor of Medieval Literature. "You're doing what you did with Papa before you went to that la di da college," they'd say.

"For the moment," Tony would answer, hoping it wasn't forever. But with each passing rejection, his doubts grew.

"And the kids?"

"Ready to go back to school when it finally reopens. I think Samantha will have a small scar here." He touched the middle of his forehead.

"Laurel?"

"Stressed out." An understatement, he thought. Terrified she'd lose her job, frazzled over losing something, worried about not being paid during the storm. Short tempered with the kids. And him. Not to mention that crazy search for her mother.

"I'm old fashioned. She should be home. You should be working. Time you forgot about teaching. They don't want you." Mama opened the refrigerator which would have supplied a small restaurant. "Let me give you some minestrone to take home."

Tony was alone on the T as he rode back to the other world. He found a newspaper, thinner than usual, when he changed at Park Street. It was full of storm stories: of people trapped in cars on Route 128, of oil not delivered, of looting.

He wanted to be home. His special table awaited him. He'd found a book with cherubs in black and white and had painstakingly colored them with soft colored pencils he had splurged on from the art store near Fenway Park. He could have dropped a whole month's rent in that store, if he'd let himself, but like a good responsible father and husband, limited himself to the pencils. Never had he worked so slowly on any piece, both from prolonging the joy and fear of ruining it.

As they pulled into Kendall Station he saw the wall photos of people and inventions from M.I.T. and Harvard. Prestige schools with hundreds of employed professors. All he wanted was one tenure track post. So why couldn't he get it? What was wrong with him? It didn't matter that he got satisfaction out of taking a thrown away item and making it beautiful. That he could spend a lot of time with his kids.

As the subway train pulled out of Central Square he relived sanding the surface of the table until he almost had an orgasm when he stroked its oak surface. A good piece of wood that had been desecrated. He would make it loveable again.

In Harvard Square two students got on and swung around on the pole before settling in the red hard plastic seats. Care free. Like he used to be. Students who would graduate and get jobs. Probably computer majors. Not liberal arts. Nothing for the preservation of culture. Just for money.

Even his wife worked in her field—or did at the moment. She had insisted they come up with a budget in case she were fired. Pared what was already pared. The best thing would be for him to find work. Flea market sales filled a gap, but a steady paycheck would take the pressure off.

He sighed. He shot too high wanting to be a college professor. Maybe it was time to hunker down and build a business. Support his family. Stop dreaming. He could still read about London conduits built in 1345, to trace the history of food as shown in the *Canterbury Tales*. What was left for him to say about the Middle Ages anyway that hadn't already been said?

Who was left to teach? Kids didn't care what happened 600 years ago.

The subway car chugged into Porter Square. He got out and entered the cavernous station with its red pipes and safety messages flashing. The long escalator crept up toward the street. Bronze mittens and gloves rested in the middle railings between the up and down stairs. Each time Tony saw them he admired the originality.

The cold slapped him as he went through the revolving door. The quiet streets were eerie, but he couldn't stop but think that every now and then a blizzard shutting down the city was good. Gave people a chance to slow down, clear their heads. It recreated the hardship of olden days.

As he headed toward Chestnut Street, he glanced up to see a billboard with a feel good message. A photo of Robert Kennedy was next to the words: "Some men see things as they are and ask why. I dream things that never were and ask why not?" He walked backwards a few steps to get another point of view. If he believed in omens, which he didn't, he would take it as a sign to keep sending out CVs.

Although Mass Ave. had been cleared of snow, Chestnut Street remained uncleared. He forced his way through, feeling a bit like a human snow plow. Three times he looked back at the billboard.

CHAPTER 20

Laurel DiDonato dressed in her jogging suit and fuzzy socks, played fish with her son and daughter. Their faces, scabbed from chicken pox, previewed what they might look like as pimpled teenagers. The threesome sat on the floor, the cards in the middle.

"When's Daddy coming back?" Robbie asked.

"Soon. Have you got any . . ." Before she could say fours, Tony's footsteps pounded up the stairs.

As he bent to kiss each of them in turn he said, "Granny sent some minestrone."

"With lots of macaronis?" Samantha asked. She grabbed the bag to peek.

"If it hasn't enough, we can add some," Laurel said just at the phone rang. She stretched to reach the receiver on the table next to the couch and pulled her hair back freeing her ear.

A man's voice asked, "Laurel DiDonato?"

"That's me."

"Rick Ames, Attorney General's office. Environmental Strike Force. Matt Rossi said there's a problem where you work. Can I come over to talk?"

"Aren't the roads still closed?" she asked.

"Not to cops. The ESF has police status."

"We're outside of Porter Square."

"I know where you are. I grew up around the corner."

"Let's play cards until that man comes," Robbie said to his

mother who alternated between pacing, peering out the window and glancing at her watch. If the other clocks in the apartment hadn't advanced at the same turtle rate, she would have sworn her watch needed batteries.

"Later. I can't concentrate."

"Good," Sam said. "The better my chances to win."

Tony started to pick up the cards. "Go play in your room. Better yet, go downstairs and play with Paige and Seth. Me? I'm hiding in my workroom."

Laurel looked outside again. At the end of the street she spied a white sedan with the blue Massachusetts State seal on the side pull into the parking lot of the shopping center. A man got out and began his way down their street. He didn't wear a uniform, but jeans and a parka. Laurel answered his knock.

"Rick Ames." He displayed his badge, although she wouldn't have known a real one from a fake one.

When he took off his coat, she thought he resembled the Indian on the State seal with his high cheekbones and long black hair falling to his collar. "Coffee?"

"Thanks, but I'm coffeed out."

"Let's go into the kitchen anyway, if you don't mind. Less chance of interruptions. How long have you been on the ESF?"

"About six years. I used to be a normal cop in Woburn until I got my law degree."

"So you know about the big pollution case there?"

"It made me sick, not literally like all those people who got cancer. It was what made me shift into environment protection, even if it happened before my time on the force."

"How do you like it?"

"It's a hell of a lot better than stopping people driving five miles over the speed limit." He seated himself at the Formica table.

She folded her hands on the table top. "What do you need from me?"

He took out a caramel-colored leather notebook with a yellow legal pad inside. "Give me enough information to get a search warrant. They aren't terrorists, so we have to do it the old-fashioned way."

Laurel excused herself to get her briefcase. She returned with a stack of papers. "I've copies of manifests coming and going for a five-year period. Oh, and copies of all my E-mails to the president."

"You just made my job a lot easier." He flipped through the papers and took notes. "Usually an investigation takes three to four weeks. This should cut it in half."

"Time's important, because they might destroy files." Again, her stomach felt as if someone had tied a wire around it. "I'd like you to find the originals. The location is on the top of the copies."

"Don't worry."

Laurel wanted to say that that was like her GYN or dentist telling her to relax when they were working on her. "I worry."

"We'll take your computer too, so we've got the E-mails."

Rick capped his pen. It clicked. "Why are you doing this? Do you have a gripe against them?"

The words snapped from her mouth as fast as a frog hooking a fly with his tongue. "I do. I've a gripe against anyone polluting the environment or endangering others." Standing, she put her fists on the table and leaned towards him. "You gotta understand. My husband isn't working. I could lose my job if I'm suspected of being the whistle blower." She took a deep breath.

Rick nodded. "We'll try and protect you."

"That doesn't stop me from losing sleep. No matter what I do, someone is in danger. It's just that my family's finances are less important than poisoning others."

"I can only guarantee we'll do everything we can, but it isn't a hundred percent." He patted her hand.

"I know. What's next?"

"I'll take down your exact words," he said. "But maybe you'll have to see the judge."

"If it's necessary I'll take a day off." She shuddered thinking of filling out the form that said "reason for request" and her answer "to go to court so the Attorney General can get a search warrant and nail your asses for being scum."

"Most of the time the judge accepts my sworn testimony. At least ninety-nine times out of a hundred." He spent another hour questioning her. When they were finished his notebook was on the last page.

After he left, she thought that maybe the vendor with whom she had cancelled the pick up order might back her up. She called Rick's voice mail and left a detailed message. Then she crossed herself and said a Hail Mary.

The pots clattered as Laurel submerged them in the hot, soapy water. Unusual to have a Sunday at home instead of at her mother-in-law's. Nice. The sense of having to be there annoyed her when some Sundays, she would have preferred to stay in her night clothes and read the Sunday papers. As she scrubbed each pan, she kept going over yesterday's conversation with Rick. Should she have told him anything else? Had she done the right thing? It didn't matter, because she couldn't take it back.

After giving the sink a final wipe with her sponge, she went into the living room. Tony lay stretched on the couch, an old quilt over him. He made soft little putt putt noises. Maybe as he aged his snoring would get louder, but right now she found it comforting.

No noise from the kids' room. Samantha, who had proclaimed

she wasn't the least bit tired and that naps were for babies, had fallen asleep within seconds of Laurel tucking her in. She'd left Robbie thumbing through a book, but from the quiet, she was sure he'd nodded off too. The amount both kids slept convinced her they were still suffering the aftermath of chicken pox, only without temperatures.

The Sunday paper rested across Tony's chest, rising and falling with his breath. She decided not to wake him, and slumped into the chair at right angles. It squeaked.

"Want to share the paper?" he mumbled.

"Give me the help wanted. Might be good to send out some resumes."

"Wouldn't hurt." He turned so his face was against the couch back and tucked his hands into his armpits.

"Does that mean you think I will be fired?"

"It means nothing more than I said. Don't ruin a nice day, honey." His eyes stayed closed.

"You're so laid back," she said. The tone was warm not challenging.

"As a matter of fact, I'm laid back right now, although I'd like to get laid."

She threw a pillow at him. It landed on his chest. His eyes opened long enough to put it under his head and hand her the want ads.

Running her finger down the help wanted columns she read lots of ads for computer analysts/programmers who knew SAP, SMGL, C++ and lots of other letters. At least fifty percent of the engineering posts offered temporary, not permanent contracts. Translated, it meant no health insurance, no vacations. She saw nothing in her own category, permanent or temporary. "Not good," she said.

"Hmm."

"Maybe I should update my resume anyway. I can always

send it on spec. Be proactive." She kissed his forehead and liked the smile that flickered across his face.

In the bedroom she turned on the computer to check E-mails. This time she didn't give into her procrastination trick despite an urge to water the plants and even consider doing the ironing or the mending in the basket on the floor. She discarded several messages. The seventh almost made her stop breathing. She jumped up, knocking the chair over. "Tony, come quick."

The urgency in her voice sent him careening into the bedroom. "What?"

She pointed to the screen. "R-read it." She paced as he sat.

Maria.corrente@gmail.com Re: Mom, I'd love to meet you Mar. 13

"Someone answered my Web page. What should I do?" She stopped behind him and put her hand on his shoulder.

"This is what you've waited for." He stood up and pushed her into the chair. "Open it."

"I can't. What if it's fake? What if she's awful? What if she hates me?"

"What if it's real? What if she's wonderful? What if she loves you?" He started to hit the key that would open the message then stopped. "This is your moment."

"Don't leave me."

He put both hands on her shoulders.

Laurel touched the keyboard but still didn't open it. She looked at Tony, who nodded. She double-clicked on the line with the message.

Dear Laurel:

I gave birth to a baby girl July 24, 1974 in Baton Rouge Hospital LA and a private adoption was arranged through St. Anne's. I'm almost 50 years old and live in Englewood, Florida

(Gulf side). I have prayed for years that I might find you. Please contact me. You should know my husband is your father. You've a sister. We've so much to talk about.

"My God, my God, my God." Laurel walked in circles. She ran her hands through her hair. Her bottom touched the bed, but she got up before she could sink into the mattress. "What am I going to do?" She felt as if she were flying apart with specs of her all over the room. Only by wrapping her arms tight around herself could she control her feelings at all, but she still couldn't stop shaking.

Tony pulled her to him. "I've only seen you like this once before and that was when you told your parents you wanted to look for your birth parents. You were a basket case then too."

She could see her adopted mother's face and heard the words, clipped and cool. "We always feared this would happen."

Her father had stepped in and taken her mother's hand. "And we decided to support you, if you really want it."

Laurel remembered babbling something about she wanted to know more about the woman who gave birth to her, did she have any illnesses that Laurel should worry about if not for herself then but for Sam and Robbie.

Her adopted parents kept saying, "Of course you do," to each reason but her mother's voice stayed tight and she hid her hands the way she always did when upset.

Laurel had not even been as upset when her cousin Mikey called to say that her parents had been killed in a car accident. That had been a year ago.

She'd gone through the funeral on automatic. Only afterwards had she allowed herself to wish she hadn't told them about her search. Irrational, yes, but a part of her felt that if she had kept silent, they would still be alive. Knowing guilt was stupid didn't make it evaporate.

Robbie stuck his head around the corner. "Can I go play

with Seth?" He rubbed sleepers from his eyes. He looked closely at his father with his arms wrapped around Laurel. "Is Mommy sick?"

"Just a headache. Go downstairs," Tony said.

The little boy turned then stopped and came back. "Should I shut your door?"

"Leave it open." Then he gently directed her to the bed. "Do you want me to call Carol?"

"Yes, no, I don't know. I mean Tony, what do I do?"

"Answer her."

CHAPTER 21

From: Ldidonato392@hotmail.com
To: Maria.corrente@gmail.com
Subject: Re: Mom, I'd love to meet you
I want

Laurel could not get beyond the first two words on the E-mail to her birth mother. The red wine Tony had brought sat untouched next to her keyboard. She never heard him leave the bedroom.

Staring at the screen, she thought how somewhere in Florida a woman had touched a keyboard earlier that day, the same woman who had given her away like used clothing. Not fair. She must have had reasons, just like there was a reason she was frozen, unable to answer. If she only knew why.

She'd always been like this. When she'd graduated from the University of Maryland, she'd turned her bed into a whirlwind of paper until she found a job. The same desolation had hit her first morning as Mrs. Tony DiDonato. After months of talking bridesmaids' dresses, menus and music, she wasn't sure what was next. This feeling was a thousand times worse as if her brain had been shot full of Novocain. She never knew how to react when she reached a goal, and this quest had begun the minute she'd learned she was adopted. Wanted or not, that moment came back so strong she could even hear the street noises.

★ ★ ★ ★ ★

During the feast of St. Anthony, the summer she was five, Laurel tied her new sneakers, just like Papa had taught her. Turning in front of her mirror, she knew, she just knew, she looked like a big girl in her violet plaid shorts. Mama had bought them in Filene's basement. Laurel would start kindergarten next month. Thanks to Sesame Street she knew her letters and numbers and could read simple words like Dog, Cat, Run and Sit.

Two open windows didn't help the heat, thick with humidity, pervading every inch of the living room. Two fans moved the hot air without cooling it. Noise from the crowd waiting for the parade one story below drifted up with the heat. When she peeked out of one of the windows earlier, she'd seen Papa at the edge of the crowd. Two cameras were draped around his neck.

Photos he'd taken hung all over the apartment almost as dense as wallpaper. Some were printed out on canvas making them look a little like paintings. Many of them were of her: splashing in the tub, peering over the bumper guard on her crib, wearing a yellow ruffled dress for Easter Mass, her black curls tucked under a bonnet, hanging a stocking on the mantle. Others were of ships, clouds, a plant, Cobb's Hill tombstones with water dribbling over the skull and crossbones.

Nonnie sat at the other window, fanning herself with a piece of cardboard. Her grey hair was covered with a hair net. Nonnie didn't like her. Once Laurel had heard Mama yelling that if Nonnie gave her other grandchildren gifts, she'd better give one to Laurel. Nonnie said she only had so much money. That made sense to Laurel but why not take turns?

"Can I go outside to watch the parade? Can I? Can I?" Laurel tried hard not to whine, because that would make Mama say no. Her mother, rail thin as Nonnie called her, turned from where her elbows rested on the window sill. The big rubber tree, which usually sat in the window, had been pushed to one corner. The gauze curtain was pulled back and held by the braided cord holding back the drape.

"It's a better view here, and besides, I don't want you getting lost," Mama said.

"I won't get lost."

Her cousin Mikey came in. Because he was going into third grade, Laurel thought of him as almost grown up. He lived in the flat upstairs.

"Can I go with Mikey?"

"What about it, Mikey?"

He rolled his eyes. "You have to promise not to run off, Laurie."

She crossed her heart. "And hope to die."

Mama dug into her pocketbook for some money. "That's enough for one treat for each of you."

Laurel jumped up and down. Not only would she be close to the parade instead of watching people's heads, she could buy something. But what? Pistachio gelato so the green cold would freeze her tongue? Maybe pink spun candy smelling like toasted sugar? A sausage roll to be held in her mouth until she sucked the flavor out of it? Or a balloon that floated over her head? A pinwheel?

"Hold onto my belt," Mikey said as they merged into the crowd. The world turned into a sea of hips and thighs as he swiveled and swerved through the crowd until they came to the food carts. "What'd ya want?"

"Cotton candy."

"Me too."

The children watched the man pour pink granules from a silver scoop into a swirling white dish. He twirled a white paper cone, catching the strands until it was thick pink fluff and handed it to Laurel.

Laurel preferred pulling off puffs to pop in her mouth, but

Mikey made her hold onto him, so she bit into the fluff making her face sticky. Before she knew it, he'd found a place at the curb.

The crowd heard the drum and bugle corps before it turned the corner. Teenage boys were dressed in matching green pants with yellow stripes down the legs. The girls wore knee length green skirts. Cadet hats were topped with yellow plumes. Yellow T-shirts replaced their normally heavy military jackets.

Girl Scouts followed pushing decorated doll carriages. Then the first float appeared. Mr. Palzone's fish truck was decorated with a pole in the center and a cascade of tissue flowers. One of the girls standing in the truck bed holding a huge paper fish had babysat Laurel twice.

When a man waved from a convertible, Laurel asked, "Who's that?"

"Some politician," Mikey had to yell to be heard.

"What's a politician?" she yelled back.

"Don't be stupid. Everyone knows what a politician is."

She didn't say "I don't," but "I was just testing you."

"Well don't."

Looking up she saw Nonnie and Mama in their apartment window. She waved, but they were watching the statue of St. Anthony being carried down the street. Strings ran from all around his collar to the platform on which he was being carried. Pinned to the string were one, five and ten dollar bills. St. Anthony's progress was slowed by believers reaching out to attach money.

Nonnie called to the men, who lifted the statue to the first floor window. The old woman caressed the saint's face before pinning a five to a string. Laurel wanted to cry with the realization that her grandmother loved the statue more than she loved her.

Once the parade has passed and the crowd had thinned, the

children shared a strawberry gelato. Laurel wanted pistachio, but since it was Mikey who had the money, he got to choose. They sat on the steps leading to Cobb's Hill Burial Ground facing Boston Harbor. Pleasure crafts sailed in the light wind. The U.S.S. *Constitution* was to their left, but neither child knew its name, but they knew they liked to look at the old boat, especially as it turned around on the Fourth of July.

"Nonnie hates me." She dipped her flat wooden spoon into the ice cream and handed him the paper cup.

"Of course she does. It's normal." His bite was bigger than hers.

"She likes you."

"That's 'cause I'm her real grandchild. You're adopted."

She cocked her head. Adopted was what they did with kittens from Angell Memorial Hospital.

"I was born from my mother's stomach. You came from some other woman's tummy. She didn't want you so Auntie Elaine and Uncle Mario adopted you."

Laurel began crying. She pictured herself in a cage the same way her kitten had been. Nothing Mikey said could make her stop. He took her home. Mama rocked her and told her how much she and Papa had wanted a baby, and how they went to a special place and picked her to bring home to love.

"Was I in a cage?" Laurel asked.

Her mother hugged her. "Of course not."

"But why didn't my other mommy want me. Was I a bad baby?"

"This is just the beginning, I've always said you'll regret adopting her," Nonnie said from the corner of the room where she was rocking and still fanning herself.

"Please," Mama said.

The old woman stomped into her bedroom, hitting the floor with her cane. The door slammed.

Mama smoothed the strands of hair that were stuck to Laurel's forehead. "She did love you, but she couldn't bring you up, so she let you come to us. It was because she loved you, she gave you up."

Laurel wiped her nose with her sweaty forearm. Her skin had a sun-warmed musty smell. "I'd never give up my baby."

Mama held a Kleenex to her nose. "Blow. I wouldn't either, but she was an unmarried student. A baby needs a mama and a papa."

Laurel blew. Someday, she vowed she would find her real mother. She wanted to make her sorry she'd given her away.

Laurel jumped as Tony touched her back.

"You haven't moved since I left." He pressed his thumbs against the vertebrae in her neck, moving them in a semicircle. Her eyes stayed shut until he stopped. He kissed her head and patted her shoulder before leaving her alone to face the blinking cursor.

I'm so glad you answered my message. My number is 1 617 555-3474.

Instead of hitting the "send" key, she backspaced, erasing character by character and started over.

I want to know why you gave me up. I asked my adopted mother. She always answered but I knew the topic made her uncomfortable.

Laurel deleted that message. It sounded whiny and she wanted to make a good impression. Not a false one, just truthful. For a moment she wondered if two women had given babies up in Baton Rouge, but then remembered she'd been the sole adoption that week. The woman who'd sent the message through cyberspace had to be real—unless she was a con artist. Stupid. Laurel had nothing to be conned out of.

Did you know my adopted grandmother hated me? She was always scared I had black blood. She thought Papa was stupid to agree to the adoption. She died when I was ten. Papa told me to ignore her, that he loved me just as much as if he were my genetic father. He was a wonderful photographer. That's why they were in Louisiana. Papa had a special assignment. I don't know what it was, because they came back to Boston. He worked for Sheraton Hotels. Their offices were on Atlantic wharf and he loved to walk to work so he could get home sooner.

That message was even worse. What was she trying to show? That her grandmother made her suffer? That her father loved her? Did she want to make Maria jealous? She deleted the text. Getting up she paced as best she could in the limited space. Suddenly she sat down and started to write.

I've written many messages and deleted them because I'm really confused and scared, but I don't know of what. I've spent two years actively looking for you, and I've made a bunch of friends, other adoptees like myself who are searching for their birth parents. We all have one thing in common: we want to know more about ourselves. Not about when we were little. Our adopted parents have told us that. More like:

1. What are our ethnic backgrounds?
2. Did anyone in the family have diabetes or other conditions that can be inherited?
3. Who in my birth family has tangled black curly hair like mine?
4. Were you good in science and math? Or did I get that from my father? Do you have to fight to stay thin like I do? And fail like I do?

My adopted parents died. They knew I was looking for you. It hurt them, but they didn't stop me. They were good to me. Mama said it was a private adoption, although she never met you. She said you had to love me to give me away, but everyone in my support group was told that.

Sometimes at night when I can't sleep, I wonder if you're awake and thinking of me. When Robbie (he's my son) was born seven years ago, I held him for the first time, and I couldn't imagine letting him go. Even the idea that he will grow up and go to school or into the army bothers me.

And my little girl, Samantha, there are nights after her bath, when she sits on my lap, I could drown in the waves of love for her. My adopted mother Elaine (maybe you knew her name, but then again maybe not because otherwise you could have found me earlier) said it wasn't giving birth that made a mother, but the everyday caring. She once slept on the floor next to my bed at Mass General when I had pneumonia. Parents weren't allowed to stay, but she wouldn't leave and they gave in.

You said you had another child. Does she know about me? What next? Laurel

Before she lost her nerve she hit the "send" icon without rereading it. Then she put her head down on the keyboard and cried.

Tony rushed in. "Why are you crying?"

"I don't know."

A week had passed since Laurel had e-mailed her mother. "Laurel, calm down," Carol said. Tony, not knowing what to do when his wife's agitation passed his ability to cope, had gone in search of Carol. He and Jay took the kids sledding, leaving the women in Laurel's kitchen.

Lunch dishes were piled in the sink, because Laurel refused to leave the house to go to the traditional Sunday dinner at her mother-in-law's. Laurel's sporadic attempts to wash them made Carol force her friend into a chair.

"I need to do something," Laurel said. "Want some more pie?" When Carol said no, she picked up a fork and ate the remainder directly from the pie plate. "Why hasn't she answered?"

She'd left the computer on all night; every night so she could hear a click if a message arrived, ignoring Tony who claimed the sound would never wake her. She dreamed repeatedly about a click. When she jumped out of bed, nothing was in her mail box except Viagra, sex and loan ads.

Carol poured soapy water on a spaghetti-encrusted dish. "Could be hundreds of reasons: like . . . like . . . she had company, or was away . . . or . . . or . . . her computer was down."

"That's three not hundreds. To make matters worse, tomorrow I go back to work. And last week was a bitch. More stuff keeps disappearing. Not from the safe room, but the labs." Laurel jumped up. "Let's go check the computer."

Carol followed her down the corridor and settled in the easy chair ignoring the piles of laundry. "Last week was nuts for me too."

Laurel was listening, but staring at the screen. "She's answered."

"Read it."

"I can't."

"Do you want me to?"

"Yes." She stepped back and as Carol started to get up she said, "No, I'll do it. She brought up the message.

I'm so sorry I haven't answered you sooner. My computer went on the fritz, and we just got it working. Things go bad at the worse time. I took it to the dealer and he said he had to keep it a couple of days. I nearly cried. Only today did I think I could have used the internet at the library. Usually I am not that stupid, but this is not an ordinary situation. What next you ask. Call me at 941 555 8757 collect.

Carol peered over Laurel's shoulder. "Well?"

"Well, what?"

"Call her, dummy."

Laurel got the phone from the hall and hit four buttons then stopped. "What do I say?"

"Try hello."

Laurel finished dialing.

A man answered. After she said who she was, he said, "Hold on. Maria, come quick. It's her. It's our daughter. Laurel. At last."

"Thank God," Maria said when she came on the line. She was crying. Laurel was crying.

Carol tiptoed to the kitchen to wait for her friend to finish.

CHAPTER 22

"Nice basket, Mark. You're getting there." Leo patted the kid on the back as he came off the court. "Showers everyone. Early to bed. You want to be in top form for the game Friday." Ten sweaty boys filed out of the gym.

Mark Hanson let water pour over him, its heat washing away the muscle pain. He soaped the small tuffs of hair growing from his shaved head.

When his probation officer suggested he play basketball, he thought she was nuts, but surprise—he enjoyed it. Leo worked them hard. Even his teammates accepted him, no sweat.

Meeting with Carol Marsh wasn't as bad as he thought it would be, either. She was super nice. Kept black chocolate for him in her drawer. She claimed it was her favorite, too, but he didn't believe her.

Even life at June's was okay. At least no one beat up anyone else.

As he left the Y, he saw Richard's car parked across the street. Glancing over his shoulder, he made sure he was alone. He crossed and jumped in. "Let's get out of here, Commander."

"Hey man, you missed our last four meetings." Richard revved the car.

"Curfew."

"Still with us?"

"Gotta lay low for a while."

"Don't let them lull you into thinking things are okay. The

police, the courts are as much the enemies of America as the towel heads."

Mark nodded. His father had been fired. He wasn't supposed to talk to his family for another month, but he'd called one day anyway. His father sounded drunk when he grabbed the phone from his mother. He ranted about God damned nigger judge that put his brother into foster care. Then he yelled at Mark for getting caught in the cemetery. Mark had hung up.

Richard parked a block from June's. "Get out here. I'll let you know when we need you. If you pretend they're winning, you'll be more valuable to us. Undercover agent. Our first."

Richard held his arm straight out, and as he left the car, Mark returned the salute.

The smell of beef and onions welcomed Mark as he opened June's kitchen door. She stirred a pot, and held out a spoon with liquid. "What does it need?"

"Good like it is."

"What time's your game Friday?"

"Four thirty."

"Good, I can make it."

As he headed toward his room, he wondered why she wanted to go, and how long Richard would be patient with him.

CHAPTER 23

"And we kept saying, 'I don't know what to say,' over and over until Gino, that's my father's name, finally yelled, 'Say something, these are long distance rates,' but we still didn't know what to say, but finally Maria told me how long she'd been searching and waiting, and I told her how long I'd been doing the same, and she cried because she has grandchildren she hasn't seen, and she wants us to come to Florida, even if I don't know where I'll get the money, but I didn't say I couldn't afford four airline tickets, but she said she'd pay for us all and we should fly United because we'll be united . . . she has a wonderful voice that sounds like she's laughing even when she isn't . . . and oh, my God, how will I get time off?"

During this barrage Laurel, dressed in jeans and one of Tony's red plaid flannel shirts, stood at the ironing board, an iron in her hand. The killer pile of laundry/mending was next to her.

Tony licked the envelope containing his latest CV and cover letter and said for the umpty-umpth time "mmm" as he wondered when her adrenaline would drop. Blah, blah blah. She'd told Carol. She'd told six members of her support group. In between, they'd eaten supper and put the kids to bed. Was she even aware she'd started ironing? Not that he begrudged her the joy. Made her look beautiful even if she'd grown pudgy. At least it was something to hold onto in bed.

"Should we take the kids out of school? Maybe we should wait for the April vacation; everything's probably booked."

Should he tell her she'd put Robbie's shirt on a hangar without one sleeve ironed and a button missing? No, he could put it back in the killer pile later when she wasn't looking. "A week from school won't kill them. It's educational seeing someplace else."

"But what if the DEP comes?" She poured water into the iron.

"Reservations can be changed."

"The cheapest flights are non-changeable. This isn't our money, what'll they think if we cost my par . . . er . . . *them* extra money. Gino was worried about long distance rates. Oh my God. It's hard to call them my parents. Elaine and Mario were my mama and papa."

"LAUREL! Give me a chance to answer. Take a step at a time. Of course Elaine and Mario were your parents. They raised you, loved you. Find a date and let Gino arrange for the tickets. He works, doesn't he?"

"I don't know. I've so much to ask them. Can you believe my real parents are married . . . unusual." She picked up a blue blouse with a ripped seam. "Damn."

He used the remote to find CNN. "Hey, Laurel, your phone call didn't make the news."

She put down the iron and walked to where he was sitting. "It should. It would make a great TV show. Can you imagine the announcer asking, 'What happened next to Laurel DiDonato and the Correntes? Find out after this announcement.' "

Tony went to the DVDs they'd recorded, tracing the titles: made for television movies, PBS specials and *National Geographic*s saved for when the kids would no longer cry at a photo of a lion capturing a gazelle. He found *Love Train to Paris*. God, they'd bought that—hmm. He didn't remember when.

"I mean what if my sister hates me. I don't know anything about them. Maybe Gino wanted a son. They'll adore Robbie."

143

Tony remembered. He'd bought it on graduation night after eating at Bartley's. The first meal out in three years. Instead of going home to watch it, they'd wandered down to the Charles. Made love on the river bank. Like undergrads. His crimson gown was their blanket. Not wanting the evening to end, they'd walked arm in arm as Boston slept. Everything had been magic. He had his Ph.D., Laurel had her dream job. They made love again with her back against the tree and his body shielding hers. Magic should be normal. Maybe the past year had been a blip. He shoved the DVD into the player.

Camera long shot: high speed orange train speeding through little French villages. Long, low whistles.

Camera zooms in: swinging blond hair. Concentration on a woman's buttocks, as she sways down the aisle. At the end of the car is door marked toilet. She knocks. A hand pulls her inside. A blond God kisses her. She responds. Close up. Tongues flicker together.

Laurel stopped talking and looked at the television as the couple tore off their clothes. His shirt unbuttons automatically. He pulls up her lime green dress. The camera shows white stockings with three-inch lace tops. A flash of pubic hair. Laurel sinks into the sofa next to her husband.

The blond man pushes the woman against a tiny white porcelain sink, reaches between her breasts and unclips her bra, a wisp of white lace.

Tony put his arm around Laurel. His hand stroked her breast through her cotton bra. She opened her plaid shirt. His skin was warm on hers. He turned her so he could undo her bra.

The man on the train kisses the woman's neck, working his way down her tanned breasts. Her nipples, raspberry red, against her white skin stood at attention.

So did Laurel's.

The train woman pulls at the man's belt and opens his fly's

four buttons. His encouraged organ emerges.

The unzipping of Tony's zipper could hardly be heard as Laurel freed him, but not quite as easily as on the DVD. When he was liberated from his jockey shorts, Laurel took him into her mouth. He arched his back, shut his eyes and forgot the television.

Just before Laurel fell asleep a couple of hours later she asked Tony, "How do you think they filmed it in that tiny area without the camera man showing in the mirror?"

"What mirror?"

CHAPTER 24

Jay Marsh watched Carol grip the steering wheel. Her problem was destination, not traffic. At 2:30 more people jogged along the banks of the Charles River than drove on Memorial Drive.

"You can still change your mind." She braked at the lights by the Hyatt. "We'll have a drink at the hotel instead."

"Just keep driving," he said.

"I could get my tubes tied."

"You've done more than your half already. My turn."

"What time did Dr. Snelling say?" she asked.

"Three."

They both had confidence in Snelling—a throwback to the old family doctor, not a bottom-line HMO creation. Jay especially identified with the tall, rangy physician who, like himself, fought the system. During their pre-vasectomy meeting, they'd spent more time discussing ethics than vas deferens.

"We're not Luddites. We want the best from the past added to the best of the present," Snelling had said.

"Don Quixote wasn't all wrong. Windmills have their place, but we must earn a living," Jay said.

"No doubts?" Snelling has asked. "Sometimes they can be reversed, but no guarantee. You have to plan on it being permanent. If your marriage breaks up . . ."

"No doubts." Jay had done a mental check before the appointment. Carol got pregnant so easily that they joked it was like shaking hands. She'd had four miscarriages, but he didn't like her on the pill. As for a divorce, no way. He would not desert his family like his father had done.

"Nervous?" Carol brought him back to the car.

"The idea of a knife touching my balls scares the hell out of me."

When he was little, his mother told him what to expect before going to the doctor. She'd never lied about something not hurting. Before some allergy tests, Anna had taken off his shirt and run a pencil over his back in little strokes duplicating the test. The allergist wasn't quite sure what to make of the little boy who directed him on how to do it rather than cry.

The white plastic molded chairs in Snelling's waiting room were empty. Carol picked up a magazine then put it down.

As he hung up their coats, Jay wondered if he shouldn't have worn his jeans, which were tight around the crotch. He thumbed through the magazine that Carol had abandoned, although if he'd been given a quiz on content, he would have flunked.

The nurse appeared. "We're ready."

He followed her down the hall and into a small room.

She smiled, a nice smile, warm. Her figure was what any man would call lush. Lucky Snelling to have her to look at every day. "Remove everything below the waist," she said. "The doctor will be here in about five minutes." Then she left.

He worried about getting undressed. What if he got an erection when she came back in? His watch read 3:07. Then he obeyed. Wearing a shirt and sweater he felt as if he were in a French farce where the husband comes in too soon and the lover escapes half naked to the ledge.

He paced around the table in the center of the room. A cabinet with brown bottles was to one side. On a counter was a blood pressure cuff, stethoscope and tongue depressors: doctor things.

Dr. Snelling walked in. "Well this is the day, and since you're half undressed, I guess you haven't changed your mind." He stuck a digital thermometer with a plastic covering into Jay's mouth. "Did you sign all the papers?"

"No one gave me anything," Jay mumbled around the thermometer.

"We'll correct that." Snelling disappeared leaving Jay standing half naked.

When the thermometer beeped he took it out. 98.4°. Below normal.

The nurse entered with a clipboard. "I suppose as an attorney, you'll want to read everything."

He willed his penis to behave. For once it listened. Basically the document released Snelling from accidentally cutting off his penis, although it wasn't worded that way. Using the pen attached to the clip board, Jay signed it.

Snelling came back in. "Up on the table."

The metal covered only by paper felt cold under his ass.

Snelling scrubbed his hands like surgeons did on TV medical shows. He put on clear gloves and pulled a plastic visor over his face.

"Put your ankles in the stirrups. Last chance to change your mind."

Jay shook his head. With his legs splayed he thought of frogs awaiting dissection. Carol must feel like this during her GYN exams. He stared at the ceiling. Carol said her doctor had painted a smiling face on his. All Jay saw were grained acoustic tiles—probably to cut the noise of screams.

"I'm using Lydocane to numb the area, I can give you a blow-by-blow, description that is." Snelling laughed.

Jay didn't.

The liquid on his balls startled Jay. The area grew numb. He debated looking. No, some things were better not seen.

He heard things being picked up and put down, but he didn't

want to know the source. There was a click, a snap, a crunch, reminding him of the sound a knife made slicing celery.

"All done," Snelling said.

Jay thought of how a Band-Aid made his kids feel better than a kiss. Snelling wasn't going to kiss his balls.

"That's it?"

"Yup, get dressed. Have the receptionist make an appointment in about six weeks to check that the sperm is all flushed out. Until then you're still armed."

"Anything to worry about?" Like never having another erection, infection, having the tubes grow back . . .

"You might be uncomfortable for a while, that's all."

Jay looked at his watch. 3:48.

CHAPTER 25

Sneakers squeaked as the basketball players pivoted and jostled each other, passing, shooting. The gym smelled of dirty linen and sweat.

Coach-Cop Leo paced, his eyes intent on every move. He hollered encouragement, advice, orders. When one of Carol's "kids" missed his fourth shot in a row, Leo sent him to the bench. As the kid shuffled off the court he muttered, "Sorry Coach, I blew it."

Leo patted his shoulder. "More practice and it'll be better." He pointed with his forefinger at Jason and then at the court. The youth, a black kid, his hair dyed orange, jumped up from the bench.

Carol, Jay, Seth and Paige sat on the bleachers with June Finnegan. They cheered Mark Hanson's passing the ball to Jason who slam dunked it into the hoop's torn string basket. The boys high-fived each other. Their side, all of ten people, cheered.

"How's Mark doing?" Carol's eyes followed the action.

June cheered an intercept by Mark. "Strange one. He's an almost."

"An almost?"

"He obeys—almost, right to the point I can't call him on it. He joins in—almost, but stops when he looks like he is beginning to have fun."

Paige pulled on Carol's sleeve. "I want some candy."

"No."

"Why not?" the seven-year-old whined.

"You've already had your piece for the day."

"Grammy will give us some." The kids were spending the weekend with Anna while Jay and Carol escaped to New Hampshire for a get-away.

Seth straddled the bleachers as if it were a horse. "I'm bored."

Carol pulled a book from her bag. "Read this."

"Don't want to."

"I do," Paige said.

"Hey that's mine." Seth grabbed it.

This is the part where I want to use the child psych book on their little bums, Carol thought. "Seth, you didn't want it. Give it to your sister. Sit still." The five-year-old folded his arms over his chest and pouted.

"Now there's trouble," June said.

Carol thought she meant Seth. Guilt swept her for today's sins: fake patience, not taking enough time with each case and forcing her family to this game. Not only was she deserting her kids for the weekend, she wanted to get away from them. Just two days. Then June tilted her head towards the door.

Carol saw a kid with a shaved head lean against the wall. His body language oozed negativity.

"Who is it?" She missed seeing Mark freeze when he looked at the newcomer.

"Richard Yeats. Father is a right-wing nutter. I'm conservative, but the father makes Attila the Hun look liberal. Used to live next door. Whole neighborhood celebrated when they moved."

A cheer went up on the opposite side as the visitors scored, bringing them to within six points of Leo's kids. He called his last time-out. Back on the court they controlled the ball for the last fifty-nine seconds.

★ ★ ★ ★ ★

The Marshes waited outside the locker room. Mark, Jason and Tom, all Carol's kids, spotted her as they came out. Tom sidled up first. "Hi Carol, Jay, Kids. Thanks for coming." Four months before she'd had his case dismissed. She called him Leo's Miracle number 27.

"My pleasure. You guys want to go for burgers? Jay's treat."

"I'm in," Tom said.

"I could eat a whole cow." Jason said.

"I'm only paying for one for each of you," Jay said.

"Fries and shakes?" Jason asked and Jay nodded.

Mark looked at the parking lot. "I kinda like have plans, you know."

"Come on, man," Tom said.

"Maybe just for a Coke. Then I'll split."

An almost, Carol thought.

"Please slow down." Carol and Jay were late, having taken the time to see Anna's newest painting, showing children dressed in yellow slickers and boots playing on the rocks with the sea roaring in the background. Her mother-in-law had named it *Danger*. The thought of the children being swept to sea niggled at her as they roared north on Route 93.

He braked. "I want to get to the B&B before they lock up."

"I want to get there in one piece." She pulled his cell from his pocket and dialed the Blue Swan Inn to readjust their arrival time.

It was 1:07 A.M. when they pulled up in front of a white Victorian house, dominating the lot and surrounded by a snow-covered white picket fence. Light glowed through frosted window panes.

A man with a white beard appeared. "Welcome." Carol half expected him to lay a finger aside of his nose and rise up the chimney. He led them upstairs and whispered, "Bath to the left, plenty of hot water." He unlocked a door.

A fireplace with a half-burned fire warmed the room. A patchwork quilt almost covered a thick feather duvet on a brass bed. "Is this okay?"

"Perfect," they said together.

"We've only one other couple who want breakfast at 10:30. What's your druthers?"

"Perfect, I'm for a sleep-in," Carol said as she took the key.

Jay locked the door. "Even as tired as I am . . ." He pulled Carol to him and pulled off her sweater giving her little kisses as he did.

Although only half in the mood, she said, "Can't waste a fireplace."

They fell asleep holding each other, their earlier tensions calmed by orgasms. Only after the fire burned itself out did Carol pull up the duvet.

Her inner alarm went off by habit at 6:30. Shut up, she said to it. In the first light rays she could make out the outline of the antique dresser and the marble-topped nightstand with a pitcher and basin. The window was angled so the snow-capped mountains were visible. They glowed a rosy red in the sunrise. When they'd left Massachusetts it was almost spring. Now the three-hour drive had plunged them back into winter.

Jay's chest rose and fell under her hand, and she resisted the desire to pull his chest hair. A day and half with nothing they HAD to do was ahead. How long had it been since they'd had a weekend to themselves? Before Seth was born at least. Good mothers don't enjoy leaving their children. Yes they do. Working moms have too little time with their children. Quality time counts. All those folders to catch up on. They'll wait. Damn. Dusting. Ironing.

She imagined burning her to-do list and, lulled by the

imaginary flames, drifted back to sleep. An army of delinquents marched by a reviewing stand. Each stopped to yell at one of her transgressions. To one side, her mother swayed holding a half-empty scotch bottle. When the smell of coffee and baking bread floated through the hot air grate awakened her, everything disappeared in the morning light.

Jay kissed her forehead. "I'm waking into a dream. What shall we do? Cross country ski?"

Think positive, count your blessings, Carol told herself. "Cross country."

CHAPTER 26

The first thing Laurel wanted to do each night when she came home was to read her E-mail. Although she could see the computer at the foot of the bed, it seemed more distant than if it were in another city.

"Put the pasta on, Laurel."

"Mommy, Robbie hit me."

"It's Sam's turn to set the table."

"I promised my teacher I'd bring cookies tomorrow."

Even after the kids were in bed, the chores done, there were more traps.

"Can you proof this letter?"

"Make me some coffee, please."

"Did you read what Kennedy said in *The Globe* today?"

Although she understood Tony's need to talk, for she too would go nuts stuck at home all day with no one over seven to talk to, her workday world left her saturated.

Then came the blessed moment when the tendrils ensnaring her disappeared: silence, children slept, Tony engrossed in whatever. Then, and only then, could she turn on the computer. Usually it was after 10:00 P.M. How long she stayed depended on Tony wanting to sleep. He said the clicking keys kept him awake. Despite it all, she and Maria did manage to exchange at least one set of E-mails a day.

From: Ldidonato392@hotmail.com
To: Maria.corrente@gmail.com
Subject: Postponed

*ç%&/(we have to postpone our trip again. Other chemicals have disappeared from the labs. Only the janitor and I have keys to the safe room. Anderson called me to his office saying he was pleased I wasn't raising any more trouble (little does he know) and implied I could be promotable if I want to move to Cleveland. I hate this company. I need a salary. Tony says that's what happens when I rent myself out to capitalists.

Laurel

From: Maria.corrente@gmail.com
To: Ldidonato392@hotmail.com
Subject: Re: Posponed

I wish you didn't have all those problems. Although we're disappointed we understand. Heck, I am proud anyway even if I didn't do the milk and cookies after school. Just tell us when you can come, we'll get the tickets.

Your husband is not totally wrong. Money is power. I feel it less as a teacher. Your father has his own business, taking tourists fishing. His employees rent their time to him.

I need to tell you why I gave you up since Gino and I married anyway. Think of Romeo and Juliet without the suicide. Your grandfathers each had a fishing fleet. Big rivals, a stubborn Italian and a stubborn Portuguese. Both bragged they never changed their minds.

Gino and I were high school sweethearts but never told our parents. If I had, my brothers would have beaten up Gino. Old country rules. Don't worry, we're modern.

I got pregnant at 17. I went to stay with my Aunt Theresa in Louisiana who'd forged her own life. I called her, and she told my mother she needed me to help her because she'd broken her leg. At the airport she picked me up in tennis clothes and not a crutch or wheelchair in sight.

After I'd been in Baton Rouge for a week, she told me she'd given up a baby too. Never told our family. She played a mean game of Canasta. The only time I won was in the early stages of labor. She came to live with Gino and I about ten years ago and died last year. I still miss her.

Then I went to college, the first in my family. Your father was at the same one.

One day I saw him walking across campus. He said he still wanted to marry me and replace you, as if one baby could replace another. He promised to help find you.

By then our fathers were dead, our mothers more reasonable, and I told my brothers to shut up.

Love, Maria

From: Ldidonato392@hotmail.com
To: Maria.corrente@gmail.com
Subject: Tell me more

And they say the Internet separates people. Ha. Tell me more about you & Gino.

Laurel

From: Maria.corrente@gmail.com
To: Ldidonato392@hotmail.com
Subject: Re: Tell me more

God, we have so much catching up to do. We married in my senior year. I was an education/history major and had Karen two years after that. Between my Portuguese and his Italian temper, things are never dull. He's macho but sweet. You wouldn't catch him near a dishpan. Not a lot gets hidden.

We blow up. It blows over fast. You and Tony?

Love, Maria

From: Ldidonato392@hotmail.com
To: Maria.corrente@gmail.com
Subject: Re: Tell me more

Tony and I were high school AND college sweethearts. Well almost. We had a big fight the summer before my junior year at UMaryland. He went to Northeastern. We dated other people, but ran into each other when I was home the following summer. Hard not to run into each other in the North End. It was by Paul Revere's statue where old men sit and talk. He looked at me and said, "You need pistachio gelati." We've been together ever since. I helped him get his Ph.D. in medieval literature. I just wish he could get a job but meanwhile the furniture he's restoring and selling is bringing in money and it's beautiful.

Laurel

To: Ldidonato392@hotmail.com
From: Maria.corrente@gmail.com
Subject: I can't believe it

That we were in the North End probably the same time you were. We could have walked by each other. As for Tony finding a job in his field, there's so much wasted talent that could contribute to the country. Sounds like he's handling it well. Do you feel lucky?

I'm exhausted. Rough day at school. Talk tomorrow.

Love,
Maria

From: Ldidonato392@hotmail.com
To: Maria.corrente@gmail.com
Subject: Do I feel lucky?

Yes and no. I get strength from my family, from Carol (my landlady and best friend). My kids are healthy, but there's never enough time. If I lose my job, unemployment won't cover *our costs, even though Tony gets good prices for his stuff, but it is uneven. Sometimes I am just plain scared.*

Laurel

From: Maria.corrente@hotmail.com
To: Ldidonato392@hotmail.com
Subject: Scared

I understand. Gino's business can be irregular, too. I'm the stable income-earner. It was harder when Karen was little. I always taught and love it, and think if I stayed home I'd have been a worse mother. I get frustrated because I'm a hard teacher and parents complain I'm hurting the kids' self-esteem. I thought self-esteem came from accomplishment.

Sleep tight and wake happy,
Love and Kisses,
Maria

From: Maria.corrente@gmail.com
To: Ldidonato392@hotmail.com
Subject: About Karen

Karen is working on her Ph.D. You should know, she's gay and lives with a lovely woman, Robin.

From: Ldidonato392@hotmail.com
To: Maria.corrente@gmail.com
Subject: Re: About Karen

I'm glad you had confidence in me to tell me about Karen. Both Tony's and my family consider keeping secrets an art form. We don't. You can hear them all over the neighborhood.

My good news: Rick Ames called. He went before a judge today and the raid is next week. Bad News: I'm terrified.

CHAPTER 27

Laurel's restlessness kept waking Tony. Groggily, when the clock buzzed at 5:30, he pressed the shut-off button instead of the snooze alarm. Neither woke until the kids wandered into the bedroom. No pending air attack would have scrambled an air squadron as fast. Clothes and recriminations flew. No amounts of I'm sorrys appeased Laurel.

She entered the office two hours late. Rick Ames sat at her desk with another man standing shuffling through papers. "What's going on?"

Rick's hair was shorter than when he'd talked to her in her kitchen after the blizzard. They'd talked only on the phone since then.

The men flashed badges. "Sam Routhier, Massachusetts Attorney General's Office. My partner Rick Ames and we're doing an audit." Rick reached out to shake her hand.

For the best performance of a safety engineer pretending she isn't a whistle blower the nominations for the Oscar are . . .

She gave them what they asked for.

"Mr. Anderson says he wants to see you," Routhier said.

Her hands shook as she entered the executive suite. The secretary pointed to the conference room whose door was open. The stone walls had been paneled in a dark wood two months ago and red velvet drapes covered the windows. The conference table was large enough to seat the Mass. National Guard should they have wanted to all sit down for a feast. President Walter

Anderson was at the head and Dr. Bill Welch, Laboratory Chief, was seated on his left. They watched a dark-haired man, granny glasses halfway down his nose, and a suit that might as well have been made of $1000 bills it looked so expensive, study a paper.

"The search order is legal," the stranger said. "If you can't explain where the chemicals are, it could mean a hefty fine." He flipped to a second page.

Anderson spied Laurel and motioned her in. "Any idea what's going on?"

She shook her head.

"Frank Adamian, our corporate lawyer. Laurel DiDonato, our safety engineer."

Laurel put her hand out, but Adamian didn't see it. She knew of no way to make its withdrawal look natural so she clasped both hands behind her back.

"Why is the DEP here now?" Anderson didn't ask her to sit.

"It isn't the DEP, it's the AG's Environmental Strike Force." Adamian didn't look up.

Laurel used all her willpower to look natural. How many times did she have to explain it. "Every toxic substance is tracked from birth to death and . . ."

"Why didn't you tell me?"

Anderson's frown chilled her. Jesus, I'll never pull this off, Laurel thought.

"Common knowledge," Welch said.

"Not mine," Anderson said.

Laurel shifted her weight from one foot to another. "Mr. . . ."

"Enough." Anderson motioned for the lawyer to leave. After the door clicked, he tapped his pen against his hand. "You two find a believable story about where those chemicals went."

Welch, lanky and needing a hair cut, took a pen and pad from his ink-stained lab shirt breast pocket and began doodling.

161

"I'll make up usage stats."

"Laurel?"

Elephants danced in her stomach. "It's criminal."

"If we're caught . . ." Welch said.

"Bill, you've asked for a raise, more equipment, and I wasn't sure. Now I am. Name what you need. Now you two go into my office and think about it. Copies of internal forms aren't in Boston." Anderson swiveled in his chair.

Bill sat on the green damask couch in Anderson's office, his hands on his knees as Laurel paced the Oriental rug. "What a mess." Dandruff flaked his collar. "I'll create some internal forms. Use my laptop. No link to the main computer. I should be able to fiddle dates."

"I can't believe you."

"I've got two kids in college."

She suspected his salary was many times her own. She'd seen his Lincoln home with the stable and horses. "And I support a family of four. Do you know the damage we could do?"

"None of that pays my mortgage."

"Isn't your research to improve the quality of life?"

A dry laugh, more a rumble, escaped. "My research is a paycheck that improves my family's life."

"I always wondered why managers faced with moral choices didn't do the right thing."

Unfolding himself from the couch, he said, "Not me. I knew. I'm going to start falsifying records like crazy."

"You can't go in there," Anderson's secretary rose and tried to beat Laurel to the door.

"Too late." Laurel shut the conference room door in the secretary's face. Adamian and Anderson sat next to each other at the oak table. "I need to talk to you, alone."

Adamian gathered his scattered papers.

"Leave them." As Adamian left, Anderson stood and hovered over her as if to say *I could squash you like a bug if I wanted.* "What?"

"Forging papers is immoral and illegal . . ." Because she didn't know what to say for a moment she took a deep breath. "Why can't we admit a mistake and promise tighter controls?" How lame, she thought. Dorothy faced down the Wicked Witch of the West and won. The witch melted but this wasn't *Over the Rainbow.* Anderson wasn't melting.

"Laurel, Laurel. You make me sad." A vein beat in his forehead. He placed his hand on her shoulder. "All I'm asking is to give us time to find out what happened. Then we'll set up better controls."

She wanted to yell liar. She didn't. She wanted to hit him. She didn't.

Reaching for one of her hands he held it, sandwich style, between his two. "Put yourself in my place. I'm responsible for everyone working here."

Less people than before you downsized it.

"I've heard your husband isn't working. You've two small boys." His voice oozed warmth. "I'm a father too. The kids are the joy of my life."

Then why don't you have their pictures on your desk?

"Take the rest of the day off, with pay, of course, to think about it. You would hate to be responsible for anyone else losing their job . . ."

She heard *including you* as he shook her hand. She resisted wiping it on her skirt.

That afternoon Laurel marched up the stairs of the Boston Common garage. Assaulted by the smell of urine, she tried not to gag until she stepped onto the grassy area where cows had once grazed. In her funk she didn't notice the redbrick Beacon Hill houses behind black iron railings nor a gardener planting pansies. She stormed down Winter Street to the Department of Environmental Protection office.

A man, younger than she, his hair razored at the sides but long on top, sat behind the metal reception desk. "May I help you?"

"Laurel DiDonato for Matt Rosi. It's an emergency."

Matt came out and greeted her with a bear hug then led her to his office which was only slightly bigger than hers.

"The company wants me to commit a criminal act," she blurted out even before sitting.

Matt rubbed his chin. "Do you want official advice or old college–friend advice?"

"Both."

"Let's get Ames in here." He used the phone on his desk to dial. "Hey, Rick, I know you're on the Jackson audit, but can you come back in?" He listened to his protests. "It's related."

Two hours later he was there. "When you didn't come back, I thought you were fired," Rick said.

"Here's what's happening. Welch is forging papers."

For the next hour they strategized.

When Laurel arrived at work the next morning, the first thing she did was to call Anderson's office. Instead of his guard dog, he picked up the phone. Sucking in her breath, she tried to sound determined. Determined? She'd gone over so many scripts in her head, changed her mind so many times, she was sure she would sound like an idiot.

"Be in my office at 2:08."

Laurel resented his dumb game choosing off times as she headed down the corridor. She was sick of all corporate games. The secretary's desk was empty. Someone had said she was sick. Laurel knocked on the door and entered without waiting for a reply. Anderson motioned her in. She sat without being asked.

"Well, Laurel, what have you come up with?" He leaned back in his chair and played with a pencil in his hands.

"I want a two-week holiday while the audit is going on. I won't forge papers. It's okay for Welch, but I can't."

Anderson twirled his pencil, but stayed in a reclining position. "Why in God's name would I approve that?"

Here goes, she thought. "I won't have to lie, but I won't compromise the company. I see it as a win-win."

Anderson chuckled, a rarity from a man whose smiles were a rarity. "Maybe I've underestimated you. And if I refuse?"

"I'll turn over the tape I made of our meeting the other day to the strike force."

His smile disappeared. He sat upright. "That's blackmail."

"I call it self-protection."

"I *have* underestimated you." He rose from his seat. Although he wasn't overweight, he seemed to expand as he walked around the desk and sat on the corner hovering in vulture-style.

Laurel stood so they were eye-to-eye. "And . . ."

"Have a nice holiday." He stuck out his hand, which she took. "You've more guts than I would have thought."

As she closed the door, she thought, he's not so smart. The tape she had was of that day's conversation, not the earlier meeting. He hadn't admitted anything though, but he didn't deny anything either. She had a couple of other conversations to get down, before she could call her mother to book the tickets.

CHAPTER 28

A beginning, a middle and an end. I don't get many of those, Carol thought as she scooped the last of the peanut butter cookie dough from a beige ceramic bowl with a cracked blue stripe near the top. She rolled it in her hands before putting it on the cookie sheet mottled from many bakings. With a fork she made two ninety degree angles on each cookie turning the balls into tiny Frisbees. Cookies got made, baked, eaten. A project started, enjoyed, finished.

The first time she'd made cookies was with her third-grade best friend Melinda and her mother. Carol had been looking forward to it all week. As she leveled a cup of flour as instructed, the door bell had rung: her mother, drunk as usual, grabbed her daughter, mumbling she had to come home now and she wasn't to play with the child of a no-goodnick. That was a bad end. She never played with Melinda again, even though her friend had carried her share of the cookies to school in a paper bag. Carol had thrown them away.

Carol set the timer. Banish the bad. A light breeze rippled the kitchen curtain as she brushed flour from her jeans.

"I adore baking smells mixed with spring air," Anna said as she walked into the kitchen carrying a copy of *Mother Jones*. "I heard the car. Jay and the kids are back."

Seth, his sneakers untied, burst into the kitchen. "We saw their plane take off. I counted eight 747s coming in, whish, whish, whish." He zoomed his arm around like a plane landing it on a cookie cooling on the rack.

Carol grabbed it. "Too close to lunch."

He relinquished it. "Not fair."

"Pick one out for you to eat after," Anna said.

Seth walked around the table standing on tip toes to study the cookies. He ran out of the room and returned with a ruler, measured them, and chose the biggest. Carol put it to one side as Jay opened the door, a One-Hour Cleaning plastic bag slung over his shoulder. Paige followed and climbed onto her grandmother's lap.

"The DiDonatos are off to Florida and the great reunion," Jay said.

"I miss Samantha already," Paige said.

"It's easier to be the leaver than the leavee." Anna smoothed her granddaughter's curls, a useless task. "Did I tell you I signed up for a computer course? And you're invited to lunch next week at a price."

Jay hung the dry cleaning over the door. "Which is?"

"Help me set up the laptop I bought."

He sat next to his mother. "Don't you know your age group doesn't do computers."

"And when has that ever stopped me? I want to start playing with some of the art programs."

The children, uninterested in the adult conversation, left. Carol ran water into the empty dough bowl.

"Actually I drove in today to talk about your father. I've heard through the grapevine he's dying and that Jennifer visited you."

Jay said nothing.

"And you didn't want to tell me. I don't have any unsettled issues with him or her. You do, and it worries me. If he dies without you making peace . . ."

Jay walked over to the window and stared at the yard. Half

was a brick patio but toward the back was where they planted the beans, zucchini and tomatoes that the family grew each summer. To one side was a strawberry patch and to the other was a lilac tree. Up against the house, rose bushes were budding.

"Don't turn your back to me." Anna came up behind him and touched his shoulder. "You hate dealing with emotional stuff. If you don't this will come back and bite you in the ass."

"Will you ever be ladylike?" His eyes were fixed on the new leaves, still in their infant yellow green that would darken as the season went on.

"Boring. At my age I've earned the right to say and do what I want."

Jay sighed and turned. "I'm listening."

Anna herded him to a chair. "There are things you don't have to do like finding your birth mother. Although after Laurel, you might want to rethink that."

Jay studied his hands.

"Look at me, when I talk to you."

He did.

"Take care of things now. After he dies, it'll be too late."

"I'll think about it. But if I didn't know better, I'd think you and Jennifer were double teaming me." He glanced at Carol. "Or triple teaming me.

Carol held up her hands. "I'm innocent, but I agree with Anna."

Carol watered her tomato seeds in their peat pots on flats in the back hall. How many would survive? No results for months. Not like cookies.

Jay watched.

She hadn't heard him come up behind. "Where's Anna?"

"Playing computer games with the kids. I think they're letting her win to encourage her."

Carol picked up the watering can and sprinkled each pot. She expected him to say something about the earlier conversation concerning his father.

"What if we told the DiDonatos they didn't have to pay rent for six months?"

As she turned, she knocked a spade off the counter. She'd inherited the house. Their only big expense was the kid's tuition. Their car was paid for and they had no credit card debt. That was probably un-American. "They won't take charity."

"Not charity. A barter. Labor for rent. The Black Hole." He dragged her to the basement door.

The Black Hole. How she hated it. Things went down and never came back. As a kid she thought monsters lurked there. The door creaked. Odors of dust and decay swamped them. When Jay flipped the light switch, a pale bulb from a black and white woven wire, popped and died. The Black Hole was telling them it didn't want intruders.

He reached through cobwebs to a shelf, groping for a flashlight, not the compact cylinder type, but a spotlight good for major electrical disruptions. Switching it on, its dust-thickened swath of light shone into the abyss. The stairs groaned with each step. They sneezed.

The light hit her father's workbench. Baby-food jars held different-sized nuts and screws. Saws, screwdrivers and hammers hung from a cork board over the bench almost like an altar. Except for the grit, it would have been a handyman's dream. With all the extra details her father pulled at supermarkets and construction projects, he seldom had time to do repairs or complete his projects. The more her mother drank, the more jobs he took.

"This is a great idea." Jay held her hand so tight her bones felt squished.

Descending into hell wasn't a great idea. She watched as he played the light over a hand-wringer washing machine, almost hidden behind helter-skelter stacked boxes. Shelves held hand-canned goods dating from before she was born—instant ptomaine. "I've seen enough."

"Think. This could be another apartment." He sneezed several times. "Take the boards off the windows, do track lighting. Sheet rock the walls." He pointed the light. "Bathroom there, kitchen here."

She edged toward the stairs, guided by a beam of kitchen light, that reminded her of people talking about near death experiences and light tunnels. "We'll talk. Upstairs." She bounded upstairs.

Anna looked up from where she was reading at the kitchen table, a cup of tea in front of her. "Now I'll know how you'll look when you're old and gray."

The couple looked at the dust that had filtered onto their hair.

"Mom, what do you think if I asked Tony to turn the basement into an apartment in place of rent?"

"Great."

"Do you know how much work it will be to clean that place out? There's stuff from before my dad moved in and he got it from his uncle who lived here from the forties . . . and we don't know if Tony will want to."

"Convince her, Mom."

Anna held up her hands. "Mother-in-law Rule No. 1—don't interfere."

After complaining about the absence of the DiDonato children, the kids decided to play together on their own. Jay worked on a brief. With everyone occupied, Carol escaped outside to indulge in early spring sunshine on a Sunday morning. She pressed her foot hard on the pitchfork, wiggling it to break through the winter-hardened soil.

She heard a crack from the cellar. Looking over, she saw that Jay had pulled off the wood. Why couldn't he have continued on his legal stuff—well that was Jay. When he thought of something he barreled ahead. On their third date, he'd proposed, saying, "Look we can date for months, but it will end up the same."

Looking at the garden, she remembered hacking back brambles, while discovering rakes, books, a basketball hoop and other remnants of a happier life. The flagstone patio had replaced broken glass. Last year the small lawn became a croquet field. Rose bushes lined the drive. A stockade fence, not rusted chicken wire, marked their property from the neighbors.

When she and Jay decided to stay in the house, he'd promised her new memories, happy ones. He'd kept his promise. Some changes had been cosmetic: paint, wall paper, new flooring. Months would go by without something triggering a wave of sadness. Maybe if they fixed the basement, all the buried memories would stay buried.

The clotted dirt smelled spring warm. She raked its black clumps, preparing it for her plants which she would nurture. Tonight she'd ask Jay for a massage. She imagined his fingers soothing her muscles, and then she would make love to him, a perfect end to a weekend.

CHAPTER 29

Day One: Arrival

As they rode to Logan Airport, Laurel felt as if she were watching herself from a distance. Check-in and boarding were a fog. On the plane she sat with Samantha and Tony with Robbie. Laurel chanted her mantra . . . it will be okay.

Robbie pricked his finger on the pilot wings the stewardess had given him. He screamed. She reached across the aisle to give the wounded digit a kiss. It will get better.

Leaning across the aisle she said to Tony, "I know I'm finally on the way to meet my birth parents, but I feel . . . I don't know what I feel."

"Laurel, don't go weird on me. For once, just enjoy."

In the toilet she touched her reflection in the mirror. It will get better.

As the plane touched down, Samantha pointed out the window. "It's like the movies."

The disembodied attendant's voice said, "Ladies and gentlemen, welcome to the Sarasota-Bradenton Airport. Please remain in your seats with your safety belt buckled until the seat belt sign is turned off."

What if it doesn't get better? What if I don't like them? What if they don't like me? None of these things would she say to Tony.

"How'll I know Grandma and Grandpa?" Robbie asked.

It wasn't a problem. As they came past security, a woman

scanned the passengers and waved a sign "Welcome Laurel and Samantha." The man at her side had another: "Welcome Tony and Robbie."

The signs were unnecessary. Maria Corrente was a prediction of what Laurel would be like in twenty years. Gino Corrente was a masculine version of Samantha only with leathery skin and a handlebar mustache.

Tony pushed his wife into Maria's arms. The sign fell and was trampled as the women hugged and turned in a circle. Gino stood to one side sniffing, then shook Tony's hand before kneeling to greet the children.

"Good thing I don't wear mascara." Maria knelt next to the children staring into their eyes.

"Why are you crying?" Robbie touched a tear.

"Because I'm happy."

"And you're really our grandmother?"

Maria dabbed at her tears with a tissue Gino handed her and nodded.

"Now I've got three, but one died. My friend Seth has only one."

"Poor Seth. Let's get out of here," Gino said.

Twenty minutes later they pulled into a restaurant parking lot. The four DiDonatos were wedged in the back seat, like a regular family outing, only nothing was regular.

"This is Captain Bill's where we celebrate all big family events."

Laurel thought how her first communion, graduation and engagement were celebrated at the Boston Union Oyster House. It'll get better.

Robbie rushed to a window when a large sailboat angled itself next to the dock. A woman in a red bikini stepped onto the wooden planks to secure it. "A pelican," Robbie said.

"A few years from now, he'll notice the girl."

"What girl?" Robbie asked.

The air-conditioning felt good after the sticky heat. Because they were late for lunch and too early for the early-bird specials, the place was almost empty.

"I recommend the red snapper." Maria reached out for Laurel's hand. She resisted pulling it away from the woman who was her mother. Maria hadn't combed tangles from her hair nor made her Halloween costumes and headed up her Brownie group. All this stranger had done so far was to recommend a fish.

"Your sister Karen is flying in tomorrow afternoon. My whole family. Together." Tears leaked from Maria's eyes. "Don't mind me. I cry at movies and some commercials."

"And when you meet your lost daughter for the first time," Tony said.

Maria flashed a smile. "I think I'm going to like my son-in-law."

Oh great, Laurel thought, Tony is adjusting better than me.

Gino and Maria had a stucco ranch, on a well-landscaped lawn, backing up to a canal. I should have come home from school to this house, Laurel thought. I should have been yelled at when I didn't mow the grass.

"We've a man who comes to do the lawn," Gino said.

Jesus, Mary and Joseph, I didn't even know that I wouldn't have to be the one to cut the grass. Maybe it won't get better, and I will never feel like I belong.

Day Two:

Gino, Maria and Laurel waited at the Sarasota-Bradenton airport for Karen. The New York flight was two hours late. Silence dribbled between them as they sat on the red plastic seats. Finally Gino stood up. "I need to stretch my legs."

The women ambled over to the newsstand. Maria picked up

a book. "I like Joyce Carol Oates and historical stuff, too."

"I read science stuff, but also Maeve Binchey and Jody Picoult." Laurel shoved a *Time* back in its slot. She pointed to the arrivals board outside. "Karen's plane is in."

Waiting at the same spot as the day before, Laurel saw a woman wave. She resembled Gino, her black hair curling around her face. She had a backpack. Maria waved back as Laurel stood to one side.

"Welcome to the family, Sis." Karen extended her hand.

"I suppose there's no luggage." Gino had come up behind them.

"Of course not. The backpack is enough. Where are my niece and nephew?"

"They found some neighborhood kids to play with."

"Bet Mom rounded them up," Karen said.

Laurel thought of how well she knows Maria, not like me.

As they pulled out of the parking lot, Laurel, who was seated in the back seat next to her sister, asked, "What's your dissertation about?"

"You really want to know?

"Definitely."

"Okay, you asked for it. You know those mutated frogs in Vermont?"

Laurel nodded. "Probably some contaminant in the water."

"I've spent a lot of time up to my ying yang in water gathering samples."

"The same phenomena happened in Minnesota, you know."

"You're right. My thesis professor debated making that part of the project. Thank God, he limited it to Vermont. My budget is empty from field trips. Mom says you're a safety engineer."

"I'm trying to prevent those mutated frogs." Laurel launched into her work problems.

"You've got guts," Karen said.

"Maybe I should have kept my mouth shut."

"No way," Karen said. "Hey, we're home already."

Laurel watched Karen and Gino put the extension in the dining-room table without being asked, an automatic family pattern, the same way her kids knew bath order and where the peanut butter was kept.

"Laurel, no one is idle in this house. The potato peeler is in the right drawer," Maria said.

The drawer was packed with tongs, wooden spoons, can openers, but Laurel rummaged until she found it. "Got it," she wanted to say Mom, but the word wouldn't come out.

Maria opened the sliding door to the backyard. "Tony, check the barbeque, please."

"Coals are just about right, Mom," Tony said. He winked at Laurel as he grabbed a plate of chicken legs to give to Gino who wore an apron saying, "Chef in Charge of Everything." On one pocket was a drawing of a woman, her arms folded with a bubble over her head: "Wanta Bet?"

Moonlight cast soft shadows through the sheet curtains. The drapes with their sunflowers matched the spreads. Laurel could see Tony's profile in the other twin bed. "I miss you."

He created a tent with the covers to welcome her and she snuggled into him. When he put his hand on her breast, she said, "I'd rather talk."

"About what?"

"I don't know."

"Might limit the conversation."

The bed was so narrow that they both had to lie on their sides. "I don't feel as if I'm here."

"You're in California, maybe? Laurel, you're not making any sense. Why don't you e-mail Carol or something?"

"Why is it whenever I want to talk about feelings, you tell me to talk to Carol?"

"Because women are better at that sort of thing."

Laurel went back to her own bed and turned on her side where she couldn't see the moon.

Day Three:

Gino left for Lemon Bay before sunrise to take a party fishing overnight. Laurel heard him whispering to Maria how he hated to be away now.

Laurel understood. Next she heard Maria moving around in the kitchen. She padded out to join her mother. "Need help?"

"Monday mornings? Always." She sipped coffee in between attempts to make a sandwich. "I hate going to work and leaving you."

Laurel spied the last piece of Black Russian Cake. She wrapped it in Saran Wrap and dropped it in Maria's lunch bag. "Not your fault."

Maria moved her fingers pointing at her briefcase, lunch, sweater, car keys. "Think I've got it all." She kissed her daughter and was out the door.

She's as natural as I want to be, but can't. Laurel washed out her mother's cup.

Day Four:

"Edison's house is interesting," Gino said. "The kids might be too young." He'd arrived an hour before, opened a beer and tossed another to Tony.

"Ahem," Karen said.

"You gals want one too?"

The adults moved out to the screened-in porch, the Florida room, Gino called it. Large plants made it feel like a jungle.

"Can we go to Disneyworld?" Samantha called through the screen. A blue heron had landed at the edge of the canal behind her daughter.

"Too far," Karen said. "Come in and I'll show you." A few minutes later the children were looking at an atlas with their aunt. "You can't be raised by Mom without knowing geography."

I'm no good at it, Laurel thought.

Day Five:

Only Maria and Laurel were home. The others had gone to a movie. Maria threw a load of laundry into the machines, "Anything you want washed?"

Laurel sat on a stool by the dining bar between the kitchen and laundry alcove thumbing through a *Redbook*. "Got it all, thanks."

The smell of floral soap began to seep into the kitchen as the machine chugged away. "You know Gino got everyone out so we could talk."

"I suspected," Laurel said. Questions bounced around her head: how long were you in labor, would you have kept me if I were a boy, were you relieved when you gave me away, how hard did you look for me. She closed the magazine and went to the bathroom and sat on the closed toilet seat until Maria knocked.

"You okay in there?"

"Just a minute." She sniffed the toilet paper: scented and colored. Lifting the seat she stared at the blue water. Because her mother added pollutants to the Florida sewer system wasn't a valid reason to avoid a heart-to-heart talk with her mother.

Back in the kitchen, Maria handed Laurel a cup of coffee. "I've a great idea. Why don't you come to school and tell my kids about environmental problems."

"I'd love to." In the back of her head the words *Mom* and

Maria did calisthenics.

Day Six:

The white sand was almost deserted, most snowbirds having returned north. The locals were at work or thought April too chilly for the beach. For anyone accustomed to New England weather, it was heaven. The Gulf stretched to an unseen Texas. A tanker floated in the distance.

Karen swung the kids, both wearing water wings, above the water in turn, then dropped them. Their squeals made Laurel smile as she stretched out and shut her eyes. The waves whispered in her ears. A few drops of water hit her stomach. Laurel propelled herself up as Tony shook his wet curls like a dog coming out of the water. "Feeling better?"

"Yes," she lied.

When Laurel insisted that the kids take a nap, Robbie threw himself on the yellow carpet and screamed, while Sam was content to sit in the flowered easy chair with her arms folded and her lower lip stuck out.

Karen then threw herself next to Robbie and rolled around and screamed. He stopped, his eyes as wide open as Laurel had ever seen them.

"You look dumb," he said.

"So did you. Tell you what—I'm tired. Why don't you put me to bed and stay with me until I fall asleep?" She held out both her hands, which the kids grabbed. As they walked down the corridor, she winked at Laurel, who wandered out into the yard. The velvet painting intensity of the huge red flowers, a variety unknown to her, decorated the corner of the lot as if it were Christmas. Christmas should have snow, not tropical weather. They would spend Christmases in Cambridge, not here, but what if they were never invited here again? If anyone was going to be rejected she wanted to be the one doing the rejection.

Day Seven:

Maria's school was a long, low building. Laurel had forgotten the sweaty, sneaker, metal locker smell of schools. Girls huddled in bunches sharing secrets, while boys jostled each other. She wondered when boys outgrew the desire to push and shove.

Maria's classroom was decorated with maps. The back wall was divided into Europe, Asia and North America with small photos of food products and minerals lined up at the top and with lines connecting them to the countries that produced them.

The second Maria's students entered her classroom they fell silent, each taking their seats, opening notebooks and sitting with their hands folded. Next door there was noise. Thirty pairs of eyes stared at her as Laurel sat on a chair next to Maria's desk.

"Boy, are you kids lucky today," Maria said as she paced between the aisles. "No quizzes."

A collective sigh.

"And you're even luckier, because I'm not lecturing."

This time there were twitters.

"And you're luckiest still because I won't be asking any questions."

Bodies slumped into chairs.

"But you're not off the hook. We've a guest to talk about the environment. Now she's agreed to a cheap rate, another Black Russian Cake."

One boy raised his hand. "Did you bring one to class?"

"Nope, some other time when you all pass an exam with B-or better. This guest is my daughter, but she's also a safety engineer. Laurel DiDonato."

All her life Laurel had been afraid of public speaking, but

seventh graders weren't that terrifying, although having her mother there was. She cleared her throat. "How many of you recycle papers and bottles?"

A few hands went up.

"Now what would you do with 300 pounds of a chemical that would poison your parents, brothers and sisters?"

"Where can I get some?" a boy in the back with his hair cut in stripes asked.

"Probably a company near here may be pouring it into your water."

The kids sat straight up. Maria standing under the photo of diamonds at the back wall gave a thumbs-up.

For the entire hour Laurel told about cases where companies circumvented the law, how the laws had been diluted over the past few years. She told how a brewery threatened to cut an endowment to Colorado University if a professor didn't stop talking about environmental issues and ended on how corporate polluters could be caught.

"Like cops and robbers," the smallest boy in the class said.

"Except we can all be cops. Mrs. Corrente may be mad at me, but no homework tonight. I want to give you an assignment. That is to care about your world. Not just tonight, but always."

The bell rang. A new group filed in. Laurel gave her presentation three times before lunch and twice after. In the lunchroom Maria presented her daughter, the safety engineer from Massachusetts, much like a Jewish mother, might say, "my son, the doctor." It was a moment before Laurel realized that Maria had called her her long-lost daughter.

Day Eight:

"I don't want a life jacket," Robbie whined as Gino fastened it.

"My crew obeys or walks the plank," Gino said. They were

below deck. Two of the four bunks had been converted into a table where Maria was cutting celery and carrots.

"No grown up has one on."

"When you can swim, you won't wear one either." Gino's tone carried the promise of other voyages. "Let me show you how to pilot this craft. That's captain talk for steer. The cook will prepare lunch."

Above deck Karen and Laurel stretched out. Laurel noticed her sister, wearing a bikini made of denim, didn't have an ounce of flab and no cellulite. She had hidden her own body in a full black suit that covered as much as possible. There was even a matching cloth skirt to tie at the waist that hid her thighs. Too bad thin and skinny genes weren't something they shared.

Above, a sea gull floated on an air current. The waves lapped at the sides of the boat. Tony sat in a chair next to Paige. Both had poles in the water.

"Something's pulling," Paige yelled.

Tony grabbed her pole and together they reeled in a red snapper. "Paige, my daughter, you just caught lunch."

They looked at the fish flopping on deck, its scales iridescent in the sun. Laurel wondered how City Boy Tony knew what to do.

As Gino went for his knife, Paige cried, "Don't kill it." Gino threw it back into the water.

"If you want lunch above deck, set up a table," Maria called from the galley.

Within minutes a table was set with plastic dishes, glasses and forks and Maria brought up tuna sandwiches and a salad.

"We could have had fish, but your granddaughter is a softie," Gino said as he carried plates down below. A few minutes later he was back. "Clear the deck, we're heading inland."

"Why?" Karen asked.

"Just checked the radio. There's some unexpected squalls

coming in."

The breeze changed to a wind. The water donned whitecaps and began tossing the boat as the men put away cushions and chairs. "Get the kids below," Gino ordered. They scrambled down the ladder, converted the table back into bunks and settled in.

For the next half hour the boat tossed to the wind's whim. Water covered the portholes alternatively on the sides as the ship heaved.

Laurel was barely able to put on the sweatshirt that Karen had thrown her. Her stomach heaved. The world spun as if she were drunk. Up and down, up and down, up and down. "I'm going to throw up," and she emptied her stomach into the bag Maria shoved under her mouth.

"Yuck," Robbie said.

Maria forced her to eat a cracker. "The dry heaves will be worse."

Laurel groaned but obeyed, although it came up faster than it went down. Maria handed her another, reminding Laurel of morning sickness suffered during both pregnancies when she'd lived on crackers.

"Karen, bring me a damp cloth. And there's Dramamine in the head."

Karen moved to the door by holding onto the benches. She stepped on the button that pumped water to the faucet. As the boat heaved starboard, she grabbed the towel bar so as not to be thrown back into the cabin. She grabbed a towel, but as she shoved the cloth under the water, the boat listed and she missed the drizzle. The second time she corrected for the upheaval and threw the cloth to Maria, who wiped Laurel's face, folded the cloth and put it on her forehead. She took two pills from Karen and insisted Laurel swallow them.

Laurel's stomach muscles felt as if someone had sliced a section and pulled it apart. As the boat continued its endless up and down, she floated between drowsy and miserable and was unaware when sleep won. She was jarred awake followed by a second bump. Then footsteps. Gino and Tony ducked down the three steps leading to the cabin. "We're here. Can you walk Sweetie?"

Braced by Maria and Gino, Laurel staggered to the car. For the first time she understood the desire to kiss the earth. Her parents helped her crawl into bed as soon as they got home. Maria disappeared and returned with a Coke stirring the bubbles out as the spoon made click-clicking noises against the glass.

Laurel remembered how many times her adopted mother had done the same. "I'm so embarrassed."

"Lots of people get seasick," Gino said. "I'm just sorry your last day ended this way."

"I'll try again. The next time we come down, Mom, Dad," Laurel said. She was better.

CHAPTER 30

"You through fuckin' around?" Richard hovered over Mark Hanson as Mark leaned against the fender of the skinhead's car. The engine was running. The driver's door was open.

Mark felt confused. Confusion was a sign of weakness. He thought about June Finnegan and the other boys. He never realized that a home could be fun. He'd never heard so much laughter over routine shit.

"Private, this is war." Richard's face was reddening starting as his neck, running up his cheeks, and over his scalp. "The terrorists will get us, if we don't get them first. And the government is part of it. What the fuck is the matter with you?"

Mark thought about his probation officer and her hidden chocolate. She worked for the government, the state, not the federal. Probably she didn't realize how brain washed she'd been. Richard had said they did that to everyone. He talked about bread and circuses and fake celebrities. He talked about how the white male had to prevail like the Founding Fathers had intended.

"We have to, I mean we have to, man, take control of our lives. Do you have any idea what an honor it is to be part of the new wave? When my father takes over New England, we'll have our own country, and you'll be one of the leaders, right next to me. We'll show those niggers, kikes and towel heads. They can't fuck with us anymore."

Mark thought of Leo, who pushed him to be his best, better

than he ever thought he was capable of. There were black kids on his team, not like the niggers Richard talked about. They were just guys trying to win a ball game.

"If it were anyone else but you, I'd say to hell with you. But man, you can rise in rank."

As Richard's voice droned on, Mark thought of his report card, the best he'd ever had and the chocolate cake June had decorated as a book with "Congrats Mark" written in yellow frosting to celebrate. She got paid by the state. Was she part of the plot?

He thought of his father, still out of work, a nigger in his old job. That matched with white guys losing power. He was a white male. What was his future? "Tomorrow."

Richard frowned.

"Tomorrow, Sir."

"Last chance." Richard pushed until Mark lay across the hood, his feet dangling. "And keep your trap shut." He threw Mark to the ground, got into the car. The tires squealed as he took off.

When Mark got home, for he thought of June's as home, she was nowhere to be seen. No good smells of stew or spaghetti sauce greeted him. He went straight to his room and threw himself on the bed. Maybe Richard was wrong. Carol, Leo, June were good people, but maybe they were trapped in a rotten system. He reached for his trig book.

A swirling light from a police car flashed through the window. He looked out. The flowers from the cherry tree did not hide Leo helping June out. Mark took the stairs leading to the front door in three leaps arriving at the same time as June did. Her right eye was black and her arm was in a cast.

"June was mugged," Leo said.

"I put up one hell of a battle," she said.

"Her attacker is in the hospital. She broke two ribs and he won't be interested in sex for a while."

Probably black, Mark thought as he flanked June on one side with Leo on the other, to help June to her room.

"I've five hungry kids to feed," she protested.

"Tell me what to do and I'll do it," Mark said. As he cut up carrots he imagined he was slicing into the nigger that hurt June.

In the kitchen he didn't hear June talk about the white man who attacked her.

After dinner, the house was quiet. The other boys were studying. June was asleep. Mark went to the red telephone on a small round cherry table in the front hall. Since it worked, June refused to replace it with a portable. He dialed Richard's number.

"It's me, Mark. I'm in."

CHAPTER 31

"Mommy, please. Daddy, stop fighting." Robbie DiDonato forced himself between his parents as they stood in their entryway. Their luggage was scattered between the entrance and the bedroom.

"Go to your room," Laurel screamed.

The little boy looked from one to another and slunk off.

"Now you've upset our son," Laurel slammed the table.

"All I said was you acted like a perfect asshole with your mother, and you went off like a rocket." His voice was several decibels lower than before Robbie interrupted them.

"Can't you get it through your thick wop skull how hard it was for me?" Her voice trembled.

Instead of answering he went to his workroom and slammed the door.

Laurel stepped on a miniature truck as she entered Robbie's room to check on him. He was facedown on his bed. The room felt stuffy, not a surprise since it had been closed up while they were gone. It looked dark and crowded after the order and lightness of her mother's house. When she sat next to him, he ignored her.

"Will you and Daddy divorce?" he spoke into his pillow.

"No, we're just fighting. All married couples fight."

"Seth's parents don't."

She rubbed his back in a slow circular motion. "Sure they do. I keep telling you, they just do it quietly."

Laurel knocked at Tony's workroom door. When he opened it, he held a brush, the one he used to sweep the fine dust from sanding off whatever wood he was working on. "I'm sorry," she said.

He gathered her in his arms and kissed her hair. "We'd better get the kids to bed, or they'll be impossible in the morning."

Just as Laurel turned on the night light, after reading the kids to sleep, she heard the doorbell, Tony's footsteps and muted male voices. Closing the bedroom door, she saw Rick Adams and Matt Rossi.

They were dressed in jeans and sweatshirts.

"We're here to warn you."

"I've lost my job?"

Tony motioned them to sit down and went for beers. They stepped over open suitcases with clothing spilling out. "Actually, we praised your record keeping," Rick said. "Except for the forged internal ones, but we didn't let on that we knew Welch did those, but we commented how weird they were."

"So what are you warning me about?" Laurel sat on the arm of the easy chair covered with a chenille bedspread that hid the stains from too many spilled glasses of milk.

"It's bizarre," Matt said. He rubbed his eyes. "The case has been closed. We got the word just as we were halfway through the forgeries."

"Even my boss says it's strange," Rick said.

After the flight, fight and getting the kids into bed, Laurel was having trouble making sense of it.

"I can't do anything more officially, but something is really wrong. I want to follow up on my off-time, but I need your help."

In bed that night Tony propped himself on his elbow. He had a book on his chest. Laurel had already shut her lamp off. "Did you ever sleep with Matt? The year we didn't speak?"

"Good God, no. Why?"

"Just the way he looks at you."

"You're acting like the typical Italian macho man, a jealous Italian."

"Nope. It would be in the past." He brushed her hair off her neck and kissed it. "I've a great way to make up our fight."

Laurel wanted to say, "No, I took a shower to save time in the morning," but she rolled over to kiss her husband.

The first call Laurel took at the office was from the HR guy, John the Prick. "Anderson told me you need a secretary. I'll put an ad in . . ."

"Call Michelle and see if she's found anything."

"Rehiring is against policy."

Screw policy, Laurel thought. "Just do it, please," she said.

"I'll see what I can do."

"Don't see, do it."

As Laurel put down the phone, she saw Paul, the janitor, waiting at her door. "I suppose you've heard the audit results." He carried a clipboard.

"Tell me." She hoped she acted surprised enough. Hell she should become an actress.

When he'd finished, he handed her his clipboard. "Look at this requisition."

"Why does Bill Welch need a security closet?"

He shrugged. "Only he and Anderson are to have keys." He dropped a key on her desk. "Oops. I forgot, I made a third key by mistake." Laurel wondered if she'd really only been back less than twenty-four hours.

CHAPTER 32

Three professors talk. One mentions nutrition in the Middle Ages. Yeast for beer. Herb medicines. Garlic oil for warts. Elderberry tea for flu. Tony DiDonato pretended he was one of those imaginary profs as he drove down the Mass Pike in Jay's compact car listening to Gregorian chants on the CD player. He added quotes from the *Canterbury Tales*. Literature reflects life, history, he tells his unseen companions.

The real scene disappeared as he passed a church yard.

Grass overgrown, hiding gravestones. Monastery windows were slits in the Norman Style. The heavy oak door creaked open. A monk, dressed in a hooded robe tied with rope, came on sandled feet with outstretched hand to lead Tony into a study. A candle, dribbling wax and puddling on the black wood, shone on a book, two feet by one, with wooden covers and vellum sheets. "I'll leave you to your research," the monk said.

A truck horn blasted. Tony swerved back into his own lane. Stupid fantasy. Too bad that manuscripts were now in museums and monasteries, even if he could gain access to their scriptoriums, they would have electric lights and not candles. Anyway, it was his fantasy to put whatever he wanted into it.

Reality. A sign said Worcester 12 miles. Tony edged towards the right lane. No matter what his dream of being a medieval scholar, without a job, there was no chat, no research, no chance.

"Since you're so good at Latin, you can be a priest," Momma had said, when he brought home an A+ from Boston Latin in seventh grade. His acceptance as one of the lucky 450 out of 3000 had saved him from the Jesuits at Boston College High. The honor of attending the public school, Boston Latin, founded before Harvard and had produced three presidents, Leonard Bernstein and many Nobel prize winners, convinced his parents it was worth risking his immortal soul.

If his three hours of homework nightly had to be done after helping Poppa make furniture, no matter. His parents excused him to play football, but not for the Medieval Club, a group he had founded with three of his friends, who shared his passion. Fascinated with the period, he lied and said he was doing sports training. At Boston Latin to be a scholar was a proud thing.

His grades earned him a full scholarship to Boston University and then a fellowship at Harvard. But after his Ph.D. his dreams of being a lifetime scholar fell under the 328 rejections, most without even an interview.

He pulled into the parking lot where he was interviewing at Clark University in Worcester. Students dressed in T-shirts and jeans, books under their arms, mulled around.

Tony crossed himself and said his rosary ending with, "I want to be part of this."

CHAPTER 33

"Scat." Carol glared at the black cat sitting next to the pot of pink geraniums. "This is Memorial Day, not Halloween." The animal blinked into the late afternoon sun. "So stay already." It jumped across the brown spikes at the top of the stockade fence into its own yard.

Her beige ceramic bowl with the blue stripe near the top rested by her left sneaker. Her legs straddled a row of strawberry plants as her juice-stained fingers snapped a sun-warmed berry from its stem. Rather than add it to the dish, she swallowed it. Flavor exploded in her mouth.

She took the bowl and a pea-filled basket to the kitchen, inhaling her aloneness. Alone wasn't lonely. She could finish chores uninterrupted. Mostly she could complete a thought.

Laurel and Jay were at work, trying to get everything done before the long weekend started and Tony was interviewing at Clark. The children had gone to a neighborhood birthday. Anna wasn't due for another hour. Leaving work early, before traffic clogged Route 128 as people headed to the Cape for the three-day weekend, was worth more than the half vacation day she took.

Preparing a meal unrushed—that was to be savored more than a strawberry. She slit a pea pod, revealing little green balls. Last week they would have been too hard, next week too starchy. Now they were just right. Empty pods piled up on a newspaper.

Tony pulled into the driveway. So much for peace. "How'd it

go?" she asked as the top of his head passed the open window. As he entered the kitchen she tried to remember the last time she saw him wearing a suit. She couldn't.

"I'm short-listed. It's only two summer courses, but . . ." He grabbed a strawberry.

"Why don't you guys eat with us?"

The Marsh and DiDonato children ran in circles around the backyard playing a game with rules which changed by the minute. Cries of "You're out" were followed by "I'm not."

The adults were seated around the redwood table. Jay swigged his beer. "They'll be cooked tonight and hopefully they'll sleep in tomorrow."

Tony picked a lettuce leaf clinging to the side of salad bowl and ate it. "Wanta use the weekend to get the basement cleaned out. Of course, if I get the job, it will take me longer to do the apartment."

"No problem," Jay said.

"I'll take all four kids for the weekend. Starting tonight," Anna said.

"That's too much," Carol said. If the kids were there they would have an excuse to do something else, something that didn't involve the Dark Hole, something that might be fun.

"No, it's not. We'll search for shells, play Frisbee. I have a clerk in the gallery all weekend, so it will be fun." Within twenty minutes she had the kids organized. As she grabbed her car keys from her pocketbook, she shouted, "Pick up your backpacks and march to the car. Left, right, left, right."

Carol glanced at the basement window free of the boards, but so filthy they still could have been there. Her reprieve was over.

Saturday morning, the two couples, dressed in grunge clothes, descended into the basement.

Tony, turning full circle, surveyed the mess. "Maybe we should just call an archeologist."

As Jay hung one of a series of lights, Tony saw Carol's father's workbench. He picked up several tools. "Wow, you've been holding out on me."

Carol listened to their chatter. Rationally, this was a good idea: get rid of the last remnant of her past. Make it positive. Screw rational. She wanted to run away.

Jay watched her for a full minute before handing her a carton wrapped with newspaper and tied with coarse string. "Go through this."

She tore the headline talking about Roosevelt meeting Stalin and lifted out a red dress covering her fingers in dust. A flattened hat hid several skirts and blouses that Ginger Rogers might have worn. "I'll call the vintage clothing store." She ran upstairs to be told if they were clean, the store would buy them. She would have stayed upstairs, but Jay came searching for her.

Opening box after box, she fought the feeling of air being sucked out of the room, until mid afternoon when she could stand it no longer. Picking the pile of old clothes she fled out the bulkhead for the dry cleaner.

"Come back," Jay called but she had already started the car engine.

By the time she did come back, two pizzas next to her on the seat beat out the smell of musty clothes deposited at the cleaners. Getting food delayed her return. As she pulled into the driveway she was greeted by thirty-three oversized trash bags stacked against the back stairs and ready to be put out for the trash man. Instead of going to the basement, she set up the food on the patio. "Come eat."

The three workers who emerged could have posed as coal

miners. "This is going to take several weekends," Jay said.

Carol groaned.

Suds already reached the top of the claw-foot bathtub as water poured from the faucet. White bubbles reflected blue and pink highlights. Rubber flowers glued to the bottom felt rough on Carol's feet as she eased herself into the froth. A long sigh escaped as she felt her pores release the grime. She wondered why she usually opted for showers when a bath was so soothing. Time was the answer. She let her mind drift.

Could her parents have made love in this tub? Had her father given her the cracked rubber duck with one painted eye chipped away that they'd found in a box of odds and ends? A knock brought her back to the now.

"Did you drown?" Jay came in and perched on the tub's edge as she did when Seth and Paige were taking their baths. "What a perfect night to run naked through the house and make mad, passionate love, but I'm too tired."

"There's tomorrow morning. And Laurel called to say they got out of going to Tony's mother for lunch tomorrow, so we can work all day."

Although the alarm was supposed to be set for eight, the Cambridge Tabernacle Bird Chorus went off before six. Jay reached for his wife. "Who would think so many birds would live in a residential area." He buried his face in her hair. "You smell like your bath."

Their love making had a freedom impossible when their ears were cocked for children, but it was gentle in a way that made them want to say, ahhhh, afterwards. They drifted off to sleep. The second awakening was the telephone.

"Waffles. Upstairs. Real maple syrup and I stole some strawberries," Tony said.

The couple pulled on clean grunge clothes. As they sat around the table Laurel asked, "Jay, can Matt, Rick and I talk with you as a lawyer."

"Who?"

"Rick's with the AG's strike force. Matt's with the DEP. It's about my work problem."

"Come to my office Tuesday. It's good to tilt at a few corporate windmills every now and then," Jay said.

"Pass the maple syrup, Don Quixote," Carol said.

By Monday afternoon, a hundred trash bags had been filled, Tony had found dressers, tables, chairs and an armoire to refinish and half the cement floor was visible for the first time since before WWII, but there were still more boxes to go through.

"I can't believe the perfect junk you guys had down here," Tony said.

"Perfect junk is an oxymoron," Carol said. "Can we quit now?" She joined her husband, leaning over a trunk plastered with boat stickers: U.S.S. *America*, S.S. *Patriot*. Several shamrocks were on one end. On opening the trunk, she discovered papers and notebooks, arranged helter-skelter. She picked up a sheet. "Wow, a $3 phone bill."

Tony grabbed a bunch of cancelled checks. "And a $15 car payment. Maybe we should archive these?"

Laurel hugged him. "Perhaps, dear husband, but the idea is to empty the basement."

"But it's family history. Store it in the attic, some scholar . . ."

Laurel flipped through a brown leather-covered book. "It's a 1959 yearbook. What was your mother's maiden name?"

"O'Brien, Kathleen."

Laurel flipped through the pages of eager-faced seniors. "Her write up said she wanted to be a beautician or a secretary, she loved homeroom with Mr. D'Orlando and maple walnut ice cream. She doesn't look like Carol."

"The cops said I was the spitting image of my father whenever he took me into the police station," Carol said. He took her when her mother was on a rampage, using any excuse to escape the house. The chief kept lollipops in his desk drawer for her.

Carol took the book. Had the wreck she grew up with ever been that pretty. Her long hair, parted in the middle, was shiny and wavy. The red didn't show, but the freckles looked as if someone had dropped cinnamon on the page. The eyes laughed.

"You'll keep that?" Tony said.

"Definitely."

Tony pulled out a photo album with a broken binding. Two elastics at ninety degree angles held it together. He handed it to Carol, who opened it. All the photos were held in place with little white corners although many had lost their glue and the pictures were cockeyed. She settled into a chair with the others gathered around.

"That you?" Jay asked. He pointed to a naked baby except for a diaper sitting on a man's stomach. He made rabbit ears over the infant's head.

"Must be. It's Dad. But I don't remember him that young."

A second photo was in color. A bald Carol, her face smeared brown, wore a pink dress and grasped a chocolate ice cream cone.

"Piglet," Jay said. "You adored ice cream even then."

As Carol turned the pages she watched herself grow through Easter bonnets, Halloween costumes and Santa's laps. In the last she wore a mortarboard, her kindergarten graduation. After that the pages were empty.

"Maybe there's another album," Laurel said.

Carol doubted it. Her father had stopped taking photos as her mother drank more.

Jay uncovered a small aqua notebook with a lock with "My

Dia v" written on the cover. The gold r and bottom of the y had disappeared. He handed it to Carol, but the lock wouldn't give.

The crunch of tires on the driveway was followed by car door slams and children announcing their return.

CHAPTER 34

A gentle knock on the bathroom door.

"One more chapter." Tony turned the page of the book balanced on his bare knees.

The handled rattled. "It's a toilet, not a frigging library," Laurel said.

He flushed and pulled up his pants. Laurel stamped by him as soon as he opened the door. Tucking his book under his arm, he sought the sanctuary of his workroom.

His muscles ached from the weekend's work. Not his normal pace. Do something. Stop. Drink coffee. Contemplate the next step. Between the basement, furniture and maybe teaching he would become as hurried as everyone else. People weren't suppose to live the way his landlords and wife did.

The table that he wanted to decoupage had been sanded and a white veil of clean wood remained, velvet to the touch—not a flaw. A red lacquer paint can and three new brushes with clear plastic protecting their bristles waited.

His desk was next to the table. If he got the job, he would have to prepare his first syllabus. Chaucer. The second. Early English Drama. Up to when Elizabeth I packed it in.

His wife staggered in, reminding him of the children when they had stayed up too late. She kissed him absently, said good night and left.

When he joined her in bed, she was curled up like the kids, a small corner of the sheet held to her lips, her breath coming in small puffs, a complete contrast to the whirlwind of her days.

Chapter 35

Carol stared at her list.

    Lay out kid's clothes
    Sew button on Paige's jeans
    My clothes
    Make lunches
    School trip permission slip
    Iron Jay's blue shirt

Doing things the night before transformed Carol's mornings from impossible to merely hectic. Repacking her briefcase wasn't on the list. She'd left it in the car for the Memorial Day Weekend, feeling almost guilt free. She no longer assumed responsibility for everything that went wrong at work, home and the planet. It was okay not to be Super Probation Officer, Wife and Mom. She could almost accept Just-Doing-The-Best-I-Can Carol although the niggling of Maybe-I-Could-Do-More lay just behind the next door waiting to jump out at her. Her lists, mental and written, kept her organized, although she knew she would run out of day long before she ran out of list.

The items checked off, she decided to go to bed, even if it was only 9:07 P.M. When she pulled open the drawer where her pajamas were folded, she saw her mother's diary on top of the chest where she had tossed it earlier. Taking a paper clip that Jay had left on the dresser, along with his loose change, she picked at the lock. Nothing. In the bathroom she found a pair of manicure scissors and cut the small leather strap that kept her mother's secrets hidden for decades.

Climbing into bed, she punched the pillows and squirmed herself into a comfortable position. The first thing she noted was that her mother's hand writing slanted to the right. Her i's had tiny circles, nothing unusual for a teen-age girl, but the name Jimmy always had a heart drawn for the dot. Her first thought as she read the first line was, it figures . . .

Saturday—May 23

I got soooooo drunk last night. The last thing I remember was talking about going swimming. We started drinking beer on Route 128 on our way to Crane's beach. Jimmy Matthews drove. I think he likes me. I like him. His hair is redder than mine, a real carrot top with freckles. We all crammed into his mom's station wagon and sang "I Heard it on the Grapevine" as loud as we could.

Some kids don't like the taste of beer. I ADORE it. By the time we hit the beach, my eyes felt coated, but I felt wonderful. Pop said he'd ground me for life if he ever caught me drinking. So I won't let him catch me. I can hardly wait to get drunk again.

Monday—May 25

Jimmy says he loves me. We were in his car. He had a bottle of Scotch. It tastes like burnt handkerchiefs, but it made me feel good fast. When he touched my breast, I felt it all the way down THERE. I know I shouldn't let him, 'cause he'll think I'm cheap. If I don't he'll find another girl. I hope he asks me to the prom.

Tuesday—May 26

Jimmy asked that bitch Judy Alexander to the prom. She wears those stupid wide-legged pants and she once made fun of my pop-it beads. She goes three weeks without wearing the same thing. Me? I can only go a week if Mom washes the blouse I wore on Monday for Friday. Anyway, he told me he had to ask her, because her father is president in the same company where his father is vice president. Jimmy asked Vince to take me and said we'd double. When I protested, he put his tongue in my mouth.

Mom asked cousin Alice to lend me her blue prom dress, but her dyed-to-match shoes won't fit. I'll have to wear my white church pumps. And I can't afford to have my hair done, but Mom said she'll do a French braid with a blue and white ribbon so I guess it will be okay.

Saturday—June 13

The prom was a blast even with Vince. Jimmy suggested we switch partners a lot. Judy pouted. On the way home Judy kept spotting pe-diddles and saying "Kiss me Jimmy." I wanted to throw up or cut her lips off. Vince looked at me and I gave him a look that said touch me and die. None of us dared take a drink because Judy took some stupid temperance pledge. Jimmy dropped her off first, then Vince, and finally we went parking behind First National Market. He left the radio on and we danced in front of all the old thrown out boxes. Sooo ROMANTIC: He even kissed my nipples. WOW!!!!!

Friday—June 19th

Pomp and Circumstance. Mom and Pop were so proud. I'm the first in her family to graduate from high school. Jimmy introduced me to his parents. They acted as if I needed a shower or something after I said I wasn't going to college. There was an all-night party with a DJ to stop us from getting drunk. The school caf was all decorated like a beach and they gave us pancakes at 6 A.M. With blueberries. Fresh.

Wednesday—July 1

Everyone's gone ape at me. Pop's mad because I haven't got a job.

Jimmy's mad because I won't go all the way. Mom's mad because at the beach Jimmy got so drunk he couldn't drive and I snuck in early and she caught me staggering in. She didn't tell Pop. I hate hangovers.

Wednesday—July 8

I've a job interview at an insurance agency in Central Square. Jimmy picked me up and we made out like crazy but when he started to put his thing in me I began to cry. He pulled out. Most boys wouldn't. Am I still a virgin? He said he loves me anyway. I have to go to confession.

Thursday—July 9

Jimmy loves me. He called to say last night was the most important of his life and I'm not cheap. And I got the job.

Saturday—July 11

Father O'Hara said he was disappointed in me when I confessed. He made me say lots of Hail Mary's and Our Fathers. I'm supposed to mow the church lawn. You can always tell which kids messed up by who is mowing the grass.

Monday—July 13

My first day of work. I wore my blue skirt and white blouse and flats. I need office clothes. Then Jimmy will see I can look classy. Better than Judy. Mom put my hair in a French braid, more grown up than a pony tail. Miss Wilson is the office manager. I bet no one ever kissed her and if they did, I bet they turned to stone. She keeps saying "This the way WE do this," or "WE do that." I can't eat at my desk, crumbs in the typewriter, you know. It's an old Remington not an IBM like in school.

Jimmy hasn't called. He can't love me.

Wednesday—July 15

He hasn't called. I held the phone in my lap wishing he would. It didn't work.

Saturday—August 1

Miserable hangover. Jimmy called. He'd been at his uncle's at Lake Winnepesauke for some water skiing. It was a last minute thing. I've never been to New Hampshire. I'll miss him so much next month when he goes to college. Mom say he won't want me around then and don't come crying to her.

We went to see Midnight Cowboy at the Revere Drive-In. Pop would be furious. He says it's dirty what kids do there. We bought Coke and hot dogs and added rum to the Coke. One taste spoils the other.

Saturday—August 8

Jimmy took me to his parents for a barbecue. I spent a week's pay on new Bermudas and a white blouse. Everyone else wore sundresses. The Matthews have a neat pool. Mrs. Matthews was polite, but you could keep popsicles in her voice. Afterwards we went parking. Jimmy had a flask of vodka and we both got giggly. I let him put his thing in me, but he didn't move so I won't get pregnant. If making love feels so good, why is it wrong? The same about drinking?

Sunday—August 9

We went to Harvard Square and he gave me his class ring. I am afraid I will lose him to a college girl. He told me to take a night course, say at Boston State. It's never too late, he says. I can't do

*that with my record. I didn't tell him that Mom was a waitress and
my working in a office is already a big step.*

Friday—August 14

*Mr. Adler is nicer than Miss Wilson. He thanks me when I type a let-
ter or bring him coffee with his one teaspoon of sugar and one
tablespoon of milk. I'm surprised Miss. Wilson doesn't want me to stir
it a certain way. What a nag. She searches my works for mistakes. I
even have to put a paper clip exactly the same way all the time.*

Monday—September 1

*Oh God. How could you kill Jimmy? What did he do wrong? Was it
because we made love? Then it was my fault he died. I can't believe
it. He went out with Vince and the rest of the guys for a last blast
before they left for college. They got totally wasted. Jimmy drove off
the road. The car exploded. Everyone is dead but Vince. He was
thrown clear. No one knows if he'll live. I just stole a shot of Pop's
whiskey to calm me down. I didn't think people my age could die.
When Gran died Mom made me kiss her. She was so cold. But she
was old, old, old. I'm so sad I can't stop throwing up.*

Carol's hand shook. For the first time her mother didn't feel
like the enemy. She went to where Jay was finishing the
paperwork on an early morning closing. "Come into the Black
Hole with me?" When he looked confused, she said, "I need to
get the yearbook."

At the bottom of the stairs, Carol saw the pile of books they
were not throwing away. The yearbook was fourth down in the
stack. On the M page, a young boy smiled back. "Poor thing."

"Who?" Jay asked.

"My mother's boyfriend. He was killed in a car crash right
before he left for college."

"Poor kid." He followed Carol upstairs.

She wanted to keep reading, but when she climbed into bed as Jay undressed, she had trouble focusing. By the time Jay slipped under the covers, she was asleep.

CHAPTER 36

Jay fell in with the other joggers along the Charles River. The oars from a passing crew team rustled the river's surface, brown from the tannic acid—at least that's what Laurel said. The sun rose. Early commuters drove down Memorial Drive. He stretched his arms in celebration until he saw the Harvard B School clock. Clocks were modern-age tyrants. He abandoned the run to begin his day.

Battleaxe Barbara pounded her keyboard. A cigarette, more ash than tobacco dangled from her lips. No state law prohibiting smoking came between her and her habit. Her "Humph" passed for good morning as she handed Jay his messages with one hand, and kept typing with the other.

He stuck his head in Lina's office. His assistance's back was to him. "Hey, Lady, another deed to file."

She swiveled around. "Hey, Boss, got a murder case for you."

"No," he said.

"Battered wife?"

"No."

"Self-defense?"

"I'm not a criminal lawyer. We've been through this before. Call Harry at legal services."

"They stink. Humph."

"You sound like Battleaxe Barbara."

"Low blow." She turned back to her computer. "Want coffee?"

In Linaspeak it was, "I give up."

"I'll get it. You want one?" In Jayspeak that was, "You're great."

Rifling through his messages he saw one from Jennifer. He rolled it in a ball and pitched it into the bin. Another was from Tom Phipps at the People's Credit Union. He'd proposed to do closings with prices based on their income. The message said the board had approved it.

The day was looking better and better.

The intercom buzzed. "Laurel somebody," Battleaxe Barbara said.

His neighbor arrived at his door before he could say send her in. Dressed in jeans and sneakers, she looked more like a student. She was followed by a man.

"Rick Ames, AG's Strike Force."

Jay pointed to his corner circular table. When they were seated, he asked, "What's up?"

Ames leaned forward, his hands folded in front of him. "Jackson created fake paperwork to cover missing chemicals, which Laurel and I think they got rid of illegally. But that's not all."

"Rick was told to back off," Laurel said.

"By whom?" Jay asked.

"My boss said it came from the top."

"So that is unusual?"

"Hasn't happened in years."

They were interrupted by Lina bringing a pot of coffee, on a tray with cups, milk and sugar, without being asked.

"My boss didn't say I could poke around on my own time, but he didn't say I couldn't." He reached into his corduroy jacket pocket and brought out a flash drive. "Can I show you these photos?"

They moved to Jay's computer. Rick picked up a pencil and pointed at three men in shadow rolling what might have been a barrel. "That's the delivery dock at Jackson. Sadly, everything is unidentifiable. The barrels could be empty."

"Coming or going?" Jay asked.

"Both. Normal deliveries don't happen at 3:38 A.M. do they Laurel?"

Laurel shook her head. "And I don't have any paperwork. Bizarre. I'm trying to snoop around, but it puts my job in danger. Calling in sick today isn't good for job security either, but we wanted someone to know besides ourselves, and that's you Jay."

"So I'm your ear? And if you want lawyer confidentiality give me a dollar to make it official."

Both Rick and Laurel reached for their money. Laurel's wallet was empty except for change. She plunked down two quarters. Rick rummaged through his pocket and came up with a quarter, two dimes and a nickel.

Jay was tempted to say that made him a small change lawyer, but didn't. He figured he harkened back to the days when doctors and lawyers in small towns were paid in chickens and vegetables or having their driveways shoveled out.

"Every instinct tells me something is big here, but I can't back it up. We'd like you to go see Mr. Jackson," Rick Ames said.

Laurel folded her hands, almost like praying. "Even though he sold the company, he's old school. Ethics count. I can't go as an employee. But you could as my representative. I know him. If he promises silence, he won't run to Anderson." At Jay's blank look, she added, "The CEO."

Jay looked at the photo on the screen. It was almost black. Had Rick not outlined the men and barrels, they could have been anything.

"Where do I find him?"

Laurel handed him a piece of paper with a New Hampshire address.

The phone rang and Jay excused himself to hear Battleaxe Barbara say, "Line 2."

It didn't matter how many times he'd told her not to interrupt him when he was with clients. "Who?"

"How the hell should I know?" There was a click and the call transferred.

"Jay. It's Jennifer."

Shit. His stepmother's soft voice made him want to clean the receiver.

"I'm sorry to bother you, but your father is at Brigham. He really wants to see you and the children."

Laurel motioned, indicating they should leave, but Jay shook his head. Rick pointed to his watch, pulled out the flash drive and left.

"The cancer has spread. He doesn't have much time."

"Is he in a lot of pain?"

"He's refused all but minimum medication because he says he wants a clear head. Please."

The words "you can run but you can't hide," flashed through his head along with a memory of running along the Charles River that morning. "I'll get back to you." He sat the phone down to find Laurel staring at him. Before she could say anything he said, "Let's get back to your problem: Is there anyone in your company who could help?"

"They're all too scared for their jobs. It's not like when the old man was there. He ran it honorably. What an old-fashioned word."

"It's one I want in my vocabulary," Jay said.

Laurel fumbled in her jeans pocket and brought out a tissue. God don't cry, he thought. He hated women crying. Laurel was often so dramatic that it was hard to sift logic from her emotion. How could anyone so scientific in her work be such a flake in daily life? She only blew her nose.

"Let me do some detective work. Lina?" he yelled through the wall. She appeared. "I've a research project that should keep you busy."

"Better than filing deeds?" Lina asked.

"Yup. I want to find out everything about Walter Anderson, Gordon Jackson, Prospect Enterprises and Jackson Products."

Lina gave a military salute and marched out.

"I can't thank you enough," Laurel said.

He patted her shoulder as he led her to the door. "I haven't done anything yet. When you get home, would you leave a note for Carol that I may be late. I'm going to see Anna."

Jay was so engrossed in memories of his anger at his father that he forgot how beautiful the day was as he drove to Rockport. The traffic was light and in no time, or so it seemed for his mind was not on the trip, he pulled into his mother's driveway. Through her open garage door, he saw her eleven-year-old car, but she didn't answer the door. He hollered. No response. What if she'd fallen? Had a stroke? Heart attack? Long ago, he accepted that he always suspected the worst whenever someone he loved wasn't exactly where he expected them to be. He also knew it was because he felt so incredibly lucky to have the family he had. Since he wasn't expected, she wouldn't have left a note if she went to a neighbor.

The back door was unlocked. Maybe she'd been kidnapped. Good luck to the kidnappers. She would make their lives miserable. Walking to the back porch he scanned the boulders, some the size of SUVs, to see Anna perched on the biggest one behind the house. Her back was towards him as she stared out to sea.

When she did see him, her face broke into smiles that made

her few wrinkles line up. She jumped from stony surface to stony surface, sure of her footing.

Taking him by the hand, she led him to where she'd been. The rocks, cooked by the sun, felt hot through his pants. When he'd been in school, they'd often talked over problems in this spot. The harbor was calm—its water changing from aqua to deep blue as it went towards the open Atlantic.

She pointed to the tide pool where a crab, dragging a piece of seaweed, scuttled in the shallow water. "Isn't he lovely. I'd been working all morning, and suddenly I had a nature attack." Her eyes twinkled. "I'm celebrating being alive. And why are you here?"

He told her, finishing with "I don't want the kids to see a dying old man and be scared."

"Bullshit." Waves slipped into the hidden spots between the boulders.

"That's all you have to say?"

She said nothing.

"I suppose you think I don't want to face him."

Anna cocked her head.

"I hear you saying BINGO."

"Let's get some tea."

In the kitchen she placed a tea pot decorated with blue Chinese people farming, walking across bridges and pushing carts.

He remembered buying it for her birthday the year he was nine. "Not fair using this pot." He spooned honey into the tea's twisting steam. Her mother's brews were never gentle. This combined peppery Earl Grey with a good dose of gunpowder, a pungent green tea leaf rolled into tiny balls.

He glanced out the window at the rock where'd they been sitting. He remembered their last major battle when he told her he intended to commute to university. She insisted he live at school. "What will you do without me?" he'd asked.

"Cook less meals and look into your clean empty room and appreciate the lack of a pigpen," and she'd packed his clothes and sent him off.

When she asked for his thoughts, he mentioned the memory.

"After leaving you I came home to my freedom. I kicked you out of the nest, all right."

"And I went, feather by feather."

"Reminiscing does not change the topic," Anna said.

"I don't want to tell the kids about their grandfather."

Anna stirred her tea.

"Talk to me, Mother."

Click, click, click . . . the spoon hit the side of the cup.

"Mother?"

She picked up her cup and walked over to the sink. Leaning against it, she said, "Remember when I bought my last car. Even the hubcaps glowed. The first thing I did was scratch the door."

He'd thought her a bit mad at the time. Maybe she'd always been a bit crazy, albeit nice crazy. "What are you talking about?"

"Analogy, Son. Perfection never exists."

He put his hands up in the air.

"You want perfection." When he started to say something, she laid her finger against her lips. "You've been a wonderful son, a good father, husband and lawyer. You try to be perfect. But you aren't and you know why?"

He knew she'd tell him.

"You lack tolerance."

He slammed his hand on the table. "That's a lie. I fight intolerance. I have a black woman working for me. I take civil . . ."

"I'm not talking about that kind of tolerance. That's part of being good, and thank God for it. What you don't tolerate is human weakness. You're so busy eradicating your own flaws, you don't allow people to be human. Worse, it keeps them from being themselves."

Jay wondered if she were going senile.

Anna dropped her cup into the dishpan. "You've never tolerated what you see as your father's sin of leaving me."

"He never wanted me." The words brought a twitch to his stomach.

"Unfair. True, I wanted a child more than he did. Not abnormal. You weren't happy when Carol got pregnant with Seth. You said it was too soon after Paige, but you don't love Seth any less."

"We're talking adoption, not natural fatherhood."

"And that's my point. Adoption was deliberate. Your father chose to adopt you. I repeat. *Chose.* Seth was an accident." She dried the cup with a dish towel. "Ever think of giving your father credit for not living out a farce of a marriage."

He shook his head.

"How many times do I have to tell you? I thought he and his colleagues were pompous assholes. I couldn't have taken one more faculty dinner. He thought I was a crazy bohemian. This does not a happy couple make. He had the courage to leave."

Jay wasn't going to credit his father with courage.

"You try and do everything he didn't: bathe the kids, play with them. But when you were little, men didn't do that. He wasn't the father you wanted. Tough shit."

"But you . . ."

"I was what you wanted in a mother. You got fifty percent. Deal with it." She went over and put her arms around him. "You'll never be truly grown up, until you forgive him. Some things will always be wrong in this world, and how you react is what measures you." She pulled his car keys from his pocket. "Go home. I've work to do."

"She's right you know," Carol said after Jay repeated the conversation to her. "And she's your guarantee against alimony." When he looked confused, she added, "Husbands are easier to replace than fantastic mothers-in-law."

The Marshes had left the kids with Tony and Laurel and were walking to Harvard Square. At the Out of Town Bookstore they stopped to listen to Peruvian musicians play guitars and pan flutes. The men had braided hair under their hats and striped ponchos were protection against the evening wind that was blowing off the river.

"So you think I should see him."

She nodded.

"He's not my real father."

"You consider Anna your real mother."

While Carol showered, Jay lay in bed picturing Anna and Carol in boxing gloves backing him into a corner of a ring—he grabbed the telephone. Ten was a little late to call the number he had to look up. The phone rang several times then a message began: "No one can come . . ."

"Don't hang up, I'm here," Jennifer said. "Hello, anyone there?"

"It's Jay."

"I'm so glad you called. I just got in from the hospital." He pictured her perfectly dressed and pulling an earring off before putting the receiver to her ear. He didn't want to imagine her at all.

"I'll visit tomorrow night after work. In case you want to warn him or something," Jay said.

"Wonderful. I do need to warn him. He's too weak for

surprises, even good ones. Will you bring the family?"

When he'd brought home an all A report card except for one B+, his father's one comment was to try harder. His throat constricted in exactly the same way as it had then. Stupid. Nothing was ever enough for the man. "I'm coming alone."

He saw Carol smile as she slipped into bed beside him.

The next morning, Jay pounded down Chestnut Street and into his own driveway. Their car had gone. A glance at his watch told him he'd been running two hours, double his normal time. Sweat marked his T-shirt.

On the kitchen table between the cereal bowl and the orange juice, Carol had left a framed snapshot taken of all of them at Anna's last summer. The frame was silver, found during the Black Hole clean up, but the tarnish had been polished away until it gleaned. A yellow Post-it was stuck to the glass: "Take it to the hospital."

When he looked at it, he could almost hear the kids giggling, and smell the salty sea air. After tearing off the note, he put it in his briefcase.

CHAPTER 37

"Three bagels?" Michelle asked as Laurel walked by her desk again carrying food, just as Laurel's adopted mother would have asked, with the implication, watch what you eat, men don't like fat women.

"If I hadn't forgotten what a pain-in-the-ass you were, I wouldn't have rehired you," Laurel said.

Laurel placed her cream cheese slathered bagel on a piece of paper. Nothing wrong with a little comfort food on a bad day. So what if she had to fasten the skirt of her blue power suit with a safety pin.

Michelle called into Laurel's office. "Matt Rossi is in reception. Want me to get him?"

"I'll do it."

Laurel found Matt looking at the antique sewing machine on display. His back was to her so she saw the Waltham Electronics embroidered on his blue work jacket. His tan work boots were scuffed. "Mr. Rossi?"

He extended his hand. "Ms. DiDonato?"

The receptionist prepared a rectangular paper with Visitor Jackson Products written on it. She added M. Rossi and slipped it into a plastic name tag which he pinned to his shirt.

Laurel led her old friend through the building without saying anything. A smell, similar to burning hair mixed with manure, hit them as they entered the first lab. Breathing through their mouths, they walked past a long black slate lab table. A man in a white coat adjusted a microscope while dictating notes into a recorder. A woman placed test tubes into a fridge. Laurel pulled two face masks from her pocket and gave one to Rossi, which they adjusted over their mouths and noses.

Toward the back was a glassed-off office where Dr. Bill Welch sat at a paper-free desk typing into a laptop. He stood up and came over to them with a frown. "Hey, Laurel, what's up?"

"We're checking some wiring problems." Her voice was nasal because she was mouth breathing. Matt was undoing light sockets, opening cabinets, but when he poked in a storage area Welch started toward him.

The bagels felt like cement in her stomach, as she pretended to examine the new hood over the lab table. There was no hum. To distract Welch, she said, "If you're working with chemicals, the ventilators should be running."

"I don't like the noise."

"The fumes can make you sick."

"I'm finished," Matt said.

The day dragged on as they wandered from lab to lab. In each he undid sockets, reached behind cabinets, turned switches off and on, asked that chemicals be moved so he could get to walls that he tapped. His clipboard filled with notes.

Paul, the janitor, wandered in. "Can I see you, Laurel?"

She stepped into the corridor and shut the door.

"What's he doing?"

"Checking wiring."

"It was done before the company was sold."

"We've had some power surges."

Paul shrugged. "Whatever you say. This guy new at Waltham?"

"Why."

"Just thought I knew everyone who worked there."

"Temp?"

Paul looked at her carefully. "Whatever you do, I'm behind

you." He walked off, whistling, with his hands in his pockets.

"Production area is last," Laurel told Matt late in the afternoon. They'd been over almost every inch of the building. Two people worked a machine that dropped powder into containers, which marched down the conveyor belt and were sealed and labeled. The workers looked like actors in a Sci-Fi movie with their eyes hidden by goggles. Three flap apparatuses covered their noses and mouths.

Matt took a device from his tool kit along with a paper and pretended to read the directions. Only Laurel noticed him shove something in his pocket.

When they found a locked door at the end of the production area, he said, "I need to check inside." The supervisor, a man in his forties, removed his mask before unlocking the closet. It was packed with gas cylinders. "Can we move the stuff?" Matt asked.

The two men rolled the cylinders one by one. When the closet was empty, Matt went in and closed the door. While Laurel waited she listened to his tapping.

Matt emerged and Laurel walked him back to reception.

When Laurel pulled into the 392 Chestnut Street driveway after work, she found Matt and Rick Ames sitting on the stairs.

"No one is home," Matt said.

Laurel unlocked her door. "Tony must be shopping." Upstairs she offered beers and took one herself. They swigged them directly from the bottle. "So what did you find?"

"They're relabeling Methyl Bromide. That's what was in Welch's storage room. I guess he figured I wouldn't recognize the canisters, but some still had the original labels on."

"I don't remember logging any in."

"Just to make sure I was right I checked with my office. It's a chlorofluorocarbon once used as a pesticide and banned since

2001 by the UN. But the U.S. had been the biggest user. They've been sticking these labels on." He handed them the sheet of paper he'd slipped into his pocket. It said "Soil Protection." The ingredients listed were harmless. "Some of the canisters in the storage area had this label. What we've got is illegal labeling of hazardous materials and improper filing."

Rick put his beer bottle on the table. "But I still haven't enough to act on and . . ."

Footsteps thudded up the stairs. Tony kissed his wife and shook hands with the men. He carried the mail, and Laurel could see the Clark University logo on an open envelope. "I'll leave you guys to work on your problems."

They discussed all types of alternatives, but none of them came up with anything that would pin down Jackson Products' offenses. Finally the two men left.

Laurel wandered into Tony's workroom. The table he was working on was covered in the fine dust from the sanding machines. She looked at the letter from Clark and then at her husband who was rubbing the wood back and forth. His eyes told her that once again he didn't get the job.

CHAPTER 38

As Carol Marsh rushed through the probation office door, a blast of trumpets greeted her. Her boss Doug, a grin on his face, rolled out a red carpet. Only half the staff was at their desk, but those that were clapped.

"What the hell is going on?" Carol shouted over the trumpets.

"You're on time. Positive reinforcement." Doug shut off the tape deck.

"Idiots, all of you," she said.

"If I hadn't glanced out the window when you pulled in, I'd've missed my chance. You should've seen your face." He grew serious. "However, I still need to see you in my office."

She followed him down the corridor. As usual she had to remove folders from his chair before sitting. "What's up?"

"I need a project report."

After rummaging in her briefcase, she handed him a blue binder. "Funny, you should ask."

He thumbed the pages and kept nodding. Taking the pencil from behind his ear, he scribbled a note. "Good job. And call June Finnegan. She's having a problem with one of your kids."

June answered the door. Although her arm was in a sling, her smile was normal. "Thanks for coming. I still can't drive with this damned thing."

Carol followed her into the living room. No two pieces of furniture matched. The slip covers were worn. One window was almost hidden with giant plants. A card table in the corner held a jigsaw puzzle of the Boston Celtics, and a computer was open to a Red Sox page.

Carol pointed to the velvet painting of the Celtics team hanging over the fireplace. "That's new."

"Isn't it a monstrosity? Jamal bought it for me after I was mugged to make me feel better." She took off her glasses and rubbed her eyes. "Want coffee? Sandwich?"

"Thanks, but no. I need to get back. I've a lot of appointments and . . ."

"Is one of them about Mark?"

Carol nodded.

"I'm worried about him. Have been for a while."

Carol said a prayer of thanks that June was a foster mother who wasn't in it for the money. "Is this your famous instinct or something real?"

"Both. This morning when I checked to make sure all the kids had made their beds, I found this." She went through the swinging door to the kitchen and came back with several books under her good arm.

Carol scanned the titles: *Guns, a Complete Guide, The U.S. Government is Your Enemy, How to Cause a Disruption, Military Tactics.* Some papers fell out with Xeroxes.

"Right wing garbage. All I can think of is the Oklahoma bomber."

"She's got no fucking right to go through my things." Mark's pacing in the small area of Carol's office would have done a tiger in a small cage proud.

She'd started the conversation with, "So Mark, June found some books that we don't think are the best reading materials for you." Her choice of words had been deliberate to test his reaction. The intensity of his anger told her there was a problem.

Although she'd defused hundreds of angry kids, she never liked doing it, but she knew one secret. Don't show fear.

Mark had never shown any signs of physical violence, although he fluctuated from charming to sullen as fast as switching a light off or on. Shooting up from her seat she looked into his eyes, put her hands on each shoulder and pushed him into a chair.

He slumped down, folding his arms, a half-deflated balloon.

She imagined an invisible key locking his lips. "So what was it for?"

He didn't look at her.

She repeated the question.

Still nothing.

Grabbing him by the shirt, she said, "Look, Mister, when I ask a question, I expect an answer."

"It's my business."

"Wrong answer. You're on probation. That makes it mine." She let go of his shirt. "Answer me."

"I hate people going through my stuff. Even June."

"I understand that, but she cares about you. Which is why she called me. Why are you reading that stuff?"

"Term paper."

"What subject?

"For history. I saw a documentary on militias and I thought it would be cool."

"That's all?"

He cocked his head. The light switch went on. "I'm sorry you got upset over nothing."

Carol glanced at her watch as she wondered if he were trying to be charming or really sorry. She was already well into her next appointment time. "Go. I want to see you next Friday afternoon." Usually they met bi-weekly.

"I'm going to Maine after school. Camping with friends."

Red flag, red flag. Signal, signal. "You can't leave the Commonwealth without the Court's permission. I represent the Court."

He smiled. "Come on, Carol, all I want to do is some fishing with friends. I never fished before."

"It's not a good idea," she said.

"There'll be an adult."

"Who?"

"My buddy's dad. What if he calls you?"

"Maybe after school gets out, but you aren't cutting classes." She reached into her drawer and picked up a chocolate.

"I'm giving up chocolate." He turned and slammed the door.

She ran after him. "Next week. Here. Same time."

He turned and walked backward. "Okay."

Her next case slouched into the office. Because she was running late, she forgot to write a note to call Mark's history teacher.

"Mrs. Carol Marsh?"

Carol cradled the phone between her shoulder and ear as she shoved papers into her briefcase. Where was the Brunner file? On the chair. The phone almost slipped as she reached for it.

"Richard Keats, Sr., the father of Mark's friend. We'd really like him to come to our place in Maine next weekend."

"He's got school."

"We're leaving Friday about four and it's only for a weekend. There's a bunch of kids."

"And there'll be adults?"

"Me and a couple of my friends. Boys that age need supervision."

Carol glanced at the clock on her desk. She was expected home an hour before. "Okay."

As she left her office, Doug came down the corridor. He

looked as tired as she felt. They were the last two in the office. She waited as he locked the door. Together they approached their cars. She threw her briefcase onto her backseat. "By the way, I wasn't on time this morning. I was early."

"Once in a row," Doug said.

CHAPTER 39

Carol hated the week before school ended. The children fought going to bed, but if she let them stay up late, mornings were awful. So she darkened their room as much as possible, read them an extra story, and then yelled down any rebellion.

What a day. Besides Mark, one of her probationers had been arraigned for murder in New York. The only good thing was Doug's satisfaction.

She half-expected, half-wished Jay had called her to go with him to see his father. Although fleeting, her thoughts had been with him most of the day. At 9:30 P.M. she looked at her watch. He was late. She showered, went to bed and picked up her mother's diary. This time she noticed her mother didn't write in it daily, but had crossed out the pre-printed dates and added her own.

Tuesday—September 2

My first Protestant funeral. Closed casket. Mrs. Matthews had to be carried up to it. When she stroked it. I started bawling. All the kids from school were crying. At the cemetery there were chairs for family only. They put the coffin in the hole then shoveled dirt and some got on the flowers. I couldn't bring myself to add any dirt. When they gave me the shovel, I passed it onto the next person. Mrs. Wilson was nasty about me taking time for the funeral. She acted like I made it up. The bitch.

Wednesday—September 3

What a nightmare. In it Jimmy came out of his grave and grabbed the rose I left.

Thursday—September 4

Vincent is off the danger list.

Thursday—September 11

I dreamed of Jimmy. I threw up this morning and my period is late. If I'm knocked up, Pop will kill me. I'm freaking out about the possibility.

Monday—October 6

No period and I'm throwing up every morning. I'm afraid to go see the doctor and Mrs. Wilson says if my work doesn't improve, she'll fire me.

Saturday—October 10

I'm PG. I bought a wedding ring at Woolworth's and saw a Dr. Land. I picked him from the phone book. His office is across from Mass General. I couldn't go to Dr. Halligan, because he'd tell Mom. On the Longfellow Bridge, I looked at all the colored leaves along the banks of the Charles. I tried wishing on each one, but it didn't work. Dr. Land didn't believe I was really Mrs. Matthews, but he examined me anyway. I had no idea he was going to do THAT to me. It hurt. The baby is due in April.

Sunday—October 11

I confessed last night. As soon as I said "Forgive me father, for I have sinned" I started to cry and couldn't stop. Father O'Hara was nicer than I thought he'd be, but he told me not to abort. I couldn't abort Jimmy's baby . . . it would be like he died twice. Father O'Hara told me about the Salvation Army in case my parents throw me out.

I called Vince. He's the only one around. He won't start college until January. We got really drunk, even though he's still on crutches. He said I should tell Jimmy's parents. It's their grandchild.

Sunday—October 12

Columbus Day. I worked up my courage to call the Matthews and asked if I could come over. They weren't thrilled but said yes. His mother has lost tons of weight. When I told them, his father yelled that I was a liar and I'd never see a cent. I hadn't thought of asking for money. And I still haven't told my parents.

Thursday—October 15

My parents threw me out. Pop said no tramp would live in his house. Mom helped me pack and gave me some money from her coffee can bank. I don't know what to do next. My salary won't cover even a room. And when I start to show, they'll fire me. They did that to a married woman once, Miss Wilson said. Mr. Adler doesn't think customers like looking at pregnant women. We deal with most of them by phone and letter. Big stomachs don't show up on paper or over the phone.

Saturday—October 17

Hannah in the next office is letting me sleep on her couch for $8 a week. Her two roommates are Gina and Nancy. Gina's a secretary at Harvard. Nancy goes to art school nights and waitresses days.

Tuesday—November 3

I can't believe it. *Jimmy's mother called. Mom gave her my work number. Miss W. had a bird because I got a personal call, but I told her it wouldn't happen again. Miss W. harrumphed. Anyway Mrs. M. bought me a grilled cheese sandwich at Brigham's and asked if I really thought it was Jimmy's baby. I told her I knew it was. She asked what I was going to do. I said I didn't know. She suggested adoption because I can't give it "advantages" and gave me $100. "Go to the Salvation Army," she said like Father O'Hara did. If Jimmy had been my son, I'd have wanted his grandchild.*

Tuesday—November 11

I'm starting to show. I wear an old loose dress or a big sweater.

I walked by the Salvation Army near the fire station five times.

Meanwhile I like living with Hannah, Gina and Nancy. We make popcorn or play cards when they don't have dates. We laugh at silly stuff. If I weren't knocked up I could go on like this forever. They sometimes go to the movies and stuff, but I don't want to spend the money. Maybe I'll keep the baby. If I do, I'll have to pay back Mrs. Matthews. But without a job, how can I buy food for the baby and who'll take care of the baby if I do have a job?

Friday—November 13

I did it. I went into the Salvation Army. I spoke to a woman wearing an ugly uniform, but I told her everything and she didn't say how immoral I was. There's a home in Jamaica Plain, but it's full. Then she called Door of Hope in Jersey City. Full. She finally found a place in Cleveland. I've never been out of Massachusetts. I told her I only had $600, but she said there was a sliding scale. I can take a bus. I thought about hitching, but that's dangerous and we've already had snow.

Tuesday—November 17th

Nancy guessed. She walked into the bathroom as I got out of the shower. She was really nice. I cried. She cried. When the others got home they said if I wanted to keep the baby, they'd help. I don't know. He'll be better adopted, but I soooooo wish Jimmy were alive.

Wednesday—November 18

Miss W. was mad because I didn't get someone's name right on the telephone, which embarrassed Mr. Adler when he called the guy. Then I knocked over a bunch of files all stacked up. Miss W. said I did it on purpose.

Friday—November 19

I was in Star Market because it was my turn to food shop when I saw Mom and Pop. They turned their backs to me. I kept trying to get them to speak to me but Pop kept saying, "I don't know you." I will never do that to any kid I ever have.

Monday—November 22nd

When I walked in this morning Miss W. was sitting at her desk with her coffee in that stupid china cup and saucer she always uses. She thinks it's low class to use a mug. I mean, how high class is working in an insurance agency? She looked me up and down and said, "Kathleen, are you pregnant?" I just looked at the floor. "You are. I knew it." She dashed into Mr. Adler's office. I could hear them mumble. When she came out, she held his door for me. He talked about the reputation of the company, unwed mothers and all that. Then he pulled out his checkbook and wrote me one for three weeks pay. "I don't have to do this," he said, "but I feel sorry for you." Hypocrite. If he really felt sorry, he'd let me work. By the time I came out, my pen from graduation, Jimmy's photo and my lipstick were in a used Stop & Shop bag. Miss W. handed me my coat and almost slammed the door behind me.

Thursday—November 26

Thanksgiving. Nancy, Gina and Hannah took me to the bus depot by South Station. Just before I got on, Nancy shoved a package at me wrapped in paper with storks. When I opened it there was an orange and green stuffed rabbit. The eyes were cock-eyed. "Cuddle it now then give it to the baby," she said. "Funny Bunny," I said. They hugged me over and over. Nancy handed me sandwiches and two Cokes. I was worried about drinking them because I would have to pee too often BUT THERE WAS A TOILET on the bus. It smelled awful, but I didn't wet my pants. It was scary changing buses at Port Authority, but I was actually in New York after driving through Harlem with all the bombed-out looking buildings. Two drunks slept on a bench and smelled like pee. All through Pennsylvania I held Funny Bunny. He helped me feel less lonely, but I'm so scared.

Tuesday—December 1

I'm more or less settled. The home looks like a dorm. There's 28 of us in 7 rooms. We can keep personal stuff. Funny Bunny stays on my bed. My roommates are Beth, Anne and Kate. Beth is a college senior. Her boyfriend deserted her. Anne doesn't talk about who got her pregnant. She's 14. Kate's boyfriend still writes. She was a secretary and he's at West Point, but if he marries her now he's out of the Academy.

Tuesday—December 15

I was wrong about this being like a dorm. It's like a prison. I need a pass to go out. Anne, Kate and I hang out together. Beth stays in her room and reads. She was an English major and wants to be a college professor. She says she can use this time to get ahead in her studies.

She's due next month. They say she's having twins. I believe it. She's huge. She almost needs a crane to get out of a chair.

Friday—January 1

Brand new decade, same old problems. Mrs. Major, who is top dog, let us stay up past curfew to see in the New Year. She let us sneak into the kitchen to make brownies ON CONDITION we cleaned up after. We caught her tasting the batter with her finger. Did she look guilty. She's pretty nice, even if she insists we go to chapel and her sermons are boring. I tried getting out of it, 'cause I'm Catholic. No dice. We toasted in the New Year with raspberry Kool Aid. If I told her I really wanted a beer, she'd've dropped her teeth.

Friday—January 17

Beth had twin girls. She didn't look at them, but handed them over to an agency. We saw them. They had lots of black hair. I want to see my baby. Will it look like Jimmy? Me? Bet it will have red hair like both of us.

Sunday—January 31

Wow, what a blizzard. All the trees are frosted. Kate, Anne and me are having pick-up sticks tournaments, but we stopped to watch The FBI. There were ten of us in the TV room when Anne's water broke. Sounds funny, water breaking.

Friday—Febuary 12

I've been neglecting you, dear diary. I don't know why.
Anne left. She gave her little boy to the same agency as Beth did. Kate will put hers in foster care. After her boyfriend graduates they'll get married and pretend to adopt it, but I bet everyone will know it is

*really their kid. I don't like to think what I will do with mine,
although Mrs. Major keeps pushing me. Her husband is just plain
Major. I don't understand the Salvation Army, but what would I do
without them?*

*Two new roommates, Karen and Lisa from Cincinnati. They knew
each other before and boy were they surprised to see each other. They
spend all their time together and I feel lonely. I think the only friend I
have is that stupid rabbit. Sad, isn't it?*

Monday—February 22

*One of the girls told me I can arrange a private adoption. She's do-
ing it. There's a lawyer who know a couple desperate for a baby. I
always thought you couldn't meet the people adopting your baby. I
asked Mrs. Major and she looked worried and said it was true
MOST of the time. She told me to be sure of what I was doing,
because I couldn't undo it. She also told me the girl who told me
about all this was getting a finder's fee. I nearly went ape, someone
making money on my baby . . . I won't speak to that bitch again.
Mrs. Major wants to protect me. JIMMY WHAT SHOULD I
DO????*

Thursday—February 25

*I knocked on Mrs. Major's door after duty-hours. Even if it was
against the rules, I needed to talk to her. She wore a ratty old plaid
bathrobe and fuzzy blue slippers, the kind that look like mops. Their
apartment is a dinky two rooms with beat-up furniture. The walls
were covered with needlework, and she was working on another.
Anyway, she couldn't have been THAT mad at me for coming because
she gave me hot cocoa. It boiled over and burned on the stove. I like
that smell. Finally she asked me what I wanted. I blurted out, "What
would you do if you was me?"*

She said she wasn't. I pushed. "But if you was?" As she dropped

Marshmallow Fluff into our cups she said, "Well If I WERE you, I'd think long and hard." Then she held my hands. "You'll pay a big price no matter what."

For a minute I thought she meant money. She saw my frown. "I mean an emotional price." She talked about how hard it would be trying to work and not earning enough to give my child what it needed. The stigma. Then she talked about not knowing where it was and how I'd feel on its birthday.

I told her I didn't like paying prices. She said no one did, but that was the way God worked. Only she didn't say it that way. Then the Major came in from some meeting, and I left.

Thursday—March 1

I met the lawyer. He has a pot belly and looks like he should chew on a cigar. I didn't like him. He told me about a couple that couldn't have kids. They're teachers or something. She's too old to adopt through normal channels.

I asked him (the lawyer) if they could handle a baby. He said the woman loved kids. The man is a lawyer, too. I was confused until he said he taught law at some university. He wouldn't tell me where, but I bet it is nearby and if it is I guess I could find my baby again. Of course, I didn't say that. If I promise something serious, I have to keep my promise and what could be more serious then promising your kid for life???

I asked if I could meet them. He said it was best done at the hand-over and we shouldn't know names. He talked about sealed records. I told him I'd think about it.

Saturday—March 5

I've been thinking about their church. No candles. No priest. Just the Majors talking and us singing. It doesn't seem real at all, I kind of like it. I did pray I'd find the right answer.

236

Monday—March 7

I can't believe it. Another snow storm. We can't get in or out. We're doing our own cooking because the cook is stuck at home. My breasts are leaking and my bras are grungy yellow.

Mrs. Major called me into her office. She asked if I knew yet what I was going to do. I cried. She brought out tissues. She keeps some in her top desk drawer. I told her I hated giving up this last piece of Jimmy. She said it was normal. We went over the same old stuff. I can only love my baby. Nothing else. I told her to call the lawyer. She said she couldn't. I'd have to. I can change my mind until the time I put the baby in their arms. Then she left the room. I looked at the phone for a long, long time before I picked it up.

Tuesday—March 15

I wish the toilet were next to my bed. I get up twenty times a night. Karen and Lisa complain. In a couple of months they'll understand.

In one way, I feel better having decided to give the baby away and worse in another. Mrs. Major says she feels torn when she has to make hard choices. I bet she'll never have to give up a baby. I know she wanted to make me feel better. IT'S JUST NOT POSSIBLE.

Sunday—April 3

Labor was worse than they said. Twenty-two hours. I felt like a prisoner strapped down. Did they think I'd run away? I screamed. FINALLY they gave me a spinal. When I touched my lower body it was like touching a pillow. I lifted my head to see him, even though they told me not to. Bad move!!! I had a headache for two days. I want to see my son. I'm not feeding or holding him, because Mrs. Major says it will be harder later, but I hobble to the nursery. No one told me it would hurt afterwards.

Thursday—April 7

It's truly over. I was dressed when Mrs. Major put my baby on my bed. He was wrapped in a blue blanket. I asked her if I could be alone with him. She said it wasn't a good idea and stood at the door with her arms crossed. I unwrapped him anyway, although she clucked her disapproval. I don't care. He has perfect little hands. He's bald, but I bet he'll be a redhead. Mrs. Major says it's hard to tell. He never opened his eyes. I never saw my son's eyes. Jimmy's son.

Mrs. Major helped me into my coat and we rode the elevator together. She waited at the door. The rules say I have to be alone at the handover. He was still my baby at that moment. My son. No one else's.

All the snow was gone. A few buds were on the trees lining the parking lot. A crow cawed overhead. I wondered if he was telling me to keep him.

The couple have a 1969 white Chrysler. When they saw me, they got out of the car and waited for me to come to them.

I said hi.

They said hello. Her eyes went through mine. Then they dropped to my baby. It was like her face melted. Tears ran down her cheeks. She kept her arms at her side, but she kept opening and closing her hands.

Her husband came up behind her, and put his hand on her left shoulder and asked to look at my son.

From nowhere the lawyer appeared. Maybe he'd come in a different car. Or he could have been in the back seat. It's not important.

I pulled the blanket back so my baby's face showed.

"Ohhhh," the woman said as she reached for the baby. She was a little awkward, but so was I. She was crying and saying how beautiful he was.

The lawyer interrupted to talk about the papers that he put on the hood of the car. When he asked me if I'd read my set, I lied and said I had. I tried. They were too full of party of the first part and party of the second part. I didn't understand. The result is the same anyway.

I'll never see my son. I grabbed his pen and wrote my name Kathleen Marie O'Brien. "Two more things," I said.

The lawyer busted in like I was some kind of criminal and reminded me I'd already signed the goddamned papers.

I looked into the woman's eyes. I chose my words, real careful-like. "Could you make James part of his name? It was his father's. He died."

The man started to say something, but before he could speak, the woman nodded.

Then I took the bag of diapers, formula and instructions which Mrs. Major prepared. Again, I thought about my words, because I couldn't have stood it if she'd said no. "There's a stuffed animal. Funny Bunny. Can you give it to him?"

"Oh for heavens sake," said the lawyer.

"We'll tell him that his mother loved him so much, she put him first to make sure he had a good home."

I knew then I'd made the right choice.

I touched their baby's cheek one last time. It was soft, but a little cool in the spring air, so I tucked the blanket around him. There wasn't a way to make the minute last longer.

The woman thanked me.

Saying you're welcome didn't seem right. That's what you say when someone thanks you for a little gift. I'd given them my heart.

Carol wiped her eyes. She remembered her drunken mother raging about not being able to support herself and any children she might have. Carol yelled back that her mother couldn't take care of herself, much less her only child.

What if she had to give up either Paige or Seth?

Oh my God, she thought. I have a brother somewhere, a half-brother, if he is still alive. He'd be older than I am.

She wished Jay were home to hold her, but he was battling his own family demons. She fought sleep waiting for him, but sleep won, pulling her deep into the peace of a person who has forgiven both the innocent and the guilty.

CHAPTER 40

Northeastern University students poured off the Greenline for evening classes. Jay, who'd stood sardine-style since Park Street Station, sank into a plastic seat until Brigham & Women's Hospital. The brick monolith was spread over the right side of the block. On the left, triple-decker houses, painted red, antique green and federal gold, had desktop-sized lawns. When he visited a client who lived in one, he'd barely noticed the hospital. Tonight the hospital hovered, a giant that ate up one side of the street and would soon consume him too.

The lobby resembled an airport's. People bustled, sat in chairs, or browsed the gift shop. Rather than ask at Information for his father's room number, Jay ducked into the café. Robot-like, he carried a tray to a small red circular table. One look at his sandwich and his stomach padlocked as his thoughts ricocheted.

"No one will shoot me, if I don't see him. I can walk away," he muttered to himself.

The man at the next table said, "Pardon me?"

"Just thinking out loud," Jay said and tried not to see the frown creep across the man's face, probably from fear that Jay was a mental case. The distraction did not last long enough to keep Jay from returning to what he didn't want to think of, but couldn't *not* think of. What if I were to die like Louis Andrew Paul Marsh? Even the name pisses me off. He couldn't even make me a Junior—that's for blood children.

The café was filling—at least he could eliminate some guilt by vacating his table. He threw the uneaten sandwich into the trash.

In the elevator, his visitor's pass in hand, he tried to think when he'd last seen his father. They'd passed each other sometimes while he was at Harvard, nodded politely—but nothing else, and only if Jay couldn't avoid the encounter altogether. Once when he and Carol were sailing with friends in Marblehead Harbor, he'd recognized his father's build and white mane on the deck of a passing boat. They had been standing on the starboard side, and he'd been telling his friend that the word came from steer board. Sailors used the term port for left because they always docked on the left if they were facing the bow, front. He walked his friend over to the port so as not to appear to see his father in case his father saw him. The friend has asked how he knew it. Jay said he'd read it in Wikipedia. Nothing in Wikipedia would tell him today what to do or say next.

The elevator bell dinged at the seventh floor. He followed the arrows to room 738, the number on his visitor's pass. The smell of antiseptic was stronger here than in the lobby. He hated that smell. Outside he hesitated. Should he barge in? The problem resolved itself when a nurse, carrying a vial-filled tray, exited, leaving the door open.

That it was a private room did not surprise him. L.A.P. Marsh always wanted the Mercedes, the Royal Oak watch. Jay remembered lectures on quality. He saw himself kept home from kindergarten with a temperature. Crayons were spread around on the bed as he and his mother colored in his Donald Duck coloring book. They had gone outside the lines, laughing as they did, to see who could obliterate the printed design. His father scolded them both.

Jennifer looked up as she fluffed his father's pillow. "Louis, look who's here." She beckoned Jay into the room.

The bald man in the bed moved his head in slow motion towards the door. "You're late." The voice had not only lost its boom, it quivered.

Mastering every ounce of internal force possible, Jay walked to the bed thinking his mantra: *they told me to come, they told me to come. They* were the women in his life: Anna, Carol and yes, even Jennifer.

The future corpse on the bed bore no resemblance to the man he'd hated for years. Had he really given such power to that bag of skin and bones? Had this skeleton always hidden inside his father's body? Did everyone contain such fragility? To stop them shaking he rested his hands on the cold metal slats of the railing that kept his father from falling to the floor.

Jennifer drew up a chair.

"Not there. I can't see you," Louis whispered.

As soon as Jay repositioned himself, his father closed his eyes. Jay scanned the room. Get-well cards were tacked with multi-colored pins to a cork board. *Jeopardy* was being broadcast on a TV set suspended from the ceiling. $1000 was written on a board in front of a contestant whose lips moved soundlessly.

Jay's eyes, like magnets, were drawn back to his father's face. An oxygen tube ran from the old man's nose: a bottle dripped a liquid into his veins.

Snores penetrated the room. At 8:00 P.M. the nurse came in to adjust the tubes. "Visiting hours are over."

Jennifer caressed her husband where his hair should have been. The action was as intimate as if they were making love, yet Jay couldn't look away. Finally, he opened his briefcase and drew out the photograph that Carol had left framed and propped it next to the blue plastic water pitcher on the night stand.

Jennifer put on her glasses to look at it. "The kids are beautiful. I know Louis will appreciate it."

Her low heels clicked on the linoleum as she walked to the closet to gather her sweater and handbag. She waited at the door for Jay to open it.

Outside she leaned against the wall. She brushed tears away with the back of her hand as the kids did when they were trying not to cry. Bitches don't cry, he thought, then changed his mind.

"I'm sorry. I'm so tired," she said.

Had it been anyone else, Jay would have tried to comfort her. He couldn't do it.

"Will you come again?"

"I doubt it," he said.

Only when he saw the Government Center sign at the T-station did Jay realize he'd missed his stop. He jumped off just as the doors closed. Although the air was normal, he felt like he was suffocating. Must escape . . . escalator . . . step . . . watch out . . .

The flower seller was locking up her buckets, mostly empty except for a few tired carnations, wilted roses and one broken bird of paradise, its plumage drooping as he burst out of the T-door into the cement canyon of Government Center. He began to run and didn't stop until he reached Longfellow Bridge. Panting, he leaned against one of its salt and pepper shaped towers. The old man dying in the bed, couldn't have followed, but he was with Jay every step. He clutched his side. A stitch. A physical pain, he could deal with. His breathing returned to normal. If only he could dissipate his confusion as easily.

He arrived home to a darkened house except for the porch light over the numbers 392. Inside he tiptoed into his daughter's room. Paige slept, unaware he was watching. He fingered a strand of her hair. Curls, delicate as corn silk—only red—

crowned her face. She reminded him of Christmas card cherubs.

Seth slept with his head at the foot of the bed. Rather than twist him, Jay covered him with a sheet then lightly brushed his lips against his son's sweaty head. The smell of the child brought him an iota of peace.

No matter what, he would never desert his children. He would never give them reason to dread visiting him if he were dying.

Unready to face Carol's questions, he went to the bathroom to brush his teeth. Looking at the mirror he saw a man with circles under his eyes, and a nine o'clock shadow on his chin that matched the dark circles under his eyes.

"What did you want?" he asked the reflection.

"I wanted him to say he loved me, that he was sorry."

"And what did you get?"

Rather than go on with the imaginary question, he knew the answer. Louis wanted to make peace with himself. It was about his father, not him.

That night he had a nightmare. Skeletons chased him to a wood with a small cabin. Inside there was a mirror, but when he looked he saw only another skeleton. His own.

Chapter 41

The demi-bus bounced over the dirt road. As it swerved, Mark Hanson grabbed the seat in front of him to keep from being jolted to the floor. The three-hour ride to Maine had been smooth until the bus turned off Route 1.

The time had whizzed by as General Keats gave a history lecture like nothing he'd been taught in school. That has-been about America the Strong, America the Good. This lecture was about betrayal from within and, more important, what to do about it.

General Keats, who wore fatigues, was his father's age, but with a Schwarzenegger build. Periodically he asked one of the boys to repeat something. If the kid didn't snap out the answer followed by "Sir" Yeats yelled, "This ain't school. This is survival, survival of our country."

When it was Mark's turn, he repeated verbatim what he'd heard a few minutes before. The rewarding smile warmed his insides. He was part of a group of real men. Real men who would do something, not just whine, not be victims.

The bus stopped in a glade surrounded by trees. Through the windows Mark spied a cabin, the only building he'd seen for miles. The air smelled of pine.

"Out. Double time," the General hollered.

The boys scrambled into the clearing, stood in small groups, not knowing what to do next.

"Attention!"

The boys snapped straight up, their arms at their sides.

"In line!"

Tripping and pushing, they formed a row.

"Straighten it out!"

Each boy aligned his position to the kid next to him. For the first time Mark noticed the billy club, which the military man hit onto his palm every few steps until he came to Mark. "Name!" he bellowed.

Mark felt spit hit his cheek, but he didn't dare wipe it off.

"Mark Hanson."

"Private Mark Hanson, SIR!"

"Private Mark Hanson, SIR!" Mark repeated.

"I can't hear you."

"PRIVATE MARK HANSON, SIR!!"

The General moved on. Only after interrogating all of the recruits did he say, "At ease," and waited until they moved their legs apart and clasped their hands behind their backs. "Do you have what it takes to join our militia? Well this weekend will prove it one way or the other, because we are only keeping the best."

I'll be one of the best, Mark thought.

They foraged for dinner: bark, bugs. Someone caught a fish. Two boys stacked wood for a fire. One reached for a lighter.

Richard Yeat's hand grabbed it. "In a real war, the enemy could see the fire." He picked up the fish and told the kid to eat it raw. The kid bit into it—then vomited.

Mark, although he wasn't next, sauntered over to the fish which had fallen to the ground and sucked on its blood forcing himself not to gag.

The moon and stars had disappeared behind clouds leaving an eerie glow in the sky where patches were still visible through pine boughs. Mark and the others hacked their way through the undergrowth. He checked his compass whenever the moon allowed. Were there bears? The best weren't afraid of bears. He'd fight them with his machete.

They emerged through pines to see the outline of a long wooden building that they then entered. Mark was struck by the smell of cordite.

The General lined the boys up behind a wooden barrier and pointed to the paper cut-outs of men. Twelve rifles rested on a table.

Mark held his breath waiting to touch his first gun. He would shoot like in the movies, but this was real. As he approached the table he realized he couldn't inspect each one, but had to pick up the next free one. His fingertips slid over the cold, smooth metal.

His General handed each boy a box of bullets. Taking two, he rattled them in his hand like a pair of dice. Then he cracked his rifle open and inserted the bullets. "We'll shoot at 40-feet. Frozen position. Make every shot count." He snapped the rifle back, raised it to firing position and hit the forehead of the middle cut-out.

Each boy took a position. Mark lost track of time. His ears ached from the reports, but not as much as his shoulder from the kickback. The pain was worth the excitement each time he pulled the trigger, and he hoped no one noticed his hard-on.

"Ya off, Hanson."

Mark jumped. He hadn't realized that the General was behind him. Closing one eye, he squinted at the target. He pretended he was a bullet zooming into a body. His right index finger squeezed the trigger. The heart of his target turned red. He'd done it. He'd hit the blood bag hanging behind the silhouette, the first boy to score. He fired ten more times, all within an inch of the right spot. None of the others had come this close.

The General took a small pistol, and showed Mark how to load it and fire. The old man shot six bull's eyes. Then he handed the weapon to Mark. Mimicking all the General's actions from loading to stance he made four of six shots.

The next exercise was to have them shoot as they moved towards the target, staying in their own lanes as the General yelled, "kill, kill, kill." The air was gray.

"Stop," the General ordered. "Time to sleep."

They put down their guns and headed for the door, but the General blocked their path. He stared at them and they stared back. "Clean those weapons and reload. Then get a rifle to sleep with. In real life, if someone snuck up on you, you would be dead meat."

Mark oiled his rifle, learning its curves before going on to the pistol. He hefted its weight in his hand. It was power. It was his, at least for the weekend.

The troops retrieved their sleeping bags from the bus and rolled them on the grass. Mark's eyes were barely open.

"What the hell do you think you're doing?" General Keats yelled. "The enemy could stumble across you."

The boys scrambled out of their bags and moved them into the bush. Mark fell asleep almost before he finished zipping up his bag and dreamed about a Cub Scout camping trip, although he'd never gone on one. He'd heard others talk about fires and toasting marshmallows while singing dumb songs. His father had refused to let him join because there were "Chink" members and the leader was a "Nigger."

Someone shook him awake. Richard, acting as sub squadron leader, whispered, "The enemy is on the other side of the field. Follow me."

Time to forget about being sleepy, cold and hungry. He

crawled on his stomach, using his elbows and knees to propel himself through slimy mud. Water penetrated his underwear. The cold sank into his bones as he forced himself to keep his teeth from chattering. Overhead bullets zinged. I'm going to be the best soldier there is, he told himself.

Noon Sunday: they were seated at desks in the cabin. The smell of mud, sweat and wet clothing mixed with the smoke from a small fire that did nothing to dispel the dampness. One wall had a black board.

The General paced in front of his troops. His fatigues were spotless, with perfect creases. His shirt looked as if it were made of cardboard. "Listen up. We ain't talking theory. Before you leave, you'll know your weapons better than you know your assholes. You'll take 'em apart and put 'em together blindfolded. Then there'll be the test. The one with the highest score will make Specialist First Class and be given his own gun." He opened a box and took out a Glock model 40.

Mark imagined holding it, shooting. He forced his attention back to the General.

"And we'll decide who comes back to boot camp in July. If you think the U.S. Marines are fussy, we're ten times worse."

Mark concentrated as he never had before. He wanted it all, the Glock, the next camp. What if Carol wouldn't let him leave a second time? She'd have to. In one way, what he was doing was protecting her. And June. And all innocent women from dark forces. That's what soldiers did. General Keats said that would bring back the old order, when women stayed home and raised good white citizens.

At the end of the day Mark handed in his test paper. The boys were ordered to hide all traces of their presence. As Mark finished covering the latrine that they'd dug, a whistle blew. They ran to stand at attention by the bus. As the General stopped in front of one kid, Mark held his breath. The thin boy was at least six inches shorter than the General. His stomach closed. That kid was the best.

The General sneered. "You learned nothing this week. You don't deserve to serve with us. But if you ever breathe a word, we'll send our death squads after you." He grabbed the kid's shirt pulling him close enough that their noses touched. How long the General glared at the kid, Mark didn't know. Then he let him go.

The kid had tears in his eyes.

Sniveling sissy, Mark thought with an equal dose of relief that it wasn't him.

The General twirled the Glock like in cowboy movies. A bird flew overhead. The General blasted it. The wind rustled in the trees. A squirrel scampered up the tree and chattered down at them hidden by the leaves, but the General ignored it. Walking to Mark he held the pistol to the center of Mark's forehead and cocked the handle.

He won't shoot me, Mark thought. This is a test. Mark stared into the General's eyes.

The General handed the gun to Mark. "Congratulations Specialist First Class Hanson."

CHAPTER 42

Carol Marsh watched Mark talk about his weekend. He sat on the chair across from her desk, his face more animated than she ever remembered it. Not the image of a June's "almost," but something she couldn't identify bothered her.

The phone rang. Calls weren't usually put through when she was with her probationers. A problem with Paige or Seth? Shaking her hair away from her eyes, she answered it.

"Nothing's wrong," Jay said. "And don't yell at the receptionist. I insisted she put me through."

"What's up?"

"Any way you can get this afternoon and tomorrow off?"

"In your dreams."

"I'm going to New Hampshire to talk with Laurel's old boss. We could fit in some hanky panky."

She wanted to say, I would love to hanky your panky, but Mark was staring.

"Sorry Babe, you'll have to go alone."

"Can't blame a guy for trying." He hung up.

"If you didn't work, Carol, you could have gone," Mark said.

She hid her annoyance at his eavesdropping and was annoyed at Jay for not speaking more softly. "Win some, lose some. Now about those weeks in July. I'll let you know."

Mark's smile disappeared. His eyes narrowed. "Why not today?"

"I want to see your report card first."

The grin returned. "I'm making the honor roll." He put on his baseball cap and sauntered out. Or was it more of a swagger? The rapid mood swings disturbed her.

Carol saw ten other kids for an average of five minutes each: all routine. As she made notes on her computer she kept thinking of Mark. Feeling the need to consult with a colleague, she walked to Doug's office and didn't bother to close the door. "How stupid would you think I was if I said I saw a kid turning around, doing things right and it bothered me?"

He pointed to a folder-laden chair.

Had he not begun updating his part of the new database? Those folders should be gone by now, but she wasn't in his office to lecture him on his work. She was there for his advice, which she found was almost always on target.

"If it were anyone else but you, I'd talk about gift horses and mouths. In your case, investigate," he said.

Back in her office she let the phone ring several times waiting for June to pick it up. "How's the arm?"

"Physical therapy will never replace shopping, but coming along," June said. "I won't take any more kids."

"Not asking. How's Mark?"

"He's been an angel."

Leo was on patrol when Carol called the station, but she left a message. Frustrated by her feelings, she pounded the computer keys. She didn't hear his first knock, but she jumped when she looked up to see him standing there.

"Dispatcher said you wanted me. Buy ya a coffee?" The armpits of his shirt were sweat stained.

She glanced at her watch then nodded. As they crossed to the coffee shop, the early June heat shimmered off the tarmac.

When they sat she said, "Tell me about Mark Hanson."

"You're wonderfully neutral. Not 'is he doing badly or well?' " He stirred three sugars into his coffee then blew on it fluttering the steam. "So what do you want to know?"

"Anything."

Leo shrugged. He's gone into weights. Works out daily. Disciplined. Swims. Didn't go out for baseball, but after basketball it's a slow game.

"Does he get along with the others?"

Leo waved his hand back and forth, a so-so motion. "He doesn't fight. I gotta get back."

Carol threw the paper cups in the trash, went back to her office and packed up for the day.

CHAPTER 43

Jazz singer Carole Sloan's voice slid through Jay's car. Between her voice, the late-afternoon sun flickering through the pine trees and a deserted Route 93, Jay felt cocooned. He'd been travelling three hours. Three hours of no-interruptions-music-soothing calm. And his meeting wasn't until 8:30 P.M.

His mind jumped from Laurel to his father. He hadn't returned to the hospital, nor had Jennifer called. The feeling the old man had won seeped into his soul—but what was the prize? Bad thoughts didn't belong in cocoons.

Think about Gordon Sargent Jackson. Unlike most of his cases, he wasn't sure what he was looking for or how he could help his neighbor. He had read Lina's notes, packed in his brief case.

Gordon Sargent Jackson

Origin: Born North Conway NH 1931

Siblings: Third son of five boys. Other brothers all dead now, two in Korea. One of polio in the 1950s. The last of a heart attack in 1998.

Parents: Eben and Esther Jackson. Members of Congregational Church. Farmers.

Early Life: Parents made all five boys finish high school. Usual work-hard attitude typical of New England, milk cows before school. Chores after. Studied, wrapped in blanket using flashlight. (In case you think I'm brilliant boss, it's all in the book *What Makes Men Successful* that I found at the Kirchner Library. Ha Ha)

Academics: Great grades in science and math. Terrible in English. (I checked the high school.) Went to College on scholarship. M.I.T. Chemistry B.S. Graduated 1961. Stanford M.S. 1963. Ph.D. M.I.T 1965

Service: U.S. Marines Korea. Wounded twice. Purple Heart. Spent year in Veteran's hospital in Honolulu. Told he would never walk. He told the doctors they were wrong. He won. He limps.

Family: Wife Lois McKenzie, nurse in Honolulu. No children, but adopted nephew Nathan who is married and works for HP. Rumor (unconfirmed) he (Jackson) never missed a Little League game.

Jackson Products: Started 1969 after he quit DuPont over napalm. Refused any contract on the unethical side. He's a chemical Steve Jobs. Came up with a good antiseptic marketed under several brand names: Germ Free, Idocreme, Kwik Heal. By 1980 company was raking in millions. (Annual reports in blue folder.)

Misc: Sold company and Newton after wife died. Moved back to family farm. Set up scholarships. Unlike lots of men who became rich, stayed Democrat.

Walter Anderson

Origin: Born Peekskill NY 1960. Well to do family. Uncle was senator who was kicked out for kickbacks from company dumping PCG (causes mutation not a pretty sight). Area is still a toxic swamp. Uncle voted for lots of anti-environmental stuff. Said he resigned for health. Ha.

Education: Philips Exeter, Yale, Harvard B School.

Work: GE then Prospect through his father's connections. Climbed his way up fast. Was VP at Prospect by 35. Was made president of several divisions in turn. List in red folder. Three have been indicted for dumping (see yellow folder with news clippings). I suspect payoffs because court changed million $ fine to slap on wrist. (I've written for trial transcripts.)

Family: Married 1985 Angela Watts, Harvard Liberal Arts B.A. Perfect corporate wife. Three perfect kids except for the one on drugs. He's in a rehab in CT. Other two at Brown and Wellesley. He pays bills. Divorced Angela 2001. Married 2002 Tiffany White, advertising copywriter. She's the trophy wife. (only guessing—newspaper photo red folder. WOW!).

My character description: Scum bag

Misc: I'm still unlocking the entangled companies and boards. CNN just did a program on American companies creating a chemical highway in Mexico where they've dumped hazardous waste. Babies being born without brains, (No shit boss) etc.

Objectivity had never been a Lina strength. "I'm not giving up passion, no way, no how. You want neutral? Hire someone else," she'd said once waggling her finger. He didn't want to know where she'd dug up all the information.

The green sign on the left of the highway said, North Conway, next three exits. He'd find a B&B and dinner.

Gordon Sargent Jackson wore a red flannel shirt with the sleeves rolled up, jeans and work boots. He answered his own door. Nothing in his appearance said millionaire—farmer, old man would have better descriptions. Only as he drew Jay into the house, did Jay notice the cane.

The farm house was renovated. Wallpaper stopped at a chair rail. The wood below was oak. The furniture was early American, maple and braided rugs covered the floors. It would have made a great *Country Living* spread.

The house didn't smell of time like many old peoples'. It was cluttered with books, some open, spine up and others with pieces of paper sticking out, marking places.

Jackson pointed to the windows with his cane. "You can just catch the last of the view. In a few minutes the moon will come up."

Jay looked over the meadows as the sun dipped behind the mountains. Seconds later the moon peeped over the top.

"When I was boy, that field was either planted or filled with cows. I've thought of farming again. Something about touching earth, watching food grow. Right now my neighbor harvests it for hay."

Jay turned down an offer for supper. "I ate at the Golden Potato. Pretty good."

"At least it's not a goddamned chain. Ever notice the whole damn country is becoming a shopping mall?"

"Does my answer effect your cooperation?"

Jackson guffawed. "I like you, young man. You told me Laurel is in trouble. How can I help?"

As Jay outlined the problem of the missing chemicals, relabeled gas cylinders and halted investigations, Jackson's face became shadowed. The more Jay talked, the more he shook his head. "Biggest mistake I made was selling to those bastards."

Jay wasn't sure what to say.

"Ever lose anyone you loved?" Jackson's clipped New Hampshire accent made *ever* sound like *ahvah*.

"No Sir. My parents are still alive. My wife and kids are fine."

"Then you're blessed. Don't ever take it for granted. Now what can I do?"

"I'm not sure." Being at a loss for words, that was different.

Jackson scrunched up his face. "You drove all this way for that?"

"Laurel knows something is wrong. She was hoping you'd have some inside information, an idea, something, *anything* . . ."

"Relabeling is dangerous. Could of told you that over the phone." Jackson propelled himself from his chair and opened his roll top desk and thumbed through papers. "Nope, can't find it. Probably threw it out then." He paused.

"Someone proposed relabeling to me. Threw them out of my office. Not a big company, a small one. Can't remember the name to save my soul." When Jay said nothing, Jackson continued. " 'Nother thing bothers me. Pressure to stop investigations. Sounds to me like we should look at Beacon Hill."

"You think it's political?"

"Son, we're talking Massachusetts. Everything's political." Picking up a personal phonebook, Jackson flipped through the pages. He used a magnifying glass to read the numbers before dialing. "Hello Simon . . . ye-ah getting old is hell . . . Listen . . ." he told the person on the other end of the line. He spoke for some time. After he hung up he wrote a name and phone number on a piece of paper. "Tell Laurel to call him and use my name."

Maybe the trip wasn't a total waste, Jay thought as he crawled into bed. Even if nothing came of it, he'd done what he could. Strange case.

He wished Carol were there. Although tired, he was too keyed up to sleep. Before leaving home that morning, he'd put Carol's mother's diary in his briefcase. She'd urged him to read it. By the time he finished it, he cursed himself for cleaning out the basement.

CHAPTER 44

A song about a love lost yesterday drummed in Jay's brain along with Tony's hammering in the basement. He lay face down on the bed—his and Carol's bed—where they'd made love—where they'd created two children.

The telephone trilled several times before penetrating his consciousness. When he picked it up, Jennifer's voice shook. "It's over. I lost him." The rest was muffled in her crying.

Okay, God, Jay thought. You've had your jokes. Stop messing with me.

"I don't know what to do. Can you come over?"

That was the last thing he wanted. Didn't she have any friends?

"Please."

Her pain cut through his. "Where are you?"

"At the hospital. I don't have my car."

"Go to the entrance. I'll be there in about twenty minutes."

Jay entered his father's Beacon Hill house for the first time. It was everything a Bullfinch brick house should be on the outside, with original violet tinted windows. It was everything a house on the Hill should be on the inside, with the oriental carpets and antiques—so different from his mother's modern style. He must call her to tell her. Meanwhile, Jay guided Jennifer to the couch. Her face was blotched. "Is anyone here?"

"It's the housekeeper's day off." She sank into a chair.

Jay knew in more detail than he wanted how she'd sat next to her husband and then realized he wasn't breathing. "Where's the kitchen? I'll make tea."

When he came back, she was curled up on the sofa. He watched her sleep. Her Shalimar perfume mingled with the smells of old wood and leather. The room was dark despite floor to window ceilings. Heavy navy drapes cut off hopes of sunlight. The walls were covered with books. From his childhood memories of his father always with a book, Jay knew they were not for decoration but had been read.

Over the marble fireplace on the oak mantel, a photo of Jennifer and his father on their wedding day stood in a pewter frame. In other photos his father shook hands with both Bush presidents, Kissinger and Reagan. One picture of Jay in a Little League uniform stood behind the rest.

Jay had loved Little League except when his father came to games, albeit rarely, in his suit and tie instead of jeans like his friends' dads. On the way home, he pounded the steering wheel as he listed every error Jay had made. Jay would stare out the window, envying his friends, who went for ice cream with their families. The next year Jay refused to even try out.

Although he didn't want to talk with Carol, she needed to know where he was. Her mind would imagine accidents on Route 93, although it might have been better, given what he now knew, if he had died in one. They could have a double funeral, father and son dying on the same day. Carol would mourn, but she would never learn the awful, impossible, yet real, truth that she had lost both a husband and half-brother. Maybe he wouldn't tell her, but that would make an even bigger lie of their marriage.

He went into the hallway to call, hoping to catch her at the office. No answer. The answering machine responded at home as did her cell. On both he left the message, "My father died.

261

I'm with Jennifer." For the first time he didn't end with I love you. God, how he loved her.

Then he called Anna who said, "Be kind to Jennifer."

Well after midnight he opened his bedroom door. Carol slept on her side, the sheet kicked back. Moonlight filtered through the Venetian blinds leaving stripes of light on her face. Her dark hair fanned out on the pillow. Jay fought the urge to cry. A light breeze whispered through the window, but the summer heat hovered. He debated sleeping on the couch, but he didn't want to explain why. Not now. Not ever.

"The funeral is Saturday morning. King's Chapel," he told Carol.

She'd stirred awake ten minutes before the alarm jangled. The room was already too warm. After getting out of bed, she drew the curtains. "Are we going, Babes?"

Babes, that's what she calls me after an orgasm, he thought, or during special moments, like when each kid was born. Our kids should *never* have been born. He lay on his back, his hands cradling his head. "I would say no, but . . ." He sat up and grabbed the pillow and hugged it. "You won't believe what the bastard did."

"Jennifer said my father left a trust fund for the kids to be used for their education: $260,000 for Seth, $160,000 for Paige."

"Sexist."

He tightened his grip on the pillow. "Worse, if they don't go to the funeral, the money goes to Harvard."

"Why?"

"Jennifer said it was to make sure we'd be there." Even when his stepmother spoke the words, he'd heard his father's voice.

"I'll support what you decide, but think long and hard." She knelt next to him and tried to cuddle him, but he pulled away.

"Too hot."

The Marshes stood with Jennifer at the back of King's Chapel. Trust Louis Paul Andrew Marsh to choose an historic church. George Washington hadn't slept here, but he'd attended services on his way to chase the British out of Boston. The walls were white. Individual pews, covered in deep red cushions were surrounded by half walls to protect early worshippers from drafts during long winter sermons. The organ played "Nearer My God to Thee," as the rows filled.

Anna appeared with several old Concord neighbors. Jay would never understand either why Jennifer invited Anna or why Anna accepted. Their explanations of how long they'd each been married to him clarified nothing.

When he mentioned it to Carol she said, "A couple can never totally divorce . . ." He changed the subject before she could finish.

When everyone was seated, Carol led the children down the center, followed by Jennifer who rested her black-gloved hand on Jay's arm. The mourning non-family united in death not life, he thought.

Several Massachusetts governors sat behind the mayor, two members of the current presidential cabinet, three from the previous cabinet, six senators and several congressmen, enough Republicans to widen the gap even more between father and son.

Flowers hid the altar, poisoning the air. A photograph, taken twenty years before, posed on the casket.

"Is that what my grandfather looked like?" Seth asked the second the organ stopped. Titters swept through the church. Jay felt an inner satisfaction that people would know the truth and felt unchristian wishing the local television stations outside had captured the moment for the 11 o'clock news.

Three days later, *The Law Library*, his father's 44-foot cabin cruiser bounced up and down the white caps dotting the Atlantic. An occasional soft drink can floated by as the boat made its last voyage with its Captain, Louis Marsh on board, or at least with his ashes. That the grandchildren were to participate in the scattering was part of the will too.

Jay debated not going, but Carol pointed out they had already done the funeral. "Do you want to tell the kids you passed up a good part of their college tuition?"

With the uncertainty about their future, at least he could give some financial security, he decided.

Jennifer wore yellow slacks and a striped yellow shirt. "The man at the funeral home said to be sure the wind was blowing away from us or we'll be covered . . ."

Jay pictured brushing his father off his jeans.

They dropped anchor. As the boat heaved with the waves, Jennifer opened the green marble urn. When Jay looked inside he was struck by how much his father looked like kitty litter.

Jennifer carried the urn to the prow and stood looking away from the shore. "I can't do it."

Jay took it and poured out the ashes. The wind caught the ashes, blowing them over the surface of the water, lifting and dropping them, a mini-sandstorm. He watched the particles, all that was left of his father. No grey mane. No booming voice. No sneer for not measuring up. Yellowish-white grit. How had he ever given so much power to particles? The scattering had one last power. It freed him.

Jay lay under the summer blanket with his eyes closed. A summer storm had dropped the temperature into the mid-sixties.

The air coming through the bedroom window was cool. Carol, in her baby dolls, lowered the sash for the first time in a week. She crawled into bed and pressed her body to his.

He willed himself not to freeze. "I can't tonight, Sweets." He stroked her hair until her breathing told him that she was asleep. He was awake most of the night with his half-sister next to him.

CHAPTER 45

"Jay looks like hell," Laurel said to Tony as she shut the apartment door. Through the open window she heard him snap at his kids, Carol's calm muttering, car doors slamming and gravel crunching under tires followed.

"It's his father's death," Tony said over his shoulder as he went into his workroom.

"A weekend with Anna will do them good," she said to his back. She wished *she* could get away for a weekend. Staying at home was driving her nuts. She had cleaned the flat so thoroughly that a person without an immune system would be safe from germs. The killer basket of mending had been emptied, although a lot of the things had since been outgrown and were now disposed of. To control her energy, she'd weeded Carol's garden, but that she thought was only fair, since excess veggies always ended up on her table anyway.

Her being fired had come so simply; almost like a child after a tantrum giving one last whimper. Her badge hadn't worked when she swiped it through the electronic device at the entrance. The receptionist made her wait until Paul brought her things out in three cartons.

Tony, freed from his household chores, had thrown himself into more and more complicated renovations. A dresser was converted into a robot, which Robbie claimed as his, despite Tony saying he was taking it to the next flea market. He'd booked more flea markets, but moaned that there had to be a more effective way to sell his merchandise.

Laurel barely noticed that *The Chronicle of Higher Education* had disappeared from their home. She got up to pour herself yet another coffee, waiting for Tony to say yet again that the last thing she needed was to be more wired with caffeine. What hadn't disappeared was *The Boston Globe* want ad section.

Laurel sat at the kitchen table tapping her left foot without realizing it as she looked through the paper. Two folders were next to her coffee cup. The green one was for ads already answered, the blue one for those still to do. She'd checked Craig's List and monster.com daily as well as the classifieds of one of her engineering magazines. The other didn't put their classifieds up, damn it.

Some of the jobs were for godforsaken places she'd never heard of. Lord knows, she didn't want to move away from Boston, but if that was the only way to find work . . . well . . .

She jumped when she realized that Tony had come back into the kitchen. He reached into his back jeans pocket and pulled out a crumbled envelope. "I forgot to give you this."

She read the note Tony pressed into her hand.

Sorry Laurel . . .
I forgot to tell you your old boss said to call Simon Bates 555-7312, 374 Mass Ave. He might be able to help. Non profit Crusader.

Love,
Jay

"Should I call? Maybe it's too late. It's been three weeks since Jay went to New Hampshire. Maybe he can't do anything . . . maybe he'll think . . ."

"Maybe the world will end . . . maybe a dinosaur will smash the house. I'm going to go work on the basement." He slammed the door.

Laurel looked at the phone and the number for several minutes before dialing.

"Planet protection, it's the only one you have."

"Simon Bates please."

"Speaking."

Within two minutes she had her appointment.

Simon Bates' 374 Mass Ave. office was a three-story, turn-of-the-century building in the heart of Central Square. Unlike the boutiques, workplaces, restaurants and chain stores in Harvard Square surrounding the brick and ivy university, the area was downscale.

Laurel made her way across the white scuffed marble entry. Stone stairs, worn in the middle by generations of footsteps, led to his office on the first floor. Laurel knocked on a frosted door with stick-on black letters saying Planet Protection.

A man in his forties, dressed in jeans and a T-shirt saying "Take a Leek" with a picture of the vegetable, answered and stuck out his hand. "You must be Laurel." His handshake was firm. "I just hung up with Gordon. Let's go to the Charles River." When Laurel frowned, he said, "Gordon claims you walk on water. I want to see."

"He exaggerates." The muscles in her shoulders relaxed as Simon drew her into the office.

Instead of sitting behind his desk, he sat cross-legged on it. "What did you bring?"

"The result of the Strike Force audit showing how great we are . . . they were. Anyway I am not employed there anymore."

"What happened?"

"Maybe they knew I was going behind their back. I don't know. My old secretary told me they put out a memo that no one was to telephone me. She said the rumor is I faked expense reports, but of course, I didn't."

Simon leaned forward, his elbows on his knees. "And the papers you were talking about. They lie?"

She rummaged through her briefcase and added to the pile. "Here are Xeroxes of faked reports, photos of methyl bromide canisters and hydrochloric acid, a video of an illegal delivery at 3 A.M. If the investigation had been completed, if the agents had done a physical inventory, they would have found nothing matched."

"Interesting."

"Then the Strike Force was pulled out."

"Interesting." He repeated the word several times as he looked at everything. Laurel wanted to scream out, "What?" but remained silent. He handed her a Planet Protections brochure printed on recycled paper. The group handled local projects: school education, antibiotics to raccoons with eye infections, climate change, wetland protection, making Laurel want to write a check.

A young woman, dressed in shorts, bounced in.

"Laurel, meet my favorite traitor, Nancy Cohen. Would you believe just because her husband got a dream job in Geneva with the UN she's walking away from this underpaid but motivating job?"

The women shook hands.

"Simon believes in guilt trips, but no go. I want to live in the same country as my mate."

"How many on your staff?"

"One now." Simon's sigh bordered on theatrical.

"Guilt trips still aren't working," Nancy said. "We rely on volunteers and donations. Your ex-boss is one of our biggest donors." Nancy plucked Laurel's papers from Simon's hand.

"Get Hannah Pierpont, she'll help," Nancy said.

"Poor Jackson Products," Simon said. Seeing Laurel's

confused expression he added, "A *Globe* reporter. A tiger. Let's set up a meeting."

Laurel watched the reporter order two café lattés at the oak bar. Her hopes had fallen when Hannah Pierpont had walked in. She looked as if she just missed midgetdom or was impersonating a junior high kid. Someone that damned cute would be hard to take seriously. Although the pace of life now was much slower, she still hated having her time wasted.

The self-service coffee bar was filled with mismatched couches and chairs arranged in conversational semicircles. Eleven coffee choices were written on a blackboard under a sign, WE AREN'T **THAT** CHAIN. A pastry case took up half the bar space. Hannah pointed to it and to Laurel, who nodded.

A sound, something between a crow's caw and a donkey bray startled Laurel. She turned. A man, sitting at one table with three others held his finger to his lips. The other three copied him. He added sugar to one cup, put a napkin in the lap of one of the men. *He looks so sure of himself. Maybe he's faking it, like the twerp who is buying me coffee.*

Hannah placed the cups from a tray on the glass tabletop in front of their couch. Both women settled back against the cushions, tucking their feet under them. Hannah rummaged through her black cloth bag, large enough for a weekend getaway and pulled out a notebook and fountain pen.

"How long have you been a reporter?" Laurel asked.

"Your real question is—am I old enough to be a reporter. I've got an M.A. from the Columbia School of Journalism and I worked three years each at the *Madison Capital Times* and the *Miami Herald.* I've been with *The Globe* four years."

If Laurel's skin was lighter, she would have blushed. "I did wonder if I were talking to a kid."

Hannah squeezed Laurel's hand. "Happens all the time. The senators on The Hill thought I was so sweet until I started nailing them. I want to be the Bernstein and Woodward of Boston. A Pulitzer would be good, too. Now tell me about you."

Laurel gave her an abbreviated biography until she came to the investigation stopping.

"Why?"

Laurel decided there was nothing childlike about the reporter. She glanced at her watch and wondered where Rick and Matt were. She'd texted them, but had no response. "Rick Ames thinks it's Beacon Hill pressure. It's got to be high up."

Hannah tried to write it down, but her pen had run dry. She changed the cartridge as Rick walked in. After introductions, she asked, "Your version of the audit?"

"I was called into my boss's office and was reassigned. I went ballistic. He let me rage and said there was nothing that could be done."

"That happen before?"

"Never."

One of the retarded men banged the table. The three of them turned to see the leader grab the offender's hand.

"My boss said he didn't care what I did on my own time, which I took as a go-ahead." Holding up his hand, he went to get his own coffee. When he came back, he said, "I talked to Fred Beaudoin, your old colleague. Anderson fired him," he added for Hannah. "Had a very interesting story. I'll give you his coordinates, but first . . ." Both women waited as he drank some coffee.

He put down his cup. "I needed that. Anderson plans to move the plant to the western part of the state for cheaper labor and tax breaks. The land is owned by Senators Massarclli, Pettersen, and Farnsworth."

Hannah smiled. "The speaker of the house."

"That's the one. I thought you'd like this." He pulled out a sheet of paper.

Laurel handed him copies of what she'd left with Simon.

"You've done half my job, guys. Can't thank you enough."

As they stood one of the three retarded men upset the table. Liquid splashed everywhere. One of the mugs broke. The others landed on the couch. Laurel watched the leader clean up the mess and hoped Hannah would be as good at cleaning up Laurel's.

CHAPTER 46

Tony licked the last of ten oversized envelopes, each with a CD of photos of the furniture he'd redone. When he had started photographing his work, it was for no particular reason. It just felt right. He'd just finished the fifth decoupage piece, an armoire, which was the last shot on the disk. Each envelope bore the address of an interior decorator, written in calligraphy with the first letter in gold ink. Five were in Boston and five were in New York.

The accompanying sales letter looked more like a medieval manuscript, probably because it was on parchment. Probably wouldn't work any better than trying to get a job teaching. But then decorators wouldn't knock on his door if they didn't know he had a door.

"Can we go for ice cream?" Robbie asked and Samantha nodded vigorously.

Supper was done, the dishes stacked in the sink. Laurel still hadn't appeared. Hell, she was no longer working and she was still late for dinner. Okay, not fair. She'd taken over the cooking and housework chores, something Tony didn't mind at all. What was hard was never to have any time in the flat to himself. Granted it was summer. The kids were around. But another adult all the time under foot just wasn't to his liking.

The sidewalk heat warmed the soles of their sandals. Tony only half listened to the children's chatter. As they approached Harvard Square, they passed the area where almost all the individual shops had given way to chains. One small shop in an alcove had a For Lease sign plastered on the window.

As if he had fast forwarded skipping ahead several scenes, he saw it repainted and his furniture on display. Putting both hands to the dirty window pane he could make out space that would do as a work area in the back. As if by a miracle his tools and paints were there. He varnished a chair as he waited for an interior decorator to pick up a four-figure order.

Papa had called him an artist with furniture. Patting his breast pocket he realized he had neither paper nor pencil. He memorized the rental agent's number. No need to say anything to Laurel until he had some figures. Most likely it would all stay another of his fantasies.

CHAPTER 47

Waves lapping at the rocks and a blue jay fight awakened Anna Marsh. A prism dangling in her sun-filled window threw rainbows indiscriminately as the curtains stood straight out. Most days she woke smiling. Not today. Unable to remember when she last had such a fitful night, she forced herself out of bed. The digital clock on the dresser said 6:32.

Her sweats lay crumbled on her rocker. A quick sniff proved them clean enough for one more run. She felt the word run was a bit of a cheat. Somewhere around 70, she slowed her morning course to a jog. Last year the jog became a lope around the harbor road.

A few minutes later she passed Bearskin Neck before heading up Route 27. Normally she ticked off the places she passed: Motive No. 1, ruby red glasses in a store window, the white colonial house with black shutters, the rainbow-colored garden. Today nothing registered.

Although she normally waved at the waitress through the coffee-shop window as she made the first pot of the day and the news dealer, his arms full of morning papers, she didn't even see them. And for the life of her she couldn't figure out why she felt so ill at ease.

In her studio with her ever-present teacup on the stand next to her easel she grabbed her palette. The canvas was an abstract. Still lifes, seascapes sold better, but this was her soul work, not that the soul work didn't sell, but it required New York and Boston galleries, while the commercial work pandered to tourists. Nothing wrong with that at all.

She stared at the mauve, blue and raspberry wavy columns trickling down the canvas. As she mixed more raspberry, the normal surge of pleasure stayed away. Giving up, she took her cold tea to the back porch and settled in the white wicker rocker with Indian-print cushions. She gazed out to sea.

The black lab from next door bounded up the lawn and put his head on her lap, hoping for one of the biscuits she kept in a yellow ceramic jar.

"I know what it is," she said to him. Her son and daughter-in-law were huggers, staying in close range, turning their bodies to present a unit to the world. Like an explosion she realized that the last three visits when Carol touched Jay he didn't reciprocate.

For the rest of the day, Anna lectured herself about non-interference. Couples go through rough patches. That Carol and Jay had so few, probably meant they were due. "I won't meddle," she said to the dog, then got up and called Jay. "Have lunch with me?"

Blue and white tiles decorated the Grendel's Den salad bar. Jay handed his mother a clear glass dish. Once seated, he pushed his veggies around the plate as if he were a choreographer and the celery, carrots, cucumbers were his dancers on a stage of tabouli.

"We can have a contest on who makes the prettiest designs, or you can tell me what's wrong."

"Nothing Mom."

She followed his eyes as he looked at the cork brown ceiling. She watched him trace a crevice with his finger between two tiles on the table. "Is it your father?"

He made a semi-snort. "Strangely, watching his ashes fly made me realize we would never resolve our differences. I can live with not having the father I wanted. Now."

The beet strips on Jay's plate were lined up making a stockade fence.

Anna didn't move.

"Mom, tell me about the day you adopted me."

Anna spoke as she had done when he was five only with a few more grown up details such as the number of miscarriages each leading to her feeling of emptiness and of the lawyer who made the arrangements. Of the frightened young girl who came out of the Salvation Army home and put Jay in Anna's arms, then gave them an orange and green stuffed rabbit. When she finished, she saw he was looking at the wall stopping the other diners from seeing him cry. Her hand shot out to touch his arm.

When he could speak he asked, "Did Carol tell you she found her mother's diary?"

Anna shook her head.

"In it, she tells of being at a Salvation Army home for unwed mothers and walking into a parking lot to give up her baby along with an orange and green rabbit."

Anna sat back in her chair so hard that the front legs came off the floor before thudding back.

"Impossible." Things only happen like that in bad movies.

"How many babies in Cleveland are given to art teachers and law professors in a parking lot? How many Funny Bunnies are there? Ten, twenty. No. Just one. Mine."

Several diners turned to stare at his raised voice but they didn't see anyone angry, only a man holding himself with crossed arms and rocking. "Then you and Carol . . ."

". . . are half-brother and sister. I've known for about four weeks. What am I going to do? I can't leave my kids. I love

Carol so much, but every time I touched her it was . . ." The word "incest" hovered around the top of his mouth, but she saw he couldn't bring himself to force it out.

"What does she say?"

"I haven't told her. And whenever she brought up the diary, I changed the subject."

The waitress came over to ask if everything was all right, but Anna waved her away. Someone must be stealing oxygen in the room. She forced herself to breath normally. "There are societies where sisters and brothers marry. Think of the Egyptians."

"Pyramids are rather uncommon here in New England, if you haven't noticed." His tone was bitter.

"No, what I am saying is just go on as you are." At seventy-five she knew doing what others expected was a direct path to misery.

"It's illegal."

"There's nothing in the birth records. Who'd tell? You? Carol? Me?"

"I can't bring myself to tell Carol. I keep thinking that if I don't say anything, it will disappear. Stupid."

Anna could advise her son about plays or movies. She could send reports about bad politcial news and hope he voted the same she would or remind them they might use a holiday. Here she could do nothing.

Jay threw two twenties on the table. "I've got to get out of here."

She took his money to pay the bill. While they were inside, a rainstorm had come up with such fury that bubbles covered each puddle and broke, but the bubbles bursting were blurred by her tears.

CHAPTER 48

Five sharp turns of the screwdriver. Tony stepped back. The last kitchen cabinet handle was fastened. Looking good. He slipped the tool into his belt. New stove and fridge in boxes. Unpack. Set up. This area done. Bathroom left. Final paint job. Jay and Carol could advertise the place for rent. A third family at 392 Chestnut Street by September. A grandmother type? Students? Potential babysitters? Fit in?

A car pulled into the drive. Too early for anyone to be home. Out of the window he saw a Beamer. A man in expensive slacks, linen shirt, loafers and no socks got out. Muscled torso. Black wavy hair over collar. Gold chain nestled in chest hair.

Tony went upstairs.

"I'm looking for Tony DiDonato," the man said.

"You found him." Tony held up his dirty hands to show the dirt when the man stuck out his.

"I'm Raphaël LaFontaine." He pulled out a cream card with blue and gold embossing.

Tony left fingerprints on the pristine surface before he shoved it in his back pocket.

"I got your letter. The parchment . . . well that was a real come on. I think I have a client that would be interested in your Beowulf piece."

Tony froze at the door for a moment, unsure of himself. Take control, he told himself and led LaFontaine upstairs.

They had to pass a faux marble side table on spindly legs.

LaFontaine stopped. "My God, this is better than what I found in Florence on my last buying trip. Did you train in Italy?"

"My father taught me. Had to work for him. His father taught him, in Italy."

LaFontaine had bent down to look at the children's bureau with fairy tale characters decoupaged, all taken from a book that Tony had found at a flea market where he'd been selling his stuff. He put his finger on Little Red Riding Hood. He moved from piece to piece then took out a camera. "May I?"

Tony nodded.

"Let's talk business."

Tony led the man to the kitchen and made espressos. LaFontaine was bouncing high four figures around, asking about letting the pieces go to his showroom and designing to client specs.

"Might be hard. Most of this is refinished trash."

LaFontaine threw back his head and roared. "Even better. I would love to see my la di da clients pay through the nose for garbage."

"I can build from scratch."

LaFontaine put down his cup. "As long as you level with me, I'll level with you. My real name is Ralph Franco. I grew up in Revere and graduated from Mass College of Art and worked three jobs until I saved up enough to open a showroom. I changed my name, added some French allure and *voilà*. I've hustled clients from up and down the East Coast. But what is real is what I deliver to my clients and that's beauty."

Tony wasn't sure what to do with that volley of information.

"What I don't fake out is my partners. Everybody makes money. Interested?"

"I don't believe this."

"Believe."

Tony had no idea how to negotiate this. "What are you offering?"

"Split the price we get for the furniture 50/50, guaranteed $25,000 a year. Exclusive contract."

A fortune. He'd no longer be dependent on Laurel. Between the two of them they might have extra money. But, if LaFontaine offered this what would another decorator want . . . "I'm waiting to hear from other galleries. You weren't the only one I contacted."

At the end they split 25/75, $30,000 guaranteed and an exclusive. By the time LaFontaine left they were planning a showing in New York for October pending approval of the contract by Tony's lawyer. He didn't mention the lawyer was also his landlord.

LaFontaine shook Tony's now-washed hand. "Great deal. I've got to get to Lincoln. Someone just moved from California and wants an authentic Early American house but with nothing old." Both men laughed.

Tony watched the interior decorator's car back out of the driveway. Could he exchange his dreams? He saw a tombstone with the word scholar crossed out and replaced by artist. Overhead a chorus of angels painted the sky and began to sing.

CHAPTER 49

Mark Hanson shrank back to the alley. He'd staked out Jay Marsh's office for three days ever since he'd seen the black bitch hug the fucking cheating bastard outside the Waltham courthouse. He'd had his regular appointment. Poor Carol. So unsuspecting. So lovely. Of course, if she'd stayed home that son-of-a-bitch husband wouldn't have taken a nigger lover.

Nigger lover. He giggled at his own pun. Sure the black cunt worked for the bastard, but they didn't have to eat together, heads almost touching. He'd watched them through the window at a Mexican restaurant. Jay reached into the woman's plate with his fork. Imagine eating after a nigger? Just the thought made him want to puke.

He'd tested them. The nigger always parked behind the building. Mid-morning Mark had snuck up to it and let the air out of her rear left tire. An hour later she'd gone to her car and then barreled back into the office. Did she call a repair service? No, Jay played hero and changed the tire. Asshole.

Thank God for his surveillance training. And weight lifting. He was smarter, stronger than ever before. His leaders hadn't ordered him to kill Marsh and his whore, but they did say act to protect the innocents.

Carol had refused to talk about her marriage when he'd asked. She kept saying she was the counselor, not the reverse. That's when he knew that *she* knew. Brave woman, standing by her man. Bastard didn't deserve her.

His Glock model 40 gun was in its holster under his jacket. In August a shaded alley wasn't any cooler than being in the sun, but he couldn't stroll around with a gun showing. If he'd had it that day at the courthouse, he'd have plugged them both on the spot, mingling their blood in death as they toppled to the sidewalk.

Stroking his weapon gave him an erection. The odor of rotting food from the garbage filled his nostrils. Sweet smells. He liked it. Standing next to garbage to rid the world of human garbage . . . a symbol of a greater truth.

His watch said 6:30 P.M. How late were those assholes working? He needed a clear shot. He almost had it through the window this morning, but the receptionist stepped in his way.

Activity. Two people emerged with briefcases. They spoke and went in different directions. The late afternoon sun reflected off the office window, blocking his view.

6:47 P.M.

There they were. The last to leave. Jay's jacket was slung over his shoulder. He put his briefcase down, patted his pocket and pulled out keys.

The black bitch carried a huge pocketbook.

She laughed.

He laughed.

Some sex joke probably.

Mark brought the gun up. The bitch was in range. Shit. She dropped her bag, spilling the contents on the sidewalk. As she bent to scoop up her crap, Jay turned to lock the door. The first bullet hit him in the back. A red stain spread across his white shirt.

This wasn't like firing at the range. Those targets stood still. Jay whirled around. When he didn't fall, Mark shot again. Jay toppled against the door.

The black bitch reached for him. As she screamed "Help us,"

Mark emptied his gun into her. God, that felt good.

Someone looked out a window and yelled "Police."

Mark ambled out of the alley. Running would call attention. He strolled down Mount Auburn Street. A wave of sadness swept over him that he couldn't get close enough to smell the blood and see their eyes pass into death. Next time.

CHAPTER 50

"I don't like it," Paige Marsh said as Carol held up a green sweater. A price tag dangled from the sleeve.

"It looks great with your red hair." Mother and daughter stood in T.J. Maxx's children's section along with other mothers and children all buying for the opening of school next week. Carol wondered why she never waited until after school opened rather than get caught up in this turmoil every first week in September.

"I won't wear it. I want a blue one."

Carol glanced in her shopping cart. Seth didn't care if he wore a paper bag, but Paige wanted only blue. My daughter, the cat burglar, she thought.

Seth pulled on Carol's skirt. "I'm bored. Let's go home."

Carol found it difficult to believe she was already buying back-to-school clothes. Next week she'd be checking homework, getting bodies bathed and in bed for a story in attempt to create quality time. If she ever tracked down the person who first created the concept of quality time, she'd shoot them.

Carol and the kids pulled into her driveway. Summer-lush marigolds lined both sides of the cement path in sunshine. The kids jumped out and were halfway into the house until Carol yelled, "Hey. The bags."

"Yes, Mom," they said together: their tone carried the message they were humoring her.

Jay wasn't home. Not to worry. She'd feed the kids and herself, and set aside a plate for him.

The soapy dishwater made a sucking sound as it swirled down the drain followed by several glugs. Carol glanced at the black cat clock, whose pendulum tail clicked as it swung. Whenever the children asked for a kitten, Jay pointed at the clock and said, "That's your kitten."

After the children had been bathed and bedded, Carol dialed Jay's office. No answer. He must be on his way home, although it wasn't like him to be this late without checking in.

She entered the bedroom. If her kitchen was the heart of the home, the bedroom was its soul where she and Jay shared a tenderness beyond passion. Unfortunately, there hadn't been much passion lately, but she suspected it was temporary. Also, he used to listen to the small details of her day, now he brushed her aside. The list of things she wanted to share, but couldn't because of him, was growing to pages and pages. Whatever caused it would be worked out. She would tackle it directly once the kids were back in school. She had no intention of letting their couple be a secret-keeping one.

By the time she laid out her things for the next morning, showered, put on her nightie and set the alarm, she realized another half hour had passed. Jay had more than enough time to make it home. She dialed his cell. It rang and rang until a woman said, "Hello."

"Who am I talking to?" Carol asked.

"Who is this?" the woman responded.

"I asked first."

"I'm a nurse at Mass General. Now to whom am I speaking, please?"

"Carol Marsh?"

"Jay Marsh's wife?"

Carol swallowed several times before she could gasp out, "Why?"

"There's been an accident. I think you need to come down here."

"Is my husband . . ."

"Alive, but please . . ."

"I'm on my way."

As if in fast forward Carol hung up the phone, dressed in jeans and a T-shirt, took the stairs to the DiDonatos two at time and burst in without knocking.

Laurel slept on the sofa, a book across her chest. Tony, visible through his workroom door was brushing something onto a table.

"I need your help. Stay with my kids."

Laurel started awake. "What's wrong?"

When Carol told her, Laurel insisted on driving her to the hospital.

"Your husband hasn't regained consciousness," the doctor said after showing Carol and Laurel into a room with a desk and chairs plus canisters and tubes and instruments that Carol had no idea what they were for.

The doctor slapped two X-rays onto a wall light box and using a pencil pointed to two dark marks. The two women stood behind him.

How can he talk about my husband? He looks like he belongs in high school.

"This is one bullet. It missed his vitals. A hair more right or left . . ." He shrugged. "Lucky man."

What's lucky about bullets in his body?

"We were able to get it out and stop the bleeding. However, at one point his heart stopped and we had to defibrillate him."

His heart stopped . . . my husband's heart stopped. It's beating

*now. Stay calm . . . breath deeply . . . it'll be all right . . . Listen . . .
concentrate.*

The doctor tapped the other dark mark. "This one is harder.
It's lodged in his spine. We're talking major surgery, but we can
only guess at nerve damage. Dr. Blaine is on his way in to oper-
ate. He's one of the best spine men in the city."

Spine man is coming to make everything all right.

"Carol, my hand."

Carol had forgotten Laurel was there and wasn't aware how
hard she'd been gripping her friend's hand.

"Can she see him?" Laurel rubbed the circulation back into
her hand.

The doctor called a nurse dressed in blue scrubs with a
stethoscope dangling around her neck. Her thick-soled shoes
made no sound.

They passed the ambulance entrance. A siren whooped
outside, getting closer until it stopped mid whoop. From inside
one of the patient rooms, someone screamed in Spanish. Two
doctors walked by, laughing.

*How can they laugh with this suffering? How can they laugh
when I'm suffering? Is there any doctor here that doesn't look
like a child?*

She led the two women into a curtained-off area. The odor of
disinfectant bit at their noses.

*At least it's not the morgue. I couldn't do it again. Not without
Jay.*

Laurel and Carol inhaled as one. Of the four beds separated
by open smoky blue curtains only one was occupied. Jay lay on
his back with an oxygen tube pinching his nose. Two plastic
bags suspended from a metal bar hung over the bed dripping
blood and a clear liquid.

Carol took his hand. "He's cold, so very cold. Get a blanket."
She stroked his hair.

My father's coffin had roses. When we walked away leaving the casket alone, I went back for a flower to press in my Bible. A petal fell. It was so soft. Jay's hair is soft, rose-petal soft. But he's not sick. He's been shot. Of all the things I worried about, this wasn't one of them.

"The police would like to talk to you," the nurse said.

When Carol looked confused, Laurel said so softly that Carol had to strain to hear, "It was a shooting."

How could I forget? I just didn't think about the police.

"Tell them Mrs. Marsh will be out in a few minutes, please," Laurel said to the nurse. When the nurse left she whispered, "Do you want to be alone with him?"

Carol turned with animal-wounded eyes. "The only thing that's keeping me from breaking into a million little pieces is having you here."

The wall clock ticked off seven minutes as Carol whispered in Jay's ear, "Please live. Fight. I love you." Then she babbled about Paige wanting a blue sweater and the kids staying with Tony and anything else that popped into her head. "If you get well I'll buy you ice cream every day and who cares about cholesterol."

Jay's eyes did not even flicker.

The nurse came back in with a man in scrubs. "Dr. Blaine is upstairs, and Joe here will wheel your husband to surgery. It'll be a long time if you want to go home." Her eyes met Carol's. "There's a waiting room upstairs. After you talk to the police I'll show you."

Carol kissed her husband's forehead.

Don't let it be my last kiss. Control. I can't give in. God, help me do what I have to do.

Her knees buckled. She felt Laurel shove her into a hard-backed chair and push her head down. Her teeth chattered.

Laurel knelt on the floor holding Carol's shaking hands in hers. "Take it easy. I'm here."

"We can talk here," the older of the two policemen said. His nametag said Langone. He was slightly overweight and his salt and pepper hair was matted from the brim of his hat. Holding the door open as the two women walked in, he nodded to his younger partner to follow.

There were three chairs. Except for the younger cop, they sat around the small table. "I'm sorry about your husband, but Mass General has some of the best doctors in the world."

"Thank you," Carol said. *Leo tells me how it hurts to deal with the victims' families. We're victims. I can't think . . .*

"Who is this?" Langone looked at Laurel.

"Laurel DiDonato. Neighbor and best friend."

The younger cop took a notebook from his breast pocket and pulled a felt-tipped pen. "What does your husband do?"

"Lawyer."

"Is there anyone you know who would want to kill your husband and the woman? An angry client?"

As Carol tried to think of enemies, what the cop said resonated. "Woman?"

"Lina Frederickson?"

"Jay's assistant."

"She died instantly. Four bullets."

Carol's thread of control pulled tighter and as she felt Laurel grab her hand, she gave the thread some slack.

"I'm sorry, I thought you knew," Langone said.

"Lina's daughter, Syeeda. Where is she?"

"Who?"

"Lina's child. She's in day care. No one would have picked her up."

Although there was almost no room she began to pace.

"Someone must find her."

God, I'll make a deal. I'll save Syeeda. You save Jay. Focus, what's the name of the day care center . . . we discussed day care problems . . . "The day care center. It's someplace in Dorchester. Walking distance of where Lina lived." Her voice sounded hysterical even to her.

Langone turned to the younger cop. "Check it out. Get someone at the station to phone you for the address from her wallet." Then he turned back to Carol. "Is there any other family for Lina?"

"A mother. In Atlanta. She visits a lot. This will kill her. Lina's her pride and joy."

"Disgruntled husband? Lover?"

"Syeeda's father died years ago. Lina's too busy to date; she's also a part-time law student." *Was a part-time student.*

Carol wrapped her arms tight around herself. Anna. Someone must tell her. But she can't be alone when she hears.

The clock on the wall read 1:23 A.M. *Anna's sleeping. Give her the rest of the night.*

"Can you tell us what happened?" Laurel asked.

As the cops recounted what they had pieced together of the shooting, Carol gave in and began to cry. Laurel comforted her, and continued to comfort her after the cops left.

Carol's head snapped up. She'd drifted into sleep sitting in the surgical waiting room. The digital clock read 06:18. *Where am I? Oh God, it wasn't a nightmare.*

Laurel slept stretched on the floor. They were the only ones there.

The sun's rising over the river. Red sun. Red sky in the morning, sailors take warning. Jay should be jogging along the river.

She shook Laurel awake. "Did you bring your cell?" Laurel started, rubbed her eyes and dug into her bag and found the phone. "Who are you calling?"

"First Doug, then Anna's neighbor. I want her to be there when I call her." Her hands flew to her mouth. "What if she heard it on the news?"

"They don't release names until next of kin is notified."

"I'm next of kin."

Doug's sleepy voice changed when Carol told him what happened.

"Find Syeeda. I want custody temporarily."

"You can't handle it, Carol, but I'll get the grandmother up here fast. You deal with Jay."

He won't live if I don't have Syeeda.

"Give me a number where I can reach you."

She rattled off Laurel's cell number.

"If you need any of us to stay with you holler." He hung up.

Laurel walked over to the coffee machine and made Carol a cup. She clasped it without drinking. Then she took the phone from Carol and called information to get the neighbor's number and called. "You don't know me, but I'm a friend of Anna Marsh's son and there's an emergency."

As she explained, a doctor dressed in surgical scrubs walked into the waiting room. "Which one of you is Mrs. Marsh?"

Carol stood up, spilling the coffee.

"I'm Dr. Blaine. Your husband survived the operation. If he gives a good fight, he should make it."

If it's good news why is he frowning?

"But at this point, I would be amazed if he ever walked again."

CHAPTER 51

"He's not responding as we'd hoped," Dr. Snelling said. "He should be awake more." The Marsh family doctor leaned against the wall outside Jay's hospital room. An orderly darted in and out of the patients' rooms shoving food trays with food-encrusted dishes on top in a metal caddie that rattled with each thrust. Evening visitors toting flowers and magazines straggled in. He shoved his hands in his white lab coat pockets.

Carol felt as if she could pass an anatomy course at this point. She knew the name of every part of the spine, which nerve went where, how muscles work . . . Her knowledge made no difference. Jay remained paralyzed from the waist down. "He acts as if he wants to die," she said. "Normally he fights windmills."

Snelling shrugged. "I'm calling the staff psychologist." He patted her shoulder. "The sooner we pull him out of the depression, the better."

Carol liked Snelling. He didn't mince words nor talk down to her. Not like Blaine. The best spine man in the city was egotistical, obnoxious and patronizing. It wasn't necessary to like him. Jay had been within a hair's breath of being a quadriplegic. Now it looked like he would only be a paraplegic.

"When can we get the psychologist to come?" God, she hoped the insurance covered it, but if it didn't she'd find a way somehow to pay for it.

"I've talked to your insurance. They're pushing for transfer to rehab. I want it delayed."

Carol didn't know how to thank him without it sounding routine. There was no simple way to express her appreciation for her husband's care, depressed or not. To the doctors it was their job. To her, it was her life. She opened the door to Jay's ward. All four beds were occupied, one by a man in traction.

Anna stood next to Jay's bed, a white plastic dish and spoon in her hand. "I got four teaspoons of Jell-O down him. His first solids."

Like his first step, tooth, word, Carol thought as she watched her mother-in-law put another spoonful of green into her son's mouth, scraping his chin like she would a baby. Progress, but short lived. The next time she tried, he turned his head away.

For the first time Anna looked old—not surprising considering Anna had been at the hospital twelve hours a day for five days. When Carol suggested the woman go home to rest, Anna said no, softly, but delivered the word with a firmness that gave it the weight of a boulder. Carol hadn't suggested it a second time.

Jay had not spoken since he'd regained consciousness. A few times his eyes flickered, but he'd clinched them shut. Carol had resisted forcing his lids open and crying, "Anyone home?"

"Let's get some coffee," Anna said. The women wound their way through the building's bowels to the hospital cafeteria. When they were seated Anna asked, "So what did Snelling say?"

Carol told her. As she watched Anna, she wondered if she would cope as well if it were Seth. No need to create future problems. How did her feelings compare to Anna's? Not important: fear was fear, pain was pain.

Anna drew in a deep breath. "I may know part of his problem, but I'm afraid to tell."

What else? Carol thought. Another woman?

"Your mother was Jay's mother."

Nonsense! Carol decided not to listen. If she didn't let the information in, it would go away. Think about the kids. Think about Syeeda with her grandmother. Think about Leo's message that there were no leads, not that it was his territory, but he had friends on the Cambridge force who kept him updated.

Anna was saying something about the diary.

Think about Tony and Laurel holding the house together. Think about Tony having a fender-bender. Think about anything except what Anna was saying.

"Your mother was adorable. When she put Jay in my arms I saw she gave me everything she had. I wanted to take her home too." Anna's eyes never left Carol's face. "Carol!"

People from several tables looked startled.

"Carol," Anna spoke more softly.

"These things don't happen." Carol's hands flew to her mouth. *Damn my mother. Damn her! Will she never stop messing up my life? Set priorities. Jay. The kids . . . That's why he'd changed the subject whenever I mentioned the diary or my mother . . . why he wouldn't let me touch him.*

"I know it's incredible. I wish I'd never told him about the stupid rabbit, but I wanted him to have some connection to his birth mother. I wish you'd never found the diary. I wish . . ."

"That explains it, why he's been so weird before . . ." she still couldn't say the shooting.

"My son was torn apart. He loves you so much, he can't imagine being without you. And because of my divorce, he couldn't imagine deserting them. I told him it wasn't necessary."

"My husband's my brother." The words emerged in a ghastly whicper. If Carol hadn't been so afraid of undoing all her prayers she would have sworn at God. She tore at the paper napkin that she had picked up when she took her tray and utensils.

"Half brother. Remember that." Anna watched the napkin

shreds grow. "I shouldn't have told you."

Carol tried to remember the yearbook photo of her mother's boyfriend as she reached for Anna's napkin. All the passion between she and Jay had been incest. That word held no reality. Incest happened in the backwoods of Kentucky. Incest was fathers forcing themselves on daughters or big brothers on little sisters. She and Jay were consenting adults, whom even after years of marriage still loved each other. She shook her head.

Anna took off her glasses that had steamed up from her tears. "I'm sorry, I thought if you knew Jay's problem we could double team him and . . ."

Carol stopped shredding the second napkin and put her smooth hand over her mother-in-law's veined and spotted one. "What I'm trying to say is that he should have told me. We could have dealt with it together."

Now the two women sat without speaking. Carol pushed the napkin bits around the table making patterns.

Anna spoke first. "Let's go back upstairs." They stood. "I couldn't love you more if you were my own daughter."

"At the rate things are falling apart, I probably am," Carol said. "That sounded wrong. I'd be thrilled if I were your daughter."

"I feel as if I'm wading in the ocean and all the sand is washing away from under my feet," said Anna.

"Join the club." Carol pictured the two of them being swept out to sea cartoon style, bounced by dolphins further and further from shore. When she told Anna, the older woman began to giggle. Then Carol joined in. Every time one regained control, they would look at each other and be seized by another spasm. People around them stared. Carol reached for her napkin shreds and threw them in the air. They floated back, setting them off again.

"It's n-n-not funny," Carol said.

"Laughter gives strength."

"I'll need . . . I've a husband to get back on his feet. My niece needs a father." Her effort at humor felt like a stomach punch, sobering her. "What did you think I'd do when I knew?"

Anna shrugged. "I wasn't sure how much more you could take."

"I'll take whatever I have to for my family to stay together. Period." *No way would the four of them be anything but her family, together no matter what the circumstances. The rest of the world need never know.*

CHAPTER 52

The phone rang in the kitchen and Laurel picked it up. A voice said, "There's going to be a pick-up tonight and of course you never heard from me."

Before she could say, "Thank you, Paul," the phone went dead. She wondered why the janitor had risked letting her know. She didn't care why, just like she didn't care that some people, if they knew the whole story, might think she was on some private vendetta. Although she would like to stick it to Anderson et al., what she really wanted was to make sure that people didn't get sick.

Light traffic flowed into Boston via the Mass Pike in the late afternoon, although the westbound lanes were at a standstill. The long Labor Day weekend was ahead. Although the temperature hovered in the mid 80s, summer stickiness had been replaced by September dryness.

As she slowed for the tollbooth, Laurel patted the passenger seat to retrieve her cell and pushed Rick Ames's number for the fifth time since she'd left work. "Finally," she said, when he answered. "I think we've another illegal pick-up tonight."

"I'll call Hannah. With or without her, I'll pick you up as soon as I can get to your house. My camping trip can wait."

"You're nuts," Tony said as Laurel pulled on jeans and navy sweatshirt.

"Just check on Carol." She peeked out the window at the empty driveway.

Tony stood behind her. "It's dangerous. One person shot in this house is too many."

Samantha came up behind them. "Is Mommy going to get shot?"

Laurel knelt to kiss her. "Your father is joking." A car horn beeped from below. She kissed the other three children and left. A second later she was back and blew Tony a kiss. "I'll be careful."

"All the bushes and you had to find one with thorns." Hannah Pierpont sat on a sleeping bag behind the row of hedges lining Jackson Products parking lot leading to the loading dock. The smell of the Charles River hung dank and heavy in the air.

"They've all got thorns, but this is the best view. Think of it as an extra detail for your acceptance speech for the Pulitzer."

"I'll think of it when the scratches infect." Hannah slapped at a mosquito. "Aren't these suckers supposed to fly south by now?"

Rick chuckled. "Those are ducks. I guess you don't do many nature stories."

The clock tower struck 2:00. Hannah settled her head on Rick's lap and snored in small putts.

Fighting to stay awake, Laurel said, "I don't think I'll ever think of detective work as glamorous again."

A motor sounded and headlights lit the hedges over them. Rick reached for his phone. "Detective Richard Ames, Attorney General's Strike Force. I'm at Jackson Products and there's a robbery in progress. Get over here without sirens."

"What the . . . ?" Before Hannah could say more, Rick slapped his hand over her mouth.

299

The truck was positioned so it hid the threesome. Rick pulled out his gun and began his way toward the vehicle as a second car without lights drove into the parking lot.

"Stop! Police!" Rick's voice.

"Hands against the wall." Unknown voice moving from the cruiser in the direction of the loading dock.

"Don't shoot." Voice on the dock.

"We're supposed to be here." Another voice from the dock.

"At 3:30 A.M.?" Rick asked.

"Overtime." The same voice that had said don't shoot.

The two women couldn't make out the mumbles, but they saw two men handcuffed being pushed into the cruiser.

At the police station, Laurel sat on a wooden bench. Grime was embedded in the wood. Rick was in another room with the police questioning the men. She listened as Hannah spoke into her portable.

"It's not a simple heist . . . remake the damned front page . . . I saw it . . . illegal chemicals. No, I don't know what was in the damned canisters . . . yes Jackson had been under investigation, but it was stopped . . . Look, just take down the first paragraphs and we'll deal with the rest as soon as I give my statement to the police." She hung up. "They act like it's my fault the crooks didn't show up earlier."

CHAPTER 53

Jay rubbed his hips, penis and upper thigh. It could just as well have been a pillow. Every night after the hospital ebbed into stillness, he inventoried his lower torso. Every night it was the same—nothing.

God's retribution for his sins: incest for loving his sister, for still wanting her even after he *knew*. He would never have her again, or any woman. God metered out direct punishment. God was a fisherman reeling in his catch . . . let it run out, pull it in again.

Like a rosary he had a litany of if onlys . . . if only his birth mother hadn't written a diary . . . if only Carol . . . she wasn't an if only . . . how he loved her, blowing on her coffee, packing a picnic lunch, reading to the kids, snuggling against him in bed . . . bed . . . no good . . . if onlys sucked.

The room's silence was broken only by the snoring of his roommates, letting him think of the pop, which at the time he didn't know was from a gun and then the searing pain. He hadn't asked what happened: no one had said anything.

It was too much work to speak, but he knew he'd been shot.

Strange being shot, something that happened to others.

His mother and Carol talked at him through the tunnel he'd erected, keeping them at the other end. He didn't want them closer.

He wished he'd died. Get rid of the voices barraging him, the needles attacking him, spoons shoved into his mouth.

What would Carol do next? Whenever she was there, she'd whisper how she loved him. She rattled a paper with a drawing from Paige, his baby girl with red curls, so like his. He imagined her sweet breath on his cheek.

He willed his heart to stop. It mocked him by beating. He pulled the tube from his arm and slept.

"Again?" A woman's high-pitched voice followed by fiddling. "We don't want our hands tied do we?" More sleep.

"Jay?" Dr. Snelling's voice.

"Jay. Dr. Tennant. I'm here again."

The psychologist. Now they wanted to shrink him. He escaped into sleep, praying no dreams would come.

The air smelled different, unair-conditioned. The window must be open. What voice would attack next? Who'd poke him today? Who cared?

Carol and Anna weren't there. The sooner they forgot him the better.

Footsteps. "Ok, Jay. Enough's enough. Dr. Tennant and I've had a long talk. I know we're brother and sister. I don't care. I love you. We need you back. You're letting us down."

How dare she say that? He was trying to free her by dying.

"We'll work everything out. Like before. But before, you weren't a coward. Please, Jay—stop being a coward!"

He wasn't a coward. Cowards were afraid to die.

He opened he eyes and shut them again.

"Don't you dare shut me out, James Louis Marsh. I've had enough. We've got two kids and I'm not raising them alone."

He opened his eyes. The light hurt. She noticed and created a shadow between him and the window. "I'm on my way to work. I'll be back tonight." As she bent to kiss him, her face loomed in so he could see the tiny pimple next to her nose.

Anna breezed in. "Carol telephoned and said you opened your eyes. About time." Two orderlies followed. One pushed a wheelchair. Jay felt himself thrust into it. His mother tucked a blanket around his legs arranging the catheter. The room spun. He shut his eyes.

Crash. Anna had banged a plastic pitcher against the night stand. He opened his eyes.

"Good, I can't stand self pity. Never could, but that's not news to you."

"I . . . feel . . ." his voice sounded croaky to him, ". . . dizzy."

She placed a kidney shaped pan on his lap. "If you vomit, do it there. We're through coddling you. Dr. Tennant's orders. Now there's a no-shit woman running things, not one of those that blames everything on toilet training. We want you out of this hospital by the end of the week. Besides the insurance is running out."

After what seemed like hours, Anna directed the orderlies to put him back into bed.

His wife arrived after dinner with two more orderlies. "Okay Babes, we're going for a ride." She wheeled him into the reception area at the end of the hall. Two men in jeans and one woman wearing a bathrobe played cards. Ten minutes later she pushed him back into the bedroom and handed him a call cord. "When you want to get back into bed, push the button. Love you more than you could ever know."

The room was empty. His bed was mussed, the other three waiting for the next patients were made to military standards. He debated slipping onto the floor. That would show them. Show them what? His head swirled. His hand shook as he pressed the button.

CHAPTER 54

Two egg yolk eyes stared at Jay from the dish on the portable table. Unlike other mornings, no one fed him. The Amazon, who'd once mimicked a caring nurse, had shoved them at him, then left. A cup held something smelling like coffee, but was the color of tea. He picked up his fork and cut into one egg and tried not to gag as yellow gunk oozed out. He really wasn't hungry.

Who would force him to do things he didn't want to do today? They said he'd be transferred at the end of the week. He heard the door open. Was it the nurse? Or the orderlies, to make him drag himself someplace he didn't want to go? He glanced around the room. Two beds were filled with sleeping men. One was still empty.

Tony sauntered in. "Hey man, long time no see."

Jay said nothing.

"I'm your attack dog today, sent by your women. My advice? Give in."

Jay turned his head and shut his eyes.

Tony went to the other side of the bed, and put his hand on Jay's shoulder. "They told me you'd pull the don't-look-at-me trick."

Jay opened his eyes. "You don't understand."

"I understand you almost died. But you didn't. Besides, I need free legal advice on a contract."

"Ask Lina." This was the first time he'd thought about work.

The words made Tony shoot out of the room. Jay found it strange, but he was too sleepy to think about it and was just drifting off to sleep when his neighbor re-appeared.

"I had to check with your shrink. She'll be here in a minute."

Tony babbled about Laurel being fired, the weather, something about his new career and how the kids all liked their teachers this year except for Robbie. This new Chatty Tony was not the man that he rode around the streets with, each saying almost nothing.

Jay felt someone take his hand. He opened his eyes to see Dr. Tennant. "We need to talk."

"I'm sorry, I blundered into it," Tony said to the doctor. He looked at Jay. "Gotta run."

The doctor now held both Jay's hands. "I've bad news. Lina is dead. She was killed by the same person who shot you."

When Carol came in wearing her going-to-court suit and raincoat that smelled damp, Jay's first words were, "I know about Lina."

Carol pulled the curtains on each side until they were cocooned in white linen. "She died instantly."

The lucky one, he thought. "Who did it?"

"At last some curiosity. We don't know. No leads. If you were a dead white male, they'd be pushing it more. I went to the funeral. Her mother's taken Syeeda down south."

Tears spewed from Jay's eyes. Volcanoes had more control. He was crying for Lina, for Syeeda, for himself, for his sister, half-sister, his wife.

"Cry, Babes. We've a lot of work ahead of us."

Jay cried until his chest hurt. When he was empty, he said, "I don't remember ever crying like that."

"You haven't been shot, had your assistant killed, discovered your beloved wife is your half-sister nor been a paraplegic before either. Some of those things we can't change. We'll work on what we can, and notice, Babes, *we*. Our marriage vows were for the better or worse. We've had the better, now let's see what we do with worse."

"I don't want your pity."

"Who said I was giving any? It's time to put our lives back together." She kissed him and not as she would kiss a brother and left. What was this kiss-and-run therapy?

How in hell could they ignore their kinship? Love making had been such a great part of their relationship, and he might not be able to ever do that again. She was a sensual woman. Would she need lovers?

He used to joke if Carol wanted the moon, it would disappear. His wife battled against her childhood, for the kids she worked with. My God, he thought, I'm thinking of her as my wife. For the first time he felt a glimmer, a very, very small flame of hope, which he extinguished as fast as if it were a real fire.

CHAPTER 55

Each morning Jay checked off things to hate.

One: Dull green walls. Couldn't the rehab center find another color?

Two: Bars on the windows? Who'd break in? Or was capable of breaking out?

Three: Fake cheerful nurses. If one more person said, "Good morning, how are we today?" he'd deck them. Only he couldn't.

Four: wishful thinking.

Five: his physical therapist, the sadist, who pulled, pummeled, prodded and poked him.

Six: the order to develop his upper body on command. Ok, he accepted the need to be able to use his arms to propel himself from his wheelchair to maintain independence. Careful. He didn't want to let even a semi-positive reason interrupt his hate litany.

Seven: mood swings. They said it was normal. The Great God They. They didn't have to live with diapers and piss bags the rest of Their lives.

That afternoon the bright red and soft gold leaves were ripped by a storm, the end of a hurricane, which lashed at the tree as its branches beat at the window. Jay rolled his chair over to the window and stared at the stripped branches. The spectacular fall foliage show was being cut short by a few weeks as the puddles drowned them. No more colors till next year.

Where would he be next year? Living in a room somewhere?

Not according to Carol. But what could they be—friends, siblings? Never lovers.

Would he be back at work? Poor Lina. The world was poorer without her. He'd never lost a friend before who was younger than himself.

If his days were full of lists and therapy, his evenings were filled with people. Carol stopped by every night and Anna several times a week. The kids came weekends, clamoring onto his lap and asking to see his therapy equipment. Tony talked about his upcoming exhibition, Laurel about . . . well he didn't pay enough attention to know her subjects.

Some patients never had visitors—his roommate, Reggie for example. A big black guy, hit by a car. Some moments Jay envied him being left alone. To have no one with that look in their eyes that said they wanted to know how he really was, but were afraid of the answer.

The two men seemed destined to spend their days within feet of each other. Reggie was always up first, anxious to get to therapy, destroying Jay's sleepy treasured think-time. The therapists paired them in the exercise program, the buddy system, each supposed to be encouraging the other. During therapy Reggie always wanted to keep going through break time while Jay refused to give up his coffee and cruller.

"How am I going to get better man, if you keep feeding your face?" Reggie complained. "I egg you on, you just have egg on your face."

The lights were out, although the hall light left a glow around the edge of the door. Jay could make out Reggie on his back, his hands behind his head. "Man, you're never going to get better with your attitude."

Jay said nothing.

"My papa took off when I was a baby. My mama raised me

to never give up. My brain works. My fingers work. When I can get out of here I can still program the hell out of a computer."

Jay had never thought of Reggie having a profession. "So why doesn't she come visit?"

"I reckon she's here." Reggie thumped his chest. "Lord gave her a big test about two years ago. Gave her cancer."

"I'm sorry."

"Not your fault. She told me her last job was to teach me to die with dignity. Gotta live with dignity too." A few minutes later Reggie was snoring.

The next morning Jay listened to Reggie brush his teeth. The guy must use a microphone. In between he hummed. He sang while shaving. Rolling out of the bathroom he made his wheelchair dance, moving in one direction then another followed by a circle. "I can't wait to figure out how to do a wheelie. Ready for chow?"

Only when they were in the dining room and as Jay poured milk on his corn flakes did Jay realize he had forgotten to recite his hate litany.

CHAPTER 56

Laurel approached her new office twirling her umbrella as the words for "Singing in the Rain" beat in her head. The job had come from heaven. Really it had come from Simon, who had telephoned and offered her the job at, "Slave labor, slave wages. Start now?" For those reasons, she almost turned it down until Tony pointed out that, with his new patron, together they made more than she had alone at Jackson. Not a lot more, but enough that they would be all right.

The fringe benefits of being able to walk to work or go two T stops as well as believing in what she was doing made her wonder how she had survived as long as she had after Anderson had come on board. Tony had even accused her of being too relaxed the other day when she just threw on jeans to go to work, rather than change her suit a couple of times because she knew she had meetings.

Jean-Pierre, the florist on the ground floor of her building, had stepped outside to check his new window display. "Ah Laurel, do it like zees." Taking her umbrella he did a perfect Gene Kelly imitation stomping in puddles. She stared for a moment and copied him. Pedestrians walked around them scowling, but she didn't care.

As she opened her office door, her boss knelt in front of the copier. "Good morning, good morning . . . lovely morning with purifying rain," he said.

In the weeks she'd worked there she had never seen him

anything but cheerful. Getting the job had been so easy.

"People don't get jobs like that," she said on her first day.

"Some do, if Gordon Jackson recommends them at the same time as I need someone."

As she scanned her email, she laughed. "Good news from the Cambridge School system. They've approved their part of the WGBH series." Had she designed the perfect job for herself this would be it. Simon even let the kids come to the office whenever Tony had to be at the decorator's or a client's.

Her headaches and tensions had disappeared. Loving your work . . . what a concept. Even her parents and half-sister were coming for Thanksgiving.

Simon picked up the ringing phone then handed it to Laurel.

"What did you think of *The Globe* article this morning?" Rick Ames asked.

She turned to Simon. "Have we got *The Globe?*" Simon usually brought it from home and they shared it as they ate their home-made sandwiches at lunch.

Laurel cradled the phone between her ear and shoulder as she pulled *The Globe* from its blue plastic covering and unrolled it. The front page headline told her that Anderson had been indicted along with the rest of senior management and it was all under Hannah's byline.

"YES!"

"And there's more," Rick said. "Three senators and the speaker will be indicted today. Instead of pacing the halls on Beacon Hill, they'll be marching in a cell for a long list of charges."

"If they stick."

"It's a good case. They were sloppy with a money trail and E-mails."

"Wanta bet Hannah gets her Pulitzer? On another topic. Would you and Tony like to have dinner with Hannah and me?

To celebrate . . ."

"Has it gone from professional to personal?"

"Let's say I'm trying to convince her having an environmental cop in her life wouldn't be a bad thing."

At lunch, when Laurel walked into the driveway, the rain had stopped. Tony was unloading lumber that clattered to the ground when he spied his wife.

"Hi. You're early." He cocked his head at his wife in her long denim skirt, so much better than those stuffy business suits. A full skirt was feminine. Guinevere or Rosamond. Roses in her cheeks from walking in the crisp November air. Cherry lips. Black wavy hair. An unstressed Laurel was a beautiful woman, worthy of courtly love.

"I came home to have lunch with my knight in shining jeans."

"He left about an hour ago, but will I do?" He embraced her.

After lunch, when Laurel left, Tony went back to building a wheelchair ramp as a surprise for the Marshes. Jay would be home next week. Although Tony felt it was too soon, the Marshes's insurance for the rehab had run out. Insurance, what a mess. He and Laurel still had to decide whether to pay the fine that the non-insured in Massachusetts had to pay or buy the mandatory health insurance. The fine was less, but what if the kids really needed medical care?

As he pondered the problem, he set up two sawhorses, got his electric drill and the long orange extension cord and began work on the ramp.

Too bad his father hadn't lived to see what he was doing. To take a piece of wood and bring out its soul . . . To heal an abused piece of furniture . . . To make a classic design, one of a kind . . .

I've come full circle, he thought.

Chapter 57

As the car pulled into the 392 Chestnut Street drive, Jay realized that the last time he'd seen his home, the trees had been green. Now only brown leaves clung to the oak, the maple was a skeleton, its boney branches praying to an unanswering god.

Carol's normally seed-catalogue perfect garden was a mass of dead weeds. Carol saw him look at it. "Hospital visits cut into gardening time."

"Your strawberries. They need straw-packing."

"I can replant. Of course, now you're home I still might still be able to save them."

He spied the ramp leading to the kitchen door. Ramps were for cripples. Maybe the PC term was motionally-challenged. Screw political correctness. He *was* crippled.

"Tony built it." Carol hopped out of the car and brought the wheelchair around from the trunk.

Although he waited for her to help, she stood back until he manipulated himself into the chair and up the ramp. Within the apartment the furniture had been rearranged so he could roll through the rooms.

"I gotta get back to work. Can you start supper please," Carol said.

Paige and Seth blew the paper covering off their straws at each other, then plunged them in their chocolate milk and blew bubbles.

"No one blew bubbles in rehab," Jay said.

Carol blew the paper from her straw at him and then bubbled her own milk. Then she cocked her head.

He wanted to go to bed. Instead he blew the paper off his straw and bubbled his milk.

"Grown ups are weird," Paige said.

Jay lay propped on pillows. The weeks of rehab exercises had strengthened his already strong arms. He looked at the new position of the dresser. The closet door was open and a second bar had been added under her clothes for his.

Carol slipped into bed. "I never got used to sleeping alone."

"What are we going to do?" he asked.

"Live one day at a time."

"Sounds too AA."

"After all those meetings I should retain something." She lifted his arm so it was around her shoulders then rested her head on his chest. "I thought I was recovering from my mother, but I didn't realize I was learning to cope with my future." A draft from the window scuttled across the bed, and she got up to pull the drapes shut.

"I'm beginning to see one advantage. I can stay in bed while you do the work." he said.

She punched him. "Don't count on it."

"Hard bitch."

"The doctors said to make you do as much as you can on your own."

He felt her snuggle against his chest, but his lower half felt nothing. Would she get tired of a sexless life and look for someone else? The phrase "one day at a time" bounced between his worries.

"I can't find my homework," Paige whined.

"Did you sign my permission slip?" Seth asked.

"What slip?" Carol's voice sounded irritated. "Paige hurry up."

"The one in my notebook."

"You didn't give it to me."

The talk was between the radio news, doors and drawers slamming, and other sentences half lost in the confusion . . . the normal chaos in the Marsh house. To Jay it sounded like a symphony.

Carol poked her head in the bedroom. "Hurry, you'll be late for your first day back at work."

"I'm not ready."

She walked over to him and putting her hands on each of the chair sides, lowered her head until their noses were almost touching. "The doctor says you're ready. Get moving."

Jay propelled his wheelchair down Mt. Auburn Street. They'd ordered a special car with dashboard controls, but delivery was weeks away. As he passed people he wondered what they thought of him in his suit, with his briefcase on his lap. Did they pity him? Did they even notice? He'd never paid attention to cripples either before he became one.

As he approached, his eyes went to the sidewalk where he'd fallen. Although it was long gone, he imagined the white chalk outline for Lina.

Battleaxe Barbara looked up from her typing as he entered. He hadn't realized that she could dash across the reception area so fast. He motioned her away as he manipulated the chair over the slight rise. "Gotta learn to do for myself."

"Gotcha. Coffee?"

"Maybe later thanks."

She shrugged and went back to her computer. "Bobby's running late. He'll brief you when he gets in."

"Thanks." He wheeled his chair towards his office.

"Nice to have you back," she called after him.

Jay wondered if she'd had a lobotomy while he was gone. Or maybe death and mayhem was a management tool to cure grouchy employees. He forced himself to open Lina's door.

He wasn't sure he'd ever seen the desktop clear. All the folders were gone. No yellow notes hung from the computer. Clean wall marked where Syeeda's photos, Lina's university diploma and her paralegal certificate had hung. The smell of her perfume had vanished.

"Pretty sad."

Jay spun the chair around to see Bobby O'Brien, a cigar hanging from his lips and bumped into the side of his desk. "I'm not used to it yet."

"Welcome back. Let's catch up."

Jay didn't trust his voice not to break if he spoke so he followed Bobby into his office for his briefing. An hour later he snapped the last folder shut. "That's it. I handled the closings, and you won't believe how well Barbara did Lina's stuff."

"Thanks."

"It'll cost you. One third billing to me and one third to Barbara."

Bargaining took more energy than Jay had.

Bobby picked up a stack of resumes. "We put an ad out for Lina's job, but if you want my recommendation you'll hire Barbara."

"Why not." He wasn't up to interviewing anyone.

"I'm not Lina. I never will be." Barbara slammed the door so hard Jay's diplomas rattled. She'd been doing Lina's job and occupied Lina's office for the past two weeks.

His mind demanded he run after her; his body wouldn't let him. In the two weeks he'd been back to work, he'd lost count of the fights they had had. He whirled his chair around, giving the wheels furious turns.

Bobby jumped out of the way. "Whoa, we have speed limits."

Jay glared over his shoulder. He took a couple of breaths in front of Lina's now Barbara's closed door. Lina never closed it. She claimed the windowless office made her feel claustrophobic. Jay knocked.

"Go away. I'm busy."

"Wrong answer." He opened the door. His chair bumped over the doorjamb to the space he almost never entered. His avoidance had little to do with the smallness of the space. Nor was it related to the horrible smell of cigarettes. He missed the chaos. He wanted to see photos and crayon stick drawings.

Barbara turned, her face as unreadable and dark as a muddy puddle. "What do ya want?"

"Your attitude sucks."

"You want me to be a dead woman."

"I want you to be civil to me and to my clients."

"That client was a leech."

Jay couldn't speak for a moment. The client was a beaten wife of a well-to-do man. When a restraining order had failed, the woman has suffered four broken ribs. Jay had asked Barbara to drive her to a halfway house in Portsmouth, New Hampshire. His assistant had refused.

"Pardon?"

"You heard me." Barbara put her hands on her keyboard, but they remained motionless. "She's got plenty of money to pay you."

"She can't get to her husband's money, but this isn't about money. It's about helping. Try looking up the word help in the dictionary."

"You could earn so much more."

"I don't need more. I've everything I want."

She looked at his legs.

Afraid he'd throw something, he rolled back to his office where he wished he could pace.

Habit made him claim he had everything he wanted. Barbara was talking about material things.

He picked up the photo of Carol and the kids, one of those department store jobbies against a fake scenic background. Every night he spent holding her. A rap at the door interrupted his thoughts.

He took a long look at Barbara, something he rarely did almost out of fear of being drawn into the black cloud she emitted for protection. He realized she was wearing a business suit. For years she'd worn . . . he didn't know what, but it wasn't this navy blue pinstripe. Professional. For the first time he saw she had a good build. Although he'd never thought about her age, he assumed she was in her early forties. He motioned for her to sit down, which she did. "So what do you want, I don't mean now, but in general."

Her voice was soft. "Probably to be treated with some respect."

"Try treating others the same way."

"But if I shoot first, they won't get me." His eyes widened. "Oh Jay, I didn't . . . I mean . . ."

It took him a minute to think of what she meant. Shoot. He'd been shot. "Forgiven."

She stood. "If you want me to quit . . ."

Part of him wanted to say yes, yes, yes. On the other hand she was even more efficient than Lina. He hated firing people. "Why would I want that?"

"Your attitude."

He shifted in his chair, a movement that was limited and made him look slightly spastic.

"You like what you are doing?"

For the next five minutes she talked about how she loved rummaging through the deed books at the court house, tracing down information. "It's like being a detective."

"Then you should continue."

"Should I take a paralegal course?"

"Only if you want to. How about law school?"

"I'll think about it on my drive back from New Hampshire after leaving your stupid client. And I'll probably decide I don't want anything but the paralegal." Before she turned to go, he saw the closest thing to a smile he'd ever seen from her.

Jay told Carol all about his conversation with Barbara as she snuggled in his arms in bed. Her head had almost cut off the circulation in his arms. Periodically he brushed his lips against her hair. They were both too tired for the oral sex that he sometimes gave her followed by the endless discussions on the right and wrong of their relationship.

He wondered what she was getting at.

"What we're doing is worth the risk. Only there's no real risk." She rolled over and shut off her light. His was already off. As Carol snuggled against him, for the first time, he felt as if things might work out. And with Thanksgiving coming up, maybe he could think of one or two things to be grateful for.

CHAPTER 58

The Washington D.C.-bound Greyhound stood in its Boston berth. Mark Hanson moved to the head of the line, handed the driver his ticket and boarded. He looked like any kid traveling for Thanksgiving weekend. People stood in the aisles as they stored their bags in the overhead rack.

A woman with white hair and a hunched back struggled with her luggage. Mark hefted it up. When she said, "Thank you, young man, it's not true what they say about your generation," he silently cursed for calling attention to himself.

It was bad enough that so many Chinks, Niggers and Fucking Spics were on the bus. God what a stink. He almost hadn't gotten on, but he had to get to D.C. He couldn't trust hitchhiking with his limited time for reconnaissance. At the last minute a few other whites showed up.

As the bus made the *whee . . whee* sounds required by law as it backed out, he hugged his backpack with the notebook filled with photos of Timothy McVeigh, the Unabomber, Waco, Montana, and a list of public buildings in D.C.

He knew where McVeigh and all the other patriots went wrong. They'd acted alienated. The secret to fooling people was to act how they expected. Meld in with the crowd. A dose of charm didn't hurt in undercover work to protect his country. Even his General didn't know what he was doing, nor had the General ordered him to freelance.

How did it feel to kill in large numbers? The fucking Arabs

that flew into the World Trade Center never saw the results of their work. Another thing. He never understood why McVeigh dealt with a building in dumpy old Oklahoma City. For him it would be Washington D.C. or nothing. The Capitol or The Lincoln Memorial.

He'd failed in the cemetery because he hadn't planned enough. This time, he had.

CNN said D.C. would be deserted for the weekend because the asshole Congress was home. Lazy bastards.

No, this time he wasn't making the same mistake. He was smarter than anyone he knew: parents, teachers, even his General. He'd murdered Jay's nigger and got away with it. And not just because of that. In the guidance office he'd seen his folder and the IQ test showing 175. He was a fucking genius. No wonder he got so tired waiting for others to catch up with him.

The stupid government wasn't bothering checking bus stations. He put his hand on his backpack. The detonation device was in his back pocket.

He saw two major disadvantages: he had no control over who would die. Some of those that would die would be innocent, victims of the oppressors and the liberator. And there was a minor disadvantage. He wouldn't be able to see the faces of the dying.

Ah well, he'd be back in Boston in time for school on Monday.

ABOUT THE AUTHOR

D-L Nelson is a Swiss American who divides her time between Geneva, Switzerland and Argelès-sur-mer, France. She is the author of three other Five Star books, *Chickpea Lover: Not a Cookbook*, *The Card* and *Running from the Puppet Master*. Visit her blog at http://theexpatwriter.blogspot.com.